STUDY
GUIDE
FOR
MURDER

STUDY GUIDE FOR MURDER

A Master Class Mystery

Lori Robbins

LEVEL
BEST BOOKS

Author Photo Credit: Alice Kivlon

First edition

ISBN: 978-1-68512-712-1

Cover art by Level Best Designs

This book was professionally typeset on Reedsy.
Find out more at reedsy.com

To Glenn

Praise for the Master Class Mysteries

"Robbins is in a class of her own with this thoroughly engrossing, occasionally funny, wry examination of the world of teaching, students, and the special challenges of solving a murder. Very highly recommended as an exceptional stand-out powered not just by its mystery, but by a psychological atmosphere that brings characters and setting to life to keep its action fast-paced and vivid."—Diane Donovan, Senior Reviewer *Midwest Book Review*

"Exposing and pushing back against the girl-sleuth conventions makes this series both familiar and quirky. Robbins reveals just enough about her heroine's life to make her appealing while leaving enough unresolved to whet the appetite for a follow-up."—*Kirkus Reviews*

"In this fast-paced and funny mystery, English teacher, Liz Hopewell, chases murderers at a posh country club where she's begrudgingly taking golf lessons to please her husband. As the country club murders unfold, Liz is drawn into a bigger mystery from her past that hits closer to home. Lori Robbins hits a hole-in-one with this tongue-in-cheek page-turner. With a delightfully quick pace and even quicker wit, this series will have you reading well past your bedtime. Warning: once you pick it up, you can't put it down. English teacher Liz Hopewell is my new favorite sleuth!"—Kelly Oliver, Amazon bestselling author of the Jessica James Mysteries

"A twisty, wicked tale sparklingly told! Lori Robbins takes us into the dark corners of suburbia, and the scariest streets of Brooklyn, in the unforgettable voice of English teacher Liz Hopewell. Liz, a prosperous mom after a difficult childhood, finds herself tracking a killer at the country club and delving into her own dark past while dodging the slings and arrows of school life. The setting and characters are vividly drawn, including assorted Stepford wives and gold diggers, a clueless and barely literate principal, and an officious, overbearing helicopter mom of a school board chair. Not to mention an adorable police detective. With her amazing, sharp voice, Liz is a standout on the merits, and her use of English lit in detecting is a unique and delicious twist. Characters to love and root for, plenty of baddies to despise, and a plot that keeps you guessing to the end—told in razor-sharp style. Sign me up for the next class!"—Kathleen Marple Kalb, author of the Ella Shane and Old Stuff Mysteries

"Lori Robbins scores a hole-in-one with *Study Guide for Murder: A Masterclass Mystery*, a witty who-dun-it set in the pretentious world of country clubs. A foursome of interesting characters, clever plot twists woven with literary references, bodies dropping like golf balls into the rough, and a cold case personal to the gutsy amateur sleuth English teacher, heighten the tension on this championship round. Robbins' latest mystery sinks the shot with style and class."—Jodé Millman, author of multi-award-winning The Queen City Crimes series

"Anyone who loves a mystery told with humor, heart, and plot twists galore will have a blast reading Lori Robbins's *Study Guide for Murder*, which features literature-quoting high school English teacher Liz Hopewell. Her marriage is on the rocks, her career as a teacher is up in smoke, and there's evidence her long-deceased mom might have been murdered. And that's just for starters. A richly detailed story with characters you'll want to follow for many more books. Give this mystery a grade of A+."—Mally Becker, twice Agatha Award-nominated author of the Revolutionary War mystery series

"Lori Robbins has done it again! Clever, fast-paced and thoroughly engaging, the latest installment in her Master Class Mystery Series is a gripping whodunit loaded with wit and suspense. *Study Guide for Murder* takes high school English teacher Liz Hopewell from the classroom to the golf course, where she is thrust into a murder investigation when her golf club becomes an instrument of death. What begins as a shocking and tragic event quickly spirals into a complex web of crime and intrigue. I highly recommend it. You won't want to put it down."—Lori Duffy Foster, author of the Lisa Jamison Mystery Series and *Never Let Go*, a thriller

"The signature Robbins caustic wit is evident from page one of this acerbic thriller. Even the name of the suburban non-paradise in which the story takes place, Valerian Hills, smacks of irony, evoking anything but the calming effect of the well-known herb for which it is named. As the cleverest writers do, Robbins begins with conflict: an argument between a former married couple, either of whom could end up dead sooner rather than later. But that is just the proverbial tip of the iceberg. Robbins is knife-edge skilled at peeling off the layers of this multifaceted whodunit: an exceptionally astute high school English teacher investigating multiple country club murders and a dysfunctional family to end all dysfunctional families. A thought-provoking plot and characters both sympathetic and maddening keep the reader glued to the pages all the way to the twisty end. Highly recommend."—Erica Miner, award-winning author of the Julia Kogan Opera Mystery series

"It's another semester and another murder for Liz Hopewell who finds herself on the wrong end of a golf club in this fast-paced, and exciting mystery. Her birthday gift of a golf lesson on the anniversary of her mother's death was unsettling, as was discovering the body of a club member who'd been done in with one of her golf clubs. Liz's sister, Susan, sees this as a karmic coincidence and insists that their mother's death may not have been accidental, and that her father's other secret family might be responsible. As the women investigate, Liz takes to the links to unmask the killer while seeking the truth about her family."—Cathi Stoler, author of The Nick Donahue Adventures, *Nick Of Time* and *Out Of Time*

"In *Study Guide for Murder*, high school English teacher Liz Hopewell finds herself in a hole deeper than any sand trap when a murder at the country club is connected to her very own golf club. What starts as a reluctant lesson in the game of golf—taken solely to appease her husband—turns into a wild investigation when she finds the victim bludgeoned. As Liz navigates the labyrinthine world of high school drama and country club pretensions, she can't help but play detective. Her flirtatious banter with the dashing detective is as sharp as her wit, and her literary references add a delightful twist to her sleuthing. Things get even more tangled when Liz's sister insists they investigate their mother's mysterious death from years past, leading them on a nostalgic jaunt through their childhood neighborhood. With Liz's humor and literary savvy guiding her, *Study Guide for Murder* is a rollicking romp through murder and memory.Liz Hopewell makes for an unforgettable sleuth."—Nancy Good, author of the Melanie Deming mysteries

Chapter One

Nothing will come of nothing
—William Shakespeare / King Lear

I f you're in the market for bottomless pits of despair and anxiety, seek employment as an English teacher. Although misery and fear aren't specifically included in most benefits packages, high schools reliably offer them at no additional cost. More to the point, gloomy themes and complicated topics are a huge hit in the classroom.

This sunny attitude, in response to dark emotions, deserted me on the anniversary of my mother's death, and I left Valerian Hills High School feeling less optimistic than usual. Persistent grief was probably to blame, but it was more complicated than that. My husband had to know, should have known, that attending a golf lesson wasn't how I wanted to commemorate that sad day.

There were, of course, much worse belated birthday presents he could have sprung on me. Poison ivy came to mind. Or pneumonia. They were last year's surprise gifts, courtesy of a camping trip that also featured black bears and torrential rainstorms.

I pulled into the Meadowfields Country Club parking lot, wishing I was back in the classroom, where I had a fighting chance of convincing my students that Spark Notes had omitted several enjoyable bits from *The Catcher in the Rye.* Instead, I was headed to the driving range, where unathletic me was sure to fail.

My extreme nervousness about the upcoming golf lesson gained intensity

1

as I walked past lawns and flowerbeds with better manicures than mine. All of the women were wearing quite adorable outfits, and I resigned myself to the fact that I might be the only person at the lesson wearing black yoga pants, which my favorite online retailer promised would take me from work to play without anyone noticing they were unsuitable to either.

I ignored the sound of footsteps and a rustle of leaves behind me when a familiar female voice caught my attention from the opposite side of a large rhododendron.

Her words pierced the landscaped barrier. "I'm calling my lawyer. I'll see you dead before I let you get away with this."

The man laughed. "I'll see you in court before you see me dead. And if I slap a restraining order on you, it'll be a cold day in hell before you're allowed near the clubhouse."

Walking away from the unfolding drama would be like closing a book ten pages before the end. I wasn't being nosy. I was merely interested in my fellow human beings, and to that end, I squeezed inside the row of six-foot-tall flowering bushes, as any botanically-minded person might do. The quarreling couple wasn't visible, but I lingered anyway. The woman's rasping voice teased my memory, but I couldn't summon a name to go with the unpleasant sound.

In a more conciliatory manner, the man said, "Melinda, be reasonable. I'm married now, and I have other obligations. You'll have to make do with less money. It's that simple."

Melinda, still combative, answered, "There's nothing simple about this. Your first obligation is to your first son. You remember him, don't you?"

"Yeah, I remember him. The kid you spoiled and coddled and who was cut from the basketball team because he flunked three subjects."

"Jack is sensitive!" Melinda shrieked. "His problems are your fault. He needs his father. Someone who can be a good influence on him."

Melinda. Jack. Of course. The woman's voice sounded familiar, because the Melinda behind the rhododendrons was better known to me as Mrs. Tumbleson, the imperious president of the Valerian Hills Board of Education. Jack was her son, and one of the three subjects he was failing was mine.

Madam President continued her tirade. "Listen, Elliot, he's your son, just as much as that new kid you got with your new wife. Do you have any idea how ridiculous you look, with your dyed hair and your two-year-old brat? When are you going to grow up?"

"You're the ridiculous one. The whole club is talking about you and the golf pro." Although he spoke more softly than his companion, he more than matched her bitter tone.

Their voices got fainter as they moved farther away. I abandoned my clubs and edged through the bushes to the other side, breaking Club Rule #2C (Keep to the paths at all times.) In fits and starts, the Tumblesons made their way to the opposite edge of the walkway. There was no protective greenery there, so I stopped a few yards away from them and became absorbed in sending and receiving nonexistent texts.

I pulled a hot pink baseball cap lower over my forehead and, from underneath the brim, peered at the angry couple. The hat was a gift from my husband, who'd failed to note, in all the years we'd been married, I owned nothing in that garish shade.

Melinda swung her tennis racquet in short, angry bursts that matched her furious expression. "Your new wife spends more time with Ryan than I do. Trust me when I say they're not working on her short game."

Elliot edged away from her racquet before delivering another insult. "You can't even pay a guy to have sex with you."

She closed the gap between them and raised her free hand to slap him. He grabbed her wrist, shoved her back, and, with a contemptuous laugh, rounded the corner of the caddy shack. She followed him, and I followed both of them.

Melinda stormed back and crashed into me. For some reason, I apologized to her, even though she was the one who was at fault. She stared but didn't acknowledge my existence. Instead, she strode across the emerald grass, swinging her racquet in a wide arc, like Beowulf on a mission to slay an Anglo-Saxon dragon.

I returned to the rhododendrons and tripped on a protruding root, which made my reentry less decorous and stealthy than my exit. I smoothed my shirt and picked a few twigs from my hair, hoping no one had seen me break Rule #37C (Do not pick, touch, or otherwise abuse the flowers.) As I brushed stray bits of dirt from my clothing, a voice far more familiar than Melinda Tumbleson's said, "Liz! What are you doing?"

Standing a few feet away, my husband stared at me without visible affection or pleasure.

As every general knows, the best defense is a good offense. A successful offense, however, takes planning, and George caught me by surprise.

"What am I doing? Uh, I'm here to golf. Yes, golfing. That's what I'm doing." I checked my watch, which gave my face something to do besides look guilty. "What are you doing?"

George removed a leaf from behind my ear. "I'm meeting my boss and two potential clients." He poked his head into the bushes and said, "Where are your clubs?"

To my horror, the golf bag had disappeared. I was saved from having to tell him I'd misplaced the expensive gift when George's boss and their two golf partners joined us. For an inexcusably sexist reason, I assumed their clients were male. But they were quite decidedly female. And not dumpy, dressed in wide shorts and dowdy shirts female. No, these two lovelies wore tiny hip-hugging skirts and form-fitting shirts. My husband gave me one more anxious look before leaving with them. I wasn't jealous, of course. Good old faithful George would never be like Elliot Tumbleson, who traded in his first wife for a newer model several years ago. According to recent rumors, he had wife number three waiting in the wings.

I watched George's progress toward the first tee. The foursome stopped twice to laugh uncontrollably, and their hilarity kept me rooted. Two more minutes alone was all I needed to talk myself into skipping the golf lesson. I was halfway to that decision when a man with a husky Australian accent stopped me.

"Liz! Over here!" A tanned guy with sun-bleached hair and a white smile waved at me. I waved back and held up one finger to indicate the very short period of time I needed before reporting to the driving range. Hazarding one more foray into the bushes, I searched for my golf bag. The gap was now

4

considerably wider, and the clubs had inexplicably migrated ten yards from where I'd left them. Two of the silly hats that topped the clubs were askew, and the bag had a swipe of dirt across the back. Thankful that whoever mistakenly took my clubs returned them, I headed to the driving range.

George and his golf buddies were on the putting green. As I passed them, he paused in his methodical warm-up and told me to have fun, in much the same way parents tell their kids to enjoy a summer camp that offers extra credit for sadomasochistic bullying.

I took my place alongside the smartly dressed students in the golf clinic. In my black stretchy pants, black shirt, and nearly-black hair, I looked like a dark exclamation point at the end of a flowery, fair-haired sentence. The sleek lineup of perfectly coiffed pale gold heads made me self-conscious, and I tried to smooth my tangled dark brown hair into submission, which didn't improve my look or my stance.

Despite feeling absurdly out of place, I concentrated on Ryan's instructions. His patience was unforced, although it couldn't have been easy to teach the basics of the game he loved to a group of largely untalented amateurs. I knew how he felt, since I had to do the same with *Moby Dick* and *Hamlet*.

The warm and relaxed feelings Ryan inspired ended abruptly when he told us to start swinging. I closed my eyes, which wasn't one of the steps he'd recommended. When I opened them, I saw six golf balls bounce a few times until they rolled to a gentle stop. The seventh, mine, hadn't budged from the tee.

A loud laugh from the woman behind me ensured my botched attempt wouldn't go unnoticed. Sonya Tumbleson, Elliot's second wife, had slipped in so quietly I wasn't aware she'd arrived. She could barely contain her amusement. "If you want to play golf, I'm pretty sure you have to make contact." Then, she casually drove her golf ball twenty yards past the closest competitor.

I told myself that perhaps Sonya didn't intend to be mean, but it was a tough sell. I loathed Melinda, Elliot Tumbleson's first choice of a marriage partner, and it wasn't a stretch for me to feel similarly about the second. I gritted my teeth and didn't threaten her with bodily harm, which would have violated Club Rules 1A, 1B, and 1C.

Bryony Aldridge, who was as much a fixture at the club as I was an outsider, joined Sonya to watch my second attempt. "How does it feel to be the student instead of the teacher?"

I swung my club in a large enough arc to keep her at a distance. "It's a lot less work."

She found my answer funny, which wasn't the reaction I intended or expected. "Is *work* the reason why you're dressed like you're going to a funeral?"

As the rest of the ladies laughed, I swung again with all my might. The ball flew off, described a sharp arc over the snack bar, and descended somewhere near the back parking lot. I stiffened but heard no cries, groans, or broken glass.

After checking that no one had been decapitated by the ball, Ryan rushed over. "Liz, you hit the ball with a lot of force. All you have to do is straighten that out, and you'll be driving it a mile."

As a teacher, I recognized the sound of another teacher lying through his teeth in an attempt to provide positive feedback. I stretched my lips into a smile, put my head down, and, for the rest of the hour, addressed only the ball.

After the lesson, Sonya, with grudging courtesy, invited me to join her and the other ladies for a drink. I declined the honor of their company in favor of cooking dinner, sorting laundry, and grading a stack of essays on *1984*. I collected my clubs and walked out with far more zeal than I'd had going in. Feeling rebellious, I once again cut across the bushes, where I encountered an obstacle the club rules didn't cover.

Elliot Tumbleson's motionless body.

Chapter Two

Death, a necessary end, will come when it will come
—William Shakespeare / Julius Caesar

The savage dent in Elliot Tumbleson's head was a strong indication he'd sliced his last golf shot, but determining his chance of survival wasn't my call to make. I punched nine-one-one into my phone, staggered back onto the path, and yelled for a doctor. We were at a country club, for heaven's sake—there had to be dozens of physicians on site who'd opted for post-golf drinks instead of post-op complications.

The nine-one-one operator picked up my call and said, "What's your emergency?"

I needed two hands to keep the phone steady. "I-I think he's dead. Elliot Tumbleson. The blood is, it's—"

She spoke over my sobs. "Can you give me your name? Where you are?"

I choked out the words. "Liz. Liz Hopewell. The Meadowfields Country Club in Oak Ridge, New Jersey. Please hurry!"

"Help is on the way. Are you alone?"

Although the question was interesting from a philosophical perspective, loneliness was the least of my worries. I described Elliot's injuries, and the compassionate woman on the other end of the line told me not to move him. That part was easier than her next request. Shuddering violently, I slipped two fingers under his wrist to feel for his pulse, but since I couldn't find my own pulse, the evidence wasn't conclusive. His skin was warm, but his arm was limp. His face was almost completely buried in the underbrush.

The sound of concerned voices filtered through to where I knelt. I shouted, "In here! I'm in the bushes!"

Carl Bagarosa, the groundskeeper of the club, charged through to where I knelt. He looked down, stopped short of stepping on Elliot, and immediately turned the same color as the grass he tended. He barked to the growing crowd outside, "Man down. Somebody call an ambulance." He pointed a shaky finger at me. "Step away."

"I already called for an ambulance." Fighting waves of nausea and lightheadedness, I said, "H-he's not responding."

Carl, who moonlighted as an auxiliary police officer, regarded me with open suspicion. "Stand down and don't make any sudden moves." His hand moved to the front pocket of his pants, as if he were going to pull a gun from a holster, but he was unlikely to be packing anything more lethal than a few tees.

The groundskeeper's militant stance was rendered irrelevant by the arrival of the ambulance. The medics pushed us out of the way and got to work on Elliot, obliterating any clues Carl and I hadn't already destroyed. I disentangled myself from the sharp branches of a bush that encircled us, and, guided by a police officer, I exited through what was now a wide path of broken twigs and crushed leaves and flowers.

No one in the growing crowd of onlookers—except, perhaps, one person—knew what happened. Most wore a mixed expression of horror, fascination, and the secret pleasure people feel at being present at a noteworthy, if tragic, event. From that group of interested but emotionally uninvolved witnesses, my husband appeared.

George rushed to my side. "Liz! What's happening? What were you doing?" He took me by the hand to lead me away but dropped my fingers as soon as he touched them. His hand, like mine, was now sticky with blood. He brought me to a spigot outside the caddy shack, where we cleaned up as best we could.

Four cop cars, lights flashing and sirens screaming, pulled up behind the ambulance, breaking Club Rule #4A (No parking in areas marked with yellow or green stripes.) Uniformed police officers corralled the gawkers and cordoned off the parking lot. Detective Tom Harriman, who'd investigated the death of one of my colleagues several months earlier, emerged from an unmarked car. With him was a guy I didn't know, but who looked as if he could be Tom's older brother. Same lean face, short brown hair, and dark blue eyes, but time had etched faint lines across his forehead and in the corners of his mouth.

I waited, nervously shifting from one foot to the other. Given the bloodstains on my hands and shirt, it was understandable that no one directly approached me. Instead, with an absence of manners surprising in so genteel an atmosphere, people whispered and pointed. Officer Valerie Spitzak escorted us out of earshot of the mob.

George whispered, "Were you the first one on the scene?"

"Yes. At least, I think I was. I didn't see anyone else."

My husband muttered. "Let's hope the police are satisfied with that and let us go."

I wasn't as eager to leave. Having been so proximate in location and time, I felt personally invested in finding out what happened. George would have been happy to exit and never mention Elliot Tumbleson again.

I searched the faces in the crowd, looking for Melinda Tumbleson, whom I'd last seen swinging a tennis racquet, or Sonya Tumbleson, whom I'd last seen swinging a golf club. Of the two possible murder weapons, a club seemed more likely, given the sharp gash in Elliot's head.

I didn't have to wait long for confirmation. Tom Harriman walked toward us, carrying in gloved fingers a bloodied golf club wrapped in plastic. In his other hand was a familiar-looking fuzzy golf club topper. Patches of pink were visible, though most of it was soaked in red blood.

Elliot's blood. My golf equipment.

The detective gave me a wary look. "I don't suppose you know whose this is."

Nausea kept me silent, but George turned into a whirlwind of energy. He picked through the remaining clubs in my golf bag, muttering incoherently something about a driver.

"Liz! You must have had the driver with you for the golf lesson." To the detective, he said, "Plenty of women use the same brand of golf club. That driver could belong to dozens of people besides my wife."

Harriman's partner joined us and introduced himself as Detective Ben Sorkin. He ignored George and concentrated on me. When I told him the club was most likely mine, he said, "When was the last time you saw it?"

George tried to speak in my stead, but Sorkin shut him down. "Mr. Hopewell, please let your wife answer." He flashed his dark blue gaze at me. "Can you tell me if and when the bag was left unattended? When would someone have had the opportunity to take it?"

"It could have happened during the golf lesson. After I parked the bag behind me, I forgot about it. If you hadn't asked me, I wouldn't have known it was missing."

I delayed telling him someone had moved my golf bag while I was eavesdropping on Melinda and Elliot. This episode wasn't one I wanted to share in front of George., who was more upset over my failure to use the driver during the lesson than the fact that someone else had used it as a murder weapon.

Detective Sorkin interrupted what was already an uncomfortable conversation for all concerned. He turned to George and said, "Mr. Hopewell. Talk to Officer Spitzak. That way, we don't have to keep either of you longer than necessary."

Sorkin's next words made clear his motivation for removing George from the scene. "Ms. Hopewell, did you kill Elliot Tumbleson?"

"H-how could you ask me that? I'm, um, I'm an *English* teacher. His son is in my class. And I know Elliot. I mean, I know who he is. We're not exactly best buddies, but—" A fit of distressed coughing got in the way of further protests.

Detective Sorkin, unimpressed by my profession and subject, waited for the choking fit to pass. "The first Mrs. Tumbleson informed me that you're no friend of the family. It's a question I have to ask."

"I understand your point, however misguided it is. To answer your question: No, I did not kill Elliot Tumbleson. As for my relationship with Mrs. Tumbleson, she's not the one who was murdered." I wiped away a fresh river of tears and fought to match his calm demeanor. "I was the first person at the scene, and it does appear that my golf club was the murder weapon. But, as I've already explained, I'm an English teacher, not a killer. We prefer to inflict psychological damage."

He was neither amused nor convinced. To my great relief, Tom joined us. "Liz, I finished taking a statement from Melinda Tumbleson and…" He glanced at Detective Sorkin and then looked at me. "We have a few more questions. She claims you were stalking her and Mr. Tumbleson earlier in the day."

"I wasn't stalking them! I was…I wasn't…I was going to the golf lesson." I started sweating, exactly as a guilty person would when faced with evidence of her crime. Out of this panicked fog, a glimmer of hope emerged. "I can't deny eavesdropping on Melinda and Elliot, but I wasn't alone. I'm positive someone was following me. But maybe that person was following them."

Sorkin was relentless. "Got any evidence to back that up?"

I remembered blocking out the sound of footsteps and the rustle of leaves in an effort to overhear the Tumblesons argue, but Sorkin wasn't interested in this vague recollection. I explained that someone had moved my golf bag and said, "I didn't see who did it, but maybe you can find footprints? Or fingerprints? Or something else that'll prove I wasn't the only one at the scene of the crime." Seeking a better target for their inquiries, I fixed upon the second Mrs. Tumbleson. "Have you spoken to Sonya yet?"

Tom flicked a glance at the clubhouse. "She fainted when she got the news about Mr. Tumbleson and is resting inside. We're sending her home with one of our officers, who'll wait with her until her mother shows up."

Looking fragile and beautiful, Sonya stepped out of the building and into the sunshine, leaning heavily on the arm of a stiff and red-faced cop. As she walked unsteadily down the gravel path, shrill screams rang out. Melinda Tumbleson lunged at Sonya. "You killed him! I know you did it! And now I'm going to kill you!"

Sonya, despite her apparent frailty, viciously shoved Melinda, who fell backward into a bed of petunias. The younger woman sneered as her rival clumsily got to her feet. Before Melinda could plant her fist in Sonya's face, two officers pinioned her.

Melinda screeched, in a most unhinged manner, "That filthy homewrecker stole my husband. And then she killed him. Take her away! She's crazy!"

Sonya was remarkably steady, given her recent swoon. "I think we all can see which one of us is crazy." She looked up at the two detectives through long lashes I was certain were not her own. Tom seemed mesmerized by her, but Sorkin's expression was more difficult to read. He gently took her arm and led her toward a waiting cop car. She leaned into him.

It was quite a performance. Sorkin returned to us so bewitched, he agreed to let me go home, but not before informing me that since the murder weapon belonged to me, and since I was the one to find Elliot, and since I had a history of bad faith dealings with the Tumblesons, I was his pick as the prime suspect.

Chapter Three

Had we but world enough and time
—Andrew Marvell / "To His Coy Mistress"

"How did you do it?" George spoke softly, but there was so much anger behind his words I felt as if he were shouting at me.

"Do what? Are you asking me if I murdered Elliot?"

"How did you manage to get involved in a second murder case? What am I going to tell my boss or our clients? Or the kids? This is a disaster."

"It's a worse disaster for Elliot and his kids." I didn't mention the other person he'd left out of his damage assessment. Me.

"I suppose you're going to start hanging out with that Detective Harrison again." He heaved one of his I'm-trying-to-be-patient sighs.

"It's Harriman, not Harrison, as you well know. Although I think we're all on a first-name basis at this point. Are you jealous of Tom?" I thought about mentioning the two pretty women he'd golfed with but decided this was beneath me.

George pressed his lips into a thin line. "I am not jealous of *Tom*. Should I be?"

I switched my handbag to my left shoulder, which put more distance between us. In truth, it wasn't Tom who occupied my thoughts but the enigmatic Detective Sorkin, with his deep-set eyes and composed manner. "You're acting as if I deliberately found a dead body as a way to spend time with Tom."

George muttered, "You looked so happy to see him. Happier to see him than me."

"I was happy to see Tom because he's a cop, and I was with a dead guy. A murdered guy. George, it was terrible. And terrifying. I was worried the killer would come back." I clicked the remote control to unlock the car, pretending, for George's sake, that I'd remembered to lock it.

"For all we know, the murderer did come back. Or maybe he never left. Who had the opportunity to take your golf club? I'm assuming, of course, that you aren't the one who gave Elliot the kibosh. It's no secret that he is, or was, the least popular guy at the club." With an effort, he added a few sympathetic words. "Not that he deserved to die for it."

"It can't be easy to top the list of boorish men at the Meadowfields Country Club. The competition was fierce, even before you signed up to become a member." I lightly smacked his shoulder. "Put your mind at rest. If I swing a golf club at anyone, it will be you."

George embarked upon a lecture about how lucky we were to have been accepted as members and followed up with tips on how to overcome the social stigma of finding a murder victim. I nodded at appropriate intervals, but my mind was occupied with trying to identify likely suspects. It was, paradoxically, the only way for me to subdue the lingering horror of finding Elliot's dead body.

When my bright pink golf bag disappeared, I assumed someone mistakenly took it, but perhaps the killer saw it and realized she could remove the club and frame me. Given the color, a woman was more likely than a man to have taken it. But if the theft didn't happen then, several people could have swiped my driver at almost any point during the hour-long golf lesson. Two or three left for a bathroom break, and others purchased a drink from the snack bar. Ryan Walker, on his trip to get more golf balls, was absent long enough to have attacked Elliot. Another mark against the golf pro was his widely admired and lethally accurate swing.

Elliot's two ex-wives seemed the most likely suspects, mostly because anyone who was married to him had to have wanted to kill him. I myself occasionally fantasized about life without George, although I'd never been tempted to do him in. Perhaps Melinda or Sonya lost her temper and killed

Elliot in a fit of anger. He had a vile disposition, and the usually redoubtable Melinda winced whenever anyone mentioned his name.

I realized, a few seconds too late, that George was waiting for an answer. After agreeing to everything I hadn't heard him tell me, I said, "The time of death is already narrowed pretty decisively since the body was warm when I found it. It's such a hot day, though. That had to affect the rate of—" George flinched, but before he could disparage my forensic analysis, I switched gears. "Sonya was late to the lesson. I have no idea when she arrived. She sort of sneaked in behind me. As for Melinda Tumbleson, she had a fiery argument with Elliot shortly before he was killed."

George stared at me. "How did you know they were fighting?"

I mentally cursed my careless words. Why couldn't I leave my internal monologues where they belonged? I reached for my cell phone and acted as if I'd gotten an emergency text from the Mommy Police. "Wow! The kids are almost home. Let's talk later."

I jumped in the car and left before George, but he beat me home by a good five minutes. I was so nervous I slowed at every yellow light, allowed too many cars to cross the four-way stop signal before darting across the intersection, and drove five miles below the speed limit. It was a miracle no one got out of his car and attacked me. New Jersey drivers weren't known for an abundance of patience.

When I arrived, George was in the shower, and our kids, fifteen-year-old Ellie and seventeen-year-old Zach, had yet to arrive from their afterschool activities. I contemplated the benefits of cooking dinner versus doing laundry or grading papers. In the end, I did none of those things and ordered two large pizzas.

I wasn't planning on telling the kids about the murder, but news traveled fast in small towns. Many members of the Meadowfields Country Club lived in neighboring communities, and although we maintained a fierce rivalry in every sport, we cooperated quite amiably when it came to gossiping about each other's personal business.

Ellie struck a dramatic pose. "Mom! I heard what happened to that kid in your class. First, his parents get divorced, and then his father is murdered.

15

Are you and me and Aunt Susie going to investigate again?"

Zach looked horrified. "There is no way Mom is going to get involved in another murder." He turned to me. "Right?"

I hastened to reassure my son. "Believe me, I'm not going to get involved. It was the merest coincidence I was there when it happened."

Ellie smirked. "That's not what Mrs. Castleton said. She said the murder weapon belonged to you."

George slammed his glass on the counter. "That woman is a menace. Ellie, I don't want you riding with Mrs. Castleton ever again."

Before Ellie could burst into tears or stalk up to her room, before George could make any more upsetting pronouncements, and before Zach could register his daily complaint about starving to death, the pizza arrived. I calculated the probable number of calories I'd burned as a consequence of the golf lesson and the murder and decided I could afford to eat the cheese off the top of two slices of pizza. I vowed to forego the carbohydrates in the crust, so I left those until after everyone went upstairs.

The insomnia that hit me a few hours later was probably a reaction to Elliot's death and not the greasy dinner. Unable to sleep, I began writing as a means to exorcise the violent images that plagued me. Freed from the pressure of having to give immediate answers to the cops or George, I laid out a factual account of my day. Unsatisfied with this dry summary, I added possible suspects and motives.

It was a cruel coincidence that on the anniversary of my mother's death, another kid's parent met an untimely end.

Chapter Four

There pass the careless people / That call their souls their own
—A.E. Housman / "There Pass the Careless People"

At 6:45 am the room that housed the copy machine at Valerian Hills High School was reliably deserted. That's why, on the morning after Elliot Tumbleson was murdered, I skipped the break room gossip and coaxed pages of a study guide on *Frankenstein* into the machine. By mid-morning, the first of the daylong paper jams would begin, and unless I wanted to spend my lunch break fixing the ancient copier, 6:45 was the only option. Should the board of education follow through on their threats to trim the English department, I could start a second career as a tech support worker for Xerox.

When I returned to my classroom, a fellow English teacher and friend, Emily Pearson, was waiting. She was eager to gossip about the previous day's events.

I delivered as little information as was consistent with friendship while scrolling through a sea of communications. In the middle of a series of emails marked High Importance, one missive stood out from the rest. I swiveled my computer so Emily could read it. The brevity of the message did not bode well for me.

Dear Ms. Hopewell,
Report to the principal's office at 3 pm.
Have a nice day,

Melinda Tumbleson
President, Valerian Hills Board of Education
[Jack's Mom]

The full horror of such a meeting hadn't sunk in before a loud *harrumph* interrupted us. Unable to wait until the three o'clock meeting she'd commanded me to attend, Melinda marched in. The president of our school board, whose preferred title was "Jack's Mom," did so with as much pomp as if an imaginary band were playing "Hail to the Chief."

Emily seemed to shrink before my eyes. My friend took a few tentative steps toward the door, but I pulled her back. She remained by my side but fixed her eyes on her phone.

Melinda planted her fists on my desk. "As you can see from my email, we'll be meeting with Timmy after school today, but I have a few other items to discuss with you that can't wait."

It didn't seem like the right time to offer condolences, so I stayed silent. Emily made a low, mewing sound, but offered no other contribution to the conversation.

Melinda probably wouldn't have listened anyway since, as promised, she had more pressing matters to discuss than her ex-husband's death. "I'll be quick. First, change Jack's grade from an F to a B+. This will allow him to focus on healing. Second, give him the lead in the school play. There's no point in waiting for an audition to assign him the part. Every single teacher who has had Jack has commented on his talent."

My mocking boast about working as a technician for Xerox was becoming more appealing the longer Melinda talked. "I don't doubt that other teachers have told you how talented Jack is, but I can't afford to give the impression of favoritism. Jack himself wouldn't want that. The auditions are coming up very soon. Let's talk then."

She pursed her lips. "I assure you, Ms. Hopewell, if you don't do as I say, it will be a very one-sided conversation."

Her threat didn't impress me. All conversations with the board president were one-sided, at least as far as she was concerned.

Melinda glowered at me with red-veined eyes. "Jack has many extra-curricular commitments. Send me the rehearsal schedule before you post it so I can make any necessary changes." She turned on her heel and, over her shoulder, informed me, "I was opposed to the decision to make you the new AP teacher. But you can prove me wrong by doing as I say. Otherwise, you may find yourself with a very different assignment next year."

"And you may find yourself in violation of board policy. I have a witness to the fact that you're abusing your power as president of the board of education." I pointed to Emily, who looked as nervous as a rabbit next to a stew pot.

Melinda put her hands on her hips. "Who are you going to complain to? Timmy? He's a nontenured principal. The superintendent? Her contract is up for renewal in June. They know the board will do whatever I tell them to do."

This was true. Melinda did all the work, and her grateful board members meekly went along with every decision she made. With fake bravado, I said, "I wouldn't waste time with either the principal or the superintendent. I'm going straight to the union to file a grievance."

This flimsy threat almost made her laugh, but laughter didn't come naturally to her. The teachers' union was so weak we worked for two years without a contract. Our hardball negotiating tactic was to volunteer at town events to prove how dedicated we were.

Nonetheless, I stayed defiant. "I won't let you get away with bullying me."

This time, Melinda did laugh. "Of course you will."

Emily followed her to the door and watched her walk down the hallway to make sure she was gone. "Liz, you're crazy! Mrs. Tumbleson will make your life miserable if you don't toe the line. Forget about keeping the AP classes. She could get you moved to the middle school."

Although getting transferred to the middle school was a version of hell all high school teachers feared, I was more interested in Melinda's failure to mention Elliot's murder, other than as a ploy to get me to change Jack's grade.

"Let her. My only regret has to do with Jack. I feel sorry for him and won't let him fail despite the aggravation of having Melinda think I did it to appease her."

At the sound of the bell, Emily scurried back to her classroom. I gulped two Excedrin with a few swallows of coffee and hoped the magic potion would ease the pain in my head.

Jack Tumbleson, as expected, was absent. I read the statement our school counselor prepared for us and followed that with a personal message regarding the tragic death of his father. In the spirit of mourning, we read Auden's poem "Funeral Blues." Given the circumstances, the kids were more attentive than they usually were during the first class of the day, although not everyone was on the same metaphoric page.

Kevin Sugarman, who earlier in the year informed me that he hated poetry, never read, and was taking the Advanced Placement class only because it would look good on his college application, said, "Hey, Ms. Hopewell, didn't you provide the murder weapon?"

The class gasped and giggled. I was in the middle of a sip of water when he delivered this mocking challenge. I swallowed, choked, and dribbled half the water down my chin.

Kevin, sensing weakness, pressed further. "My mom said you found the body, and the police are investigating you."

Few teenagers, with the possible exception of Jack, got under my skin in any meaningful way. But Kevin made me rethink my lifelong aversion to corporal punishment. I looked down at the Auden poem and, somewhat perversely, found comfort in the words, *Nothing now can ever come to any good.*

I gazed unblinkingly at Kevin and said, "I'm so pleased to know that you and your mother are concerned about Jack." Few adults, let alone kids, were strong enough to fight a cold stare, and he wasn't one of them. Seconds ticked by as his face turned dark red. Before he could recover, the bell rang. The other students rushed to the door, but Kevin gathered his books with insolent slowness, letting me know I hadn't bested him.

I waited for him to leave before locking the door and going to the office for a walkie-talkie, which was required equipment for hall duty. This job required me to check the bathrooms for vaping students and the hallways for loiterers, but I wasn't good at either task. I disliked the intrusion of a bathroom visit and harbored a sneaking sympathy for kids who needed a break from the pressure cooker we call high school.

Defending us against more potent threats was our armed guard, a scary-looking guy who sported a military-style buzz cut, a gruff manner, and a devout belief in conspiracy theories. He curtly nodded as we passed each other. I resisted the urge to salute him. He and Timmy got along famously; together, they designed security measures that made the school as impregnable and as welcoming as a maximum-security prison.

Distracted by a series of cell phone vibrations, I took an illegal break in the faculty lounge. Despite the appealing name, our break room afforded few places to relax. The tables were rickety, and the chairs were made of plastic that had been molded into curves that comfortably accommodated very few human backsides. There was a sofa for lounging, but it hadn't been cleaned in the ten years I'd been at Valerian Hills High School, and the fabric showed signs of spilled coffee, ink, and other, less easily identifiable stains.

Nurse Ronnie, who was on break, looked disapprovingly at me. "Aren't you supposed to be on hall duty?"

I mumbled something about an emergency and read two messages from my daughter and three from my sister, who had also left a voice message.

I texted Ellie first. **Don't use your cell phone at school!**

Ellie answered with three hearts and the message, **Worried about u**.

I texted back an equal number of hearts and added two smiley faces. **Don't worry about me or I'll worry about you!**

My sister's messages demanded an immediate answer. I texted a promise to call her after 3:00, but Susan insisted, **Now. We need to talk now.**

Worried that something more urgent than a dating mishap inspired her plea, I called her.

She shrieked into my ear, "Why are you at work? Aren't you a complete wreck?"

I watched the clock tick off one of the eleven minutes I had left until my next class began. "Susan, I'm in a hurry. Get to the point or wait until after I finish school."

"No can do. I'm leaving work early because I have an appointment at Excellent Eyelashes. They're having a sale for new customers. You know how expensive eyelash extensions are."

"Is the cost of fake eyelashes the vital issue you called me to discuss?" I checked the hallway, sped down the empty corridor, and entered the English office, which was, for once, without English teachers.

Pleased by the unexpected privacy, I gave Susan thirty seconds to arrive at her long-delayed point. She said, in an injured tone, "I called you because of the murder at the country club. I can't believe I had to find out about it from the newspaper instead of from you."

"What is it about that horrible event that can't wait until later?"

"This is Fate. This is Karma. This is the Universe talking to us. Or at least to you." She emphasized every other word to convey the magnitude of what she was trying to tell me.

"If you think I'm going to investigate another homicide, forget about it. Not happening." I reminded her that the last time we pursued a killer, I ended up having to wear turtleneck sweaters for many months. The scars remained, in more ways than one.

Coolly, she answered, "That episode isn't relevant to my purpose. I want us to investigate the murder you've never admitted happened. We need to know the truth about how Mom died, no matter how difficult that might be. Don't you see? You found Elliot Tumbleson's body on the anniversary of Mom's death. It's a Sign. You can't resist Fate."

"I have no idea what kind of warped vision of karma or fate you have rattling around in that head of yours, but I can assure you that I have no desire to talk about how Mom died." I bobbled the phone but managed not to drop it. "What happened yesterday was a tragic coincidence, not some cosmic reckoning. I can't. I won't. No."

Susan barreled past my objections. "Mom never took so much as an aspirin. And she never drank more than a glass of wine. Are you telling me she swallowed a bunch of pills with a vodka chaser and then went driving? Didn't happen, Liz. Not like that. You know it, and I know it."

Suddenly weak-kneed, I leaned against the wall. "The police said it was an open and shut case. What could we do? We were kids."

"We were teenagers and old enough to know that the whole episode reeked of secrets we were afraid to uncover. It happened a long time ago, so it's a cold case. But cold cases get solved. And we can do this. Together."

The bell signaling the end of class rang, which gave me five more minutes to discourage her. "Are you sure you want to know the answer? You know as well as I do who the prime suspect is. And he's dead. So what difference would it make?"

She corrected me, "We *think* he's dead. The Lousy Bastard was quite the con artist. For all we know, he faked his death and is living with his third or fourth wife in an undisclosed location in Queens. The problem with your logic is that this isn't about him. It's about us. We need to know."

The Lousy Bastard, which was the name my sister and I gave our father after he abandoned us for the second or maybe the third time, was a thief and a liar. The question I'd avoided for many years was if he was a murderer as well. He disappeared for good after my mother's funeral, telling Susan and me, with uncharacteristic candor, that we'd be better off without him. With no apparent remorse, shame, or apology, he explained that he had another wife and another family, and he was leaving us to live with them.

I remembered with painful clarity the sanctimonious expression on his face when he claimed he wanted to be a real father to his other children, who needed him more than we did. I didn't try to dissuade him and felt relief, rather than sorrow or anger when he left. It wasn't so bad. Our grandparents took us in until we graduated high school.

Shaking myself back to the present, I argued into the silence on the other end of the line. "There's nothing about our past that I want to know more about. Not two minutes ago, I got a text from Ellie. She's already worried about me. Our last investigation was tough on her and Zach. I don't want to be in a position where I have to lie to them."

"No one's telling you to lie. Our parents, both of them, made secrecy a way of life. Is that what you want for your family?" I heard the clatter of her high heels, followed by the sound of New York City traffic as she said, "Ellie and

Zach are the same age we were when Mom died. You're underestimating your kids. And yourself."

The bell rang again. I ran back to my classroom and surreptitiously checked my phone one last time.

The newest message was from Tom Harriman, the police detective my husband unreasonably disliked. His text read: **Meet today? Your classroom at 3?**

With more pleasure than most people felt in anticipation of an interview with a police detective, I texted back, **Yes.**

Chapter Five

Secrecy flows through you / a different kind of blood
—Margaret Atwood / "Secrecy"

I spent my lunch period researching cold cases, which was the kind of behavior our tech department's Orwellian-style surveillance was intended to prevent. When I began, my goal was to prove to Susan the impossibility of investigating our mother's death. Thirty minutes later, I was hooked. If these ordinary people could solve mysteries, then maybe my sister and I could as well. I was especially intrigued by a trio of elderly amateur sleuths who spent years trying to solve the decades-old murder of their high school friend. Although they hadn't yet achieved success, they refused to give up. In some ways, their story was more inspiring than if they'd nailed the killer.

Investigating our mother's death presented a set of problems that differed from any of the cold cases that topped the list on my Google search. Those involved a clear-cut case of murder, but the police had ruled Mom's car accident just that—an accident.

I think I knew, even at the time of her death, something was wrong with the story my father told me. Mom was an advocate for organic foods and homeopathic medicine. And yet, on the day she died, she loaded up on pain pills and vodka, went for a drive to a never-disclosed destination, and crashed into a tree.

I didn't challenge what I was told because I didn't want to know the answer. Of the two most likely explanations for my mother's crash, neither was pleasant. Either I'd missed signs of her suicidal depression, or someone, probably my father, orchestrated her death.

On my desk, smiling photos of Ellie and Zach reminded me of the passage of time. Susan accused me of perpetuating my family's unhealthy addiction to secrecy. She wasn't wrong. If I didn't try to uncover the truth I'd always be hiding something from them. Ellie and Zach shouldn't have to learn about their family the way I learned about random cold cases.

I eyed the clock, impatient to begin. As a consequence, the rest of the day passed with excruciating slowness. When the last bell rang, I sifted through a pile of essays on *1984*, which persisted in not grading themselves.

I was in the process of closing and locking the windows when Tom Harriman entered my classroom, bearing two cups of coffee and a paper bag from the local bakery.

Startled, I admitted, "I forgot we were meeting. I'm glad I didn't miss you."

"Very flattering, to be sure. Is that how you charmed the president of the Valerian Hills Board of Education?"

Tom and I had gotten to know each other quite well a few months earlier, when he was investigating the death of an English teacher. For most of my life, I'd been extremely risk averse, but I became obsessed with identifying the killer, perhaps because the victim was a colleague. I used literary theory to help solve the crime, which amused Tom and annoyed his partner, who had since retired. He claimed I drove him to that decision, but I think he was joking.

The detective took in my jacket, my packed book bag, and my blank computer screen. "Since when do you leave so early? Usually, it's Emily who's rushing out the door at one minute past the hour. And here I am, bringing you your favorite beverage. Black, no sugar, right?"

I took a long drink from the lukewarm brew. "I planned to work at home today. But not before seeing you, of course."

"When you're finished inhaling that coffee, I need more details about what went down yesterday. And if you want to add a few shout-outs to your favorite books, I'm all ears." He perched on the end of one of the student's desks.

If Susan hadn't spiked my interest in investigating our mother's car accident, I would have jumped at the chance to discuss Elliot's murder. Now, however, his death was less compelling than the one that had shadowed so much of my life.

"I hate to disappoint you, but I barely know these people."

If Tom sensed my reluctance, he didn't let on. "When did that ever stop you? Let's go over your statement, and then you can do your English teacher thing. Tell me what Jane Austen would say about Melinda and Sonya Tumbleson."

While he reviewed his notes, I pondered the titles on my bookshelf to see which novelists were most likely to offer appropriate advice about the murder. Although the country club setting was genteel enough to suggest Austen, it was Anthony Trollope, with his eye for dissipation and corruption, who spoke to me. I took out his doorstopper of a novel, *The Way We Live Now*, and explained one of the many subplots.

Tom weighed the book in his hand. "Never heard of the guy. Plus, it sounds boring."

I took it back and thumbed through a few pages, looking for a specific passage. "In this book, he describes the 2007 financial crash, almost a century before it happened. Bernie Madoff, the collapse of the market. All that is in here."

Tom perked up a bit. "Anything about bitter ex-wives?"

"You bet. Listen to this, *'Love is like any other luxury. You have no right to it unless you can afford it.'*"

A voice from behind broke my concentration. Detective Sorkin stood in the doorway and said, "Is that the book talking? Or is it you? You think Elliot Tumbleson bought his wives? And that when couldn't afford them both, one of them killed him?"

His detached tone irritated me. "If Elliot was killed on the spur of the moment, unpremeditated and in a fit of fury, Melinda is more likely than Sonya to have done it. Sonya, however, had opportunity as well as motive. She was late to our golf lesson and could have stolen my club while I was... er...not paying attention. I saw her in action, and she's a lot stronger than she looks."

Tom knocked back the rest of his coffee and said, "Please, Liz. Don't hold back. Tell me what you really think about Sonya."

Somewhat defensively, I answered, "You asked me. I didn't go looking for you."

Tom pulled down the corners of his mouth. "Yeah. What's up with that? You had ten different theories last time. This time, I have to drag the information out of you. Is George worried about his status at the country club?"

It's one thing to criticize your husband in the privacy of your head. Having someone else do it in front of a coolly critical guy like Sorkin was quite another.

I shoved the rest of the *1984* essays into my backpack. "George has nothing to do with my decision to steer clear of Elliot's murder. Last time, the victim was a fellow English teacher, and the murder happened on my turf. But this time around? I barely knew Elliot, and I couldn't care less about the country club. Plus, I'm already on thin ice where Melinda is concerned." Thinking about the ramifications of a guilty conviction for Melinda, I reconsidered. "Of course, if she's the murderer, she's unlikely to continue as president of the board of education. I'd have to consider that a win."

Sorkin's drew together dark eyebrows. "Neither of us wants you involved in the investigation, but you're a witness and were the first at the scene of the crime. We need to know, as best you can remember, everything that happened. Give me times, places, people. You're well acquainted with Melinda. But what can you tell me about Sonya Tumbleson? You said there was some kind of quarrel. What was it?"

The phrasing of Sorkin's questions implied a tacit admission that I was no longer his central suspect, and I obliged him by doing a second, and more nuanced, review. Despite my earlier disclaimer, once I started talking, the words came easily. "It was Melinda, not Sonya, who fought with Elliot. She wanted more alimony, but killing him would have defeated the purpose. She needed him alive and earning money. Not dead, with a heavily mortgaged house and a second wife and kid to share in the meager spoils."

Tom said, "That would make perfect sense if Elliot Tumbleson hadn't taken out a multimillion-dollar life insurance policy last Christmas."

His comment jogged my memory with a detail I'd forgotten. "Elliot said if Melinda didn't stop harassing him, he was going to take out a restraining order against her. I didn't pay much attention to it at the time, because it sounded like a way to score points. He was contemptuous, not scared. But this news about the life insurance policy does change things. Did Melinda know about it?" I sipped at the coffee and resisted the siren song of the donuts, even though the sugary carbohydrates beckoned mightily to me. "If Melinda knew that Elliot was worth more dead than alive, then perhaps the argument was the final straw."

Tom picked up a jelly donut. "She says she didn't know. Both wives will benefit from his death. And there's additional money in trust for the kids. So the financial motive is strong for both women."

Thinking of Elliot's cocky, careless, bullying manner, I said, "Don't discount the benefit of simply eliminating Elliot from their lives."

Sorkin nodded. "I already know how much Melinda and Elliot hated each other. I'm not so sure about Sonya. A couple of witnesses at the country club hinted that the second Mrs. Tumbleson was a lot like her husband when it came to extramarital affairs."

I put the coffee cup on my desk and sat down, figuring our conversation could take a while. "I don't know much about Sonya, other than the fact that I don't like her. She's as mean as Melinda."

Tom commented, "But a lot prettier."

"I agree that Sonya Tumbleson is beautiful. But if you got to know her, you might find her even less attractive than Melinda." I didn't like gossip but wasn't above using it to achieve a higher goal. "If I were you, I wouldn't put too much credence into anything Sonya says. I don't have direct knowledge of any infidelities, but as you said, there was plenty of talk around the club that she was having an affair with the golf pro. Or the tennis pro. Or both pros. At the Meadowfields Country Club, 'pro' takes on a whole new meaning."

"Are you talking about Ryan Walker? His name is popping up a lot." Sorkin looked speculatively at me. "What's your take on him?"

"There's nothing I can tell you that you don't already know. He's absurdly good-looking, and he's rumored to be sleeping with half the women at the Meadowfields Country Club."

Sorkin was sharp and quick in his response. "Are you speaking from personal knowledge? Did he make a move on you?"

I made a gagging sound, a reaction I attributed to spending too much time with teenagers. "As I've explained, I hardly knew him." Sorkin raised one of those black eyebrows at me, and I said, with greater heat, "He's not my type. I prefer a man who's not on sale or for sale."

I wasn't at my best at the end of the school day and was self-conscious under his scrutiny. Sorkin wasn't any more my type than the golf pro, but those eyes of his disturbed me. I shook my hair loose from its bobby pin prison and pretended it wasn't to shield my face from him.

Sorkin put his notebook down, picked it up, and put it down again. It was the first break in his impassive exterior. He disposed of his coffee cup in the garbage can and said, "We seem to have gotten away from the subject at hand."

A knock on the half-open door interrupted his next question. Caroline Cartwright, the chairperson of the Valerian Hills English department, entered and gave an excellent imitation of surprise.

In her upper-class British drawl, which never failed to grate on my nerves, she said, "So sorry to interrupt this little tête-à-tête, Liz, but Timmy wants to see you. I hope you haven't hurt anyone's feelings. Again."

I inwardly cursed the fate that put me in thrall to our new principal. Timmy was bad enough to deal with when he was an assistant principal, but his recent ascension to the top job in the school had brought out his latent sadism.

Like Timmy, Caroline enjoyed pulling wings off hapless butterflies. She shook her head at me when I didn't answer and said, "Timmy seems quite annoyed with you, and I wouldn't keep him waiting. It won't improve his temper or Melinda Tumbleson's." She arched thin eyebrows at the detectives as if expecting them to join in her condemnation of me.

Sorkin positioned himself between us and said, "Tell Mrs. Tumbleson, and whoever else is waiting for Ms. Hopewell, that she has been unavoidably detained."

She flounced out of the room.

In any group, the desire to eject an undesirable person tends to unite the rest, and Caroline's cattiness broke the invisible barrier between Sorkin and me. I told him to call me Liz.

The detective let his guard down enough to say, "Ben." He shut the door to prevent further interruptions and said, "Let's get back to the facts."

I took out my notebook and, after adding information about Elliot's life insurance policy, showed it to them. It had pages of writing and a layer of sticky notes. "I've already told you everything I know, but you might find this useful. I'll type it up and email it tomorrow, and if you have more questions, I'll be happy to answer them. In the meantime, I have to babysit our principal before he has a temper tantrum."

Ben flipped through the notebook. After stopping at a page written in three different colors of ink, he said, "I'd be interested to see what you come up with when you're not interested in a case."

It sounded like a compliment despite his stoic expression and dry delivery. Tom laughed and clapped his partner on the back. They headed to the parking lot, and I entered the glass-walled main office. Abigail, Timmy's secretary, stopped me. "I'm sorry, Ms. Hopewell. Mr. Dunkel is very anxious to see you, but he's with someone at the moment. How does tomorrow at 10:40 sound to you?"

"First of all, Abigail, my name is Liz. And second, I'm not giving up my lunch break to talk to Timmy."

It was a little-known fact that the bus company, in cooperation with the athletic department, had the final say on our school schedule. Those masterminds deemed 7:25 an appropriate start to the school day, which was why the first lunch period began at 10:30.

She looked flustered. "Of course, Ms. Hopewell. I mean, Liz. But Mr. Dunkel wants all of us to act more professional. So that's why I called you Ms. Hopewell."

I leaned over the newly erected, chest-high barricade that protected the secretary from the encroachments of high school life. "Let Timmy know I look forward to speaking with him at a mutually convenient time."

I turned to leave, but Timmy called me back. "Ms. Hopewell! Please come right on in. There's someone here to see you."

I entered the principal's office. Perched on the edge of a chair, wearing a black dress that matched her dark expression, was Melinda Tumbleson. The clutch of tissues with which she dabbed her eyes didn't quite mask the triumphant look on her face.

Timmy sat at his desk, clasped his hands in front of him, and said, "Now, Ms. Hopewell. What can we do—what can *you* do—to assist the Tumbleson family in their hour of need?"

Luckily, I didn't have a golf club with me. The temptation to conk both of them might have been too much to resist.

Timmy prodded me toward an acceptable answer. "Ms. Hopewell, please tell Mrs. Tumbleson that you will provide Jack with whatever accommodations he needs."

I said, "Mrs. Tumbleson, I will provide Jack with whatever accommodations he needs."

Satisfied with my words, if not my toneless delivery, he released me.

Melinda, however, wasn't done. "You can start that action plan by reviewing his work. I was very disappointed in Jack's last test grade. I don't want to make accusations of prejudicial treatment, but you gave him the lowest mark in the class. His other teachers have been giving him top marks."

I used my phone to access the school's online grade book and checked Jack's profile. Without comment, I pointed to the three subjects he was failing. She reddened and, turning to Timmy, cried, "This is what I'm talking about! How can Jack succeed with this person as his teacher?"

I bit my lip to keep my mouth from getting me into trouble. It wasn't a completely successful maneuver. "I'm very sorry for your loss. However, when I look at Jack's grades, I see that he is passing only the classes taught by non-tenured teachers. They're too afraid of you to give him the grades he deserves."

Timmy was furious. At me, not her. He instructed me to make yet another appointment to talk to him and told Melinda that he would take care of this unfortunate matter personally.

I skipped signing out for the day and drove home. Although a scant hour earlier, I couldn't wait to resume researching cold cases, my meeting with Tom and Ben, followed by the meeting with Timmy and Melinda, made it difficult to get Elliot's death out of my mind. I worried I'd forgotten to tell the detectives something important and decided to review my notes before sending them off. Although we'd thoroughly discussed all of the major players in the previous day's drama, dozens of cameo performers were also on the scene.

Chapter Six

Because I could not stop for Death — He kindly stopped for me
—Emily Dickinson / "Because I could not stop for Death"

On Saturday afternoon, the sun shone, and the New Jersey Transit gods smiled upon me. There were no delays from Oak Ridge to Penn Station, and the subway ride uptown was uneventful. Susan met me in front of the Museum of Natural History.

She greeted me with perfumed enthusiasm. *"Ma belle soeur! Je t'aime!"* Susan was a committed Francophile, and she layered her conversation, her clothing, and her body with all things French.

I offered to buy us a hot pretzel or knish for lunch, but Susan anticipated my fattening and unhealthy food choices. She produced a shopping bag full of dietetic goodies, and although I would have preferred the street food, I didn't complain about the spread, especially since I knew how much money that takeout meal cost.

We took our lunch to Central Park, where we sat on a bench and watched the kids in the playground. While I waxed sentimental about the children, Susan discussed her latest boyfriend. The last time she looked this happy, she was vowing eternal fidelity to her third husband. Her latest divorce was the worst. Susan was furious with me after I told her of my suspicions regarding her spouse and her best friend. My sister forgave me when the ex-husband and ex-best friend hot-footed it to a couples resort in the Bahamas six days after the divorce.

I cut short her detailed description of the new boyfriend and their visits to the Metropolitan Opera House. "Tell me more about him and less about the music you listened to." I popped open a Diet Coke and prepared to enjoy both the conversation and the toxic chemicals that would destroy my entire generation of women.

"His name is Georges!" she said, giving the name its French pronunciation. "How crazy is that? Now I have a George too, but he's better than your George because he's Georges! Get it?"

"Is there anything you know about him besides his first name? How can you be sure the guy you're meeting isn't a serial killer? Or a fugitive? What if he flunked British Literature and World History?"

Susan is even more thin-skinned than I am. She answered, with great dignity, "What do you take me for? I never meet a new guy anywhere near my apartment. I always propose the West Side."

Giving her boyfriend's name comedic emphasis, I said, "That's a lovely idea, but I repeat, how do you know *Georges* is who he says he is?"

Susan pouted. "I spent a ton of money signing up for an exclusive dating service, and they vet all their applicants. Believe me, if he's on the site, he's financially stable, if not emotionally stable."

"I think you need to do some vetting of your own." I used a carrot stick to dig for the more appetizing bits in my salad.

She provided several more arguments that weren't nearly as persuasive for me as they were for her. "Georges is from Montreal, so I get to speak French with him. He moved here as a kid but has a trace of an accent, which is *très* charming. He's an only child. No close relatives, which is great. No ex-wives, and no kids, which is even better. You know how I hate pretending to care about other people's children. He works for some hedge fund and is rich, rich, rich. What else do I need to know?"

I had my doubts. "All I'm saying is, take it slow. Check him out for yourself and make sure he is who he says he is."

Susan drank the last of her Diet Coke and took a few swigs of mine. "Speaking of investigating, tell me more about the murder. Do you know what the odds are of you coming across two dead bodies in less than a year? First, your English teacher friend, and now, this country club guy. The

35

number is probably astronomical. Of course, it's a tragedy. But here we are again, sisters in crime, literally!"

I ate the bread she'd hidden in the bottom of the bag. "I'm not here to talk about Elliot Tumbleson. We aren't going to get involved in that investigation because— "

"Is Detective Gorgeous on the case? Because if he is, I'm willing to rethink an exclusive relationship with Georges." Her lips curved in a smile that was wasted on me.

"Didn't you tell me that your Georges was perfect?"

"Yes, of course, he's perfect. Good looking, rich, and with season tickets to the opera. But there is no getting around the fact that he's older than I am. Not a lot older, but I'd say about ten years. Maybe more. So, not ideal. I'm in the market for a sexy young guy. Someone with a lot of energy, if you know what I mean. I suppose I could have Georges as a husband and a young, unattached guy as a fun kind of boyfriend. Sort of like committing to eating a healthy dinner and then cheating with a decadent dessert."

I hated talking about Tom with Susan and said only that he was assigned to the case.

She poked me. "Is he with the same partner?"

"Detective Brown retired. You wouldn't like the new guy any better." I gathered up our trash and walked to a nearby garbage can, but it would take a more subtle move than that to fool my sister.

Susan's eyes were wide. "I want every dirty detail, and I want it now. What's his name?"

I attempted outrage. "Elliot Tumbleson was killed with my golf club. The name of the detective investigating the case is beside the point."

"I've said it before, and I'll say it again. You have no sense of fun. I wish you'd lighten up a little."

I took her hand. "We've got a more important case to work on. I don't know what we'll find, or how far the investigation will take us, but for once, you've made the right call. We need to find out what happened to Mom. It won't be easy, and it won't be fun. As far as we know, the Lousy Bastard never went to prison, but he was a career criminal. Digging into his past could be dangerous, but mostly everyone involved is old enough to have retired years ago. It won't be as risky now as it might have been when we were kids."

"Are you sure you're feeling okay? We talked about this two days ago, and you flatly refused." She put a hand to my forehead as if checking to see if I was running a fever. "You're afraid of roller coasters, clowns, and gerbils. You get your kicks at soccer games and ballet recitals. And all of a sudden, you want to check out The Lousy Bastard's criminal gang members?"

Susan's apparent reversal exasperated me. "Now that I'm finally agreeing with you, you're changing your mind? I thought you were serious. I didn't think you were trying to needle me."

"I'm simply concerned that you've maybe hit a very rocky mid-life crisis and are using this to distract you from other, um, problems you might be having." Her tone was teasing, but her expression was grave. Although my sister and I spent hours discussing the men in her life, I rarely talked about George. Maybe there wasn't much to say.

I picked at a loose thread on my sweater. "I've been reading up on ordinary people who work on cold cases. They scour the internet and old photographs and police records, and they dedicate themselves to solving murders the police have given up on. No crazy conspiracy theories are involved."

"*Mais oui, ma chére*, I've heard of these people." She swatted my hand away from the sweater. "Don't keep pulling at your clothes. Even though you might as well throw your entire outfit in the garbage. You've had that sweater since before Zach was born, and it's positively moth-eaten."

I pulled again at the thread, which did the sweater no favors. "Don't change the subject. I'm talking about Mom. Her life, as well as her death."

"You've never talked about her before. Never. No matter how many times I tried. Why now?"

I wasn't sure of the answer. "I guess being faced with Elliot Tumbleson's murder, on the anniversary of the day she died, made me think of my own death. I don't want to leave any unfinished business behind me when I go. The way I see it, there are three possible reasons behind Mom's car accident. None of them are pleasant.

"The first is that Dear Old Dad killed her so he could collect on her life insurance and live full-time with his other wife and kids. The second possibility is that someone else did it, for reasons we don't yet know." I paused. The next words were difficult. "The third possibility is that we never knew Mom at all, and her accidental death was a suicide. That would explain why there was no investigation."

"If she killed herself, knowing we'd have no one but The Lousy Bastard to rely on...that's damned close to unbearable." Susan buried her face in her hands. "Maybe you were right all along. Maybe we should leave it at that."

I brushed spilled tears from my face and hers. "We're still giving him too much power over us. We can start by calling him Lousy instead of by a title. As for the rest, we owe it to Mom. Because I don't believe she killed herself, and she deserves better than that from us. And Ellie and Zach need more than a photo album with blank pages."

We got up from the bench in the same instant, looked at each other, and said, "Okay."

I was so sure we were doing the right thing, I forgot about the probable endpoint of a road paved with good intentions.

Chapter Seven

Like as the waves make towards the pebbled shore.
So do our minutes hasten to their end...
—William Shakespeare / Sonnet 60

My train home was forty minutes behind schedule, which put George in a foul mood. I left him to fume as I showered with military brevity, dressed in a flash, and troweled makeup on my face. I pinned my unruly locks into a passably neat French twist and grabbed my purse.

George didn't ask me about my day. Instead, he crammed twenty minutes of complaining into the ten-minute drive. When we arrived at the Meadowfields clubhouse, a valet leaped to open my door. I wasn't used to the niceties of country club life, but I remembered to tuck some cash into my purse for the parking attendants.

George's boss and his much younger wife were at a prized table on the glass-enclosed patio. A green expanse was below us, and twinkling lights from New York City's skyline echoed the stars above.

Cooper rose to his feet as we approached. "Liz. So happy to see you again." He gestured to his wife, a slim vision of expensive beauty in white-dotted pink linen. "This is Bryony."

I tripped over a nonexistent impediment but managed not to upset the immaculately set table. It was the times I most wished for the poise of Grace Kelly that I stumbled like Bozo the Clown.

Bryony half-hid her smile behind her hand. "So lovely to meet you, Lee."

Typical mean-girl ploy. As pleasantly as I could, I corrected her. "It's Liz. Not Lee." I didn't remind her we'd met multiple times.

"Of course it is." She frowned with the strain of remembering who I was. "Now let me see…I think you were in my golf clinic. Sonya Tumbleson also was there, poor thing. Who could have imagined Elliot would get himself killed?"

Cooper hitched his chair closer to the table. "Unfortunate thing to have happened to the club. Makes us all look bad."

His concern for the club, as opposed to the man, sickened me. "I believe the murder was worse for Elliot than for Meadowfields."

George kicked me under the table and said, "Do the police have any leads?"

"They're here right now." Cooper leaned in and spoke in a confidential tone. "Under normal circumstances, I would object to a police presence during the dinner hour, but the sooner they make an arrest, the sooner we can put all this unpleasantness behind us."

Bryony looked as satisfied as if she'd solved the case herself. "I tipped them off a few hours ago. They're in the kitchen, interrogating Mike. Or is it Michael? I'm not sure."

I rose from the table and muttered something that could have been interpreted as a desire to use the bathroom. Instead of heading upstairs, however, I ducked outside and circled around to the service entrance. I was ten feet from the door when it burst open. A young, tearful guy, dressed in a waiter's uniform and flanked by detectives Tom Harriman and Ben Sorkin, made his way toward the cop car.

Behind him, an older woman wailed, "Miguel! *No digas nada!* Tell them you want a lawyer!"

I was shocked to see one of my former students in custody. Although Bryony referred to him as Mike, his name was Miguel.

I appealed to the distraught woman who had shouted instructions to Miguel, but she shut me down. *"No hablo ingles, señora."*

Her rebuff was understandable but I didn't let it stop me, as I knew she spoke English with the ease and the accent of a woman born in New Jersey. "I'll dust off my high school Spanish if that's what it'll take to get you to talk to me. I was Miguel's teacher, and I want to help."

Without so much as an *hasta luego*, she re-entered the building. It was then that I became aware of our audience. A dozen or so diners had left the restaurant to watch the unfolding drama.

George broke through the crowd and took my arm. With a tender expression that didn't reach his eyes, he said, "Come back to dinner. What will Bryony and Cooper think?"

"Who cares what they think? They're not the ones who were hauled into the police station."

We returned to our table on the patio, but Bryony and Cooper were gone. They were at the tail end of a parade that trickled back into the room after the excitement of Miguel's departure.

Bryony was triumphant. "I knew from the first time I laid eyes on Mike that he had a shifty look to him, but I never imagined him capable of murder."

The Meadowfields Country Club maintained an unofficial policy of Anglicizing the names of their employees. Tamping down a rage that made me want to choke her, I said, "His name is Miguel, not Mike. The reason you didn't imagine him a killer is because he isn't one. He's a good kid who's in his last year of college and is engaged to be married. What possible reason could he have for murdering Elliot Tumbleson?"

Bryony blinked with feline enjoyment at my distress. "Why are you so bent out of shape? You only joined the club a few weeks ago. How did you get to be so friendly with the waiters?"

I longed to dump a glass of ice water down the back of her trim little pink and white dress. "Miguel was one of my students. I wrote his college recommendation letter, and George and I vouched for him when he applied for his job at the club. He goes to school all day and works here nights and weekends. So, not the criminal type."

Cooper's short laugh sounded like a nonverbal swear word. "I didn't know we had you to thank for this, George. Between you bringing Miguel to work here and Liz providing the murder weapon, maybe the police should be investigating the two of you!"

He spoke lightly, but George and I could tell he wasn't completely kidding.

My husband opened and closed his mouth like a hooked and hapless fish, so I took over. "We don't yet know if the police took him because they think he's guilty, or because they think he can provide important evidence. Miguel is innocent until proven guilty."

To Bryony, I said, "Maybe if you tell me what you told the police, I'd understand better why you suspect Miguel."

She finished her martini and, with fingers that didn't tremble, speared the remaining olive. "As treasurer of the club, Coop can't divulge any details. I, however, have no problem telling you, off the record, that there was some funny business going on. We think Mike was skimming money from the club account. Thousands of dollars are unaccounted for. Elliot, as the former treasurer, must have found out about it. That gives your star pupil plenty of motive. He could get imprisoned or deported."

"Miguel was born in New Jersey, and he's no more a thief than he is a killer. It makes more sense to investigate the members of the board. They're the ones with the knowledge and access to pull off that kind of theft." It was clear from her attitude that she knew nothing about Miguel. I wanted her to see him as I did.

Bryony looked down her expensive nose. "It's nice of you to stand up for one of your students, but him getting an A in your class doesn't count for much in the real world."

People who talked about education as something that didn't exist in the real world enraged me. George, who was well-acquainted with my feelings on the matter, cut me off before I could share those views with his boss's wife.

"Let's change the subject." George turned to Cooper in time-honored male-bonding mode and said, "What do you think of the Yankees' chances this year?"

As much as anything else that night, this statement surprised me, and I spoke without thinking. "What do you care? You root for the Mets."

George elbowed me and said, "There's nothing like a subway series." Cooper and he exchanged looks in what looked like a silent commiseration over their shared marital mistakes.

A waiter approached the table. With a collective sigh of relief, we ordered dinner.

In deference to George, I avoided controversial topics, and the rest of the meal passed with relative ease. Cooper and George discussed the condition of the grass on the golf course [good], the condition of the country [bad], and the recent uptick in the real estate market [very good.]

Bryony and I discussed Ryan Walker, the golf pro [good], the new color scheme in the women's dressing room [bad], and Bryony's new maid [very bad.] If I hadn't been so worried about Miguel, I would have been bored to death, but anxiety about him kept me alert.

At the end of the meal, while the other three waited for a valet to retrieve our cars, I sneaked back to the kitchen. As soon as I pushed through the swinging door, the loud chatter quieted. Half shocked and half resentful, a waiter whose nameplate read Ian cut me off. "Ms. Hopewell, I hope nothing is wrong. I will be at your table immediately."

I stammered, "No! I—don't go there. We don't need anything."

Ian continued to bar my way. "Then allow me to escort you back to the dining room."

"I'm here about Miguel. What's going on? Has he been arrested?"

The waiter remained outwardly polite. "We don't believe Miguel is guilty. But what can we do?"

With a confidence I was far from feeling, I said, "You can talk to me. I'll get to the bottom of this."

His suspicious attitude didn't offend me. After all, when an English teacher offers to investigate a murder, skepticism is an understandable response.

But a miscalculation, nonetheless. Underneath my smooth suburban exterior, I remained a kid from the projects. Having spent years helping my guilty father evade justice for his petty crimes, I was better equipped than most to ensure an innocent man was acquitted.

Chapter Eight

The Child is father of the man
—William Wordsworth / "My Heart Leaps Up"

On the way home from the country club, I contemplated, with growing alarm, George's new habit of zooming through yellow lights and stepping on the gas when the brake lights of the car in front of us flashed red. His driving, like his attitude toward me, bore very little resemblance to the old George.

I had no desire to join his new friends and new social scene, and after suffering through a golf lesson and dinner with the Aldridges, it was clear the social scene in question was equally disinclined to include me. Bryony's condescending attitude, from her opening gambit of forgetting my name to her disrespectful comments about teachers, underlined my status as an outsider.

I vented my frustration on George because it was his fault I had to suffer. "How big a discount did we get for the privilege of joining the country club? If dinner with Bryony and Cooper is part of the price, I think we got a raw deal. They cared more about the menu than they did about an innocent man getting arrested."

"We don't know why the cops took Miguel. We also don't know if he's innocent or guilty. You can hardly blame Bryony and Cooper for celebrating the fact that the police made an arrest." He slammed the brakes with slightly less force than was necessary to deploy the airbags.

I rubbed the back of my neck. "Miguel is innocent. I know it, and you know it."

He pulled into a strip mall and glared at me. "This murder investigation is none of your business."

"If the police arrested the wrong man, it's very much my business and yours too." I was simmering but didn't boil over. Our marriage couldn't take many more fissures.

"Let's not fight. Tonight was supposed to be a celebration of my new position at the club. The board voted me in as assistant treasurer, the same post it took Cooper years to achieve." He eased the car back on the road.

Sympathy overtook anger, and I stopped criticizing him. George had gotten a seat at the cool kids' table, and I didn't want to ruin his pleasure. In silence, we pulled into the driveway and got ready for bed. I opened a book of sonnets and was half asleep when my phone pinged with a message from Bryony, summoning me, in a rather peremptory fashion, to meet her for drinks. She was the loveliest, best-coiffed, most fashionable member of the ladies' golf and tennis teams. Bryony had no need, nor had she ever evinced any previous desire, to annex me as one of her lesser satellites.

When I read her message to George, he gave me a congratulatory slap on the back. Not my idea of a prelude to romance, but I didn't want to burst his bubble too quickly. Unlike my husband, I was suspicious of Bryony's sudden, kind attention. In all previous interactions, she made me feel like the last kid picked for the team, the one who was forced on the others at the behest of whatever well-meaning adult was in charge.

I gave George news that was bad from his perspective but fortuitous from mine. "I have auditions for the school play. I can't cancel at this late date." In response to his stricken look, I reminded him of his role in this dilemma. "You were the one who wanted me to direct the play. But don't worry about Bryony. I'll ask for a rain check." Silently, I contemplated rescheduling the meetup for the third leap year from next February.

"I admit I was wrong. You should quit the stupid play. You're too busy for that nonsense." He patted my arm as if soothing a pesky dog.

I didn't strangle him, although I did entertain visions of crushing his precious golf clubs with a cast iron frying pan. "I wish I had a recording of the conversation we had in September when you insisted we needed the extra cash. That was before you decided we had enough money to join the country club."

George slammed his book shut. "If you're in charge of the play, then take charge. Arrange your rehearsal hours so they don't impact your date with Bryony. And leave the family finances to me."

I inched closer, so Ellie and Zach couldn't overhear us. "Ever since we joined the club, you've been like a different person. You care more about your new friends than about me or the kids."

"I'm the same person I was before, except now I've got a bigger paycheck and a promotion. On top of that, Cooper fast-tracked our membership application. Considering how good he's been to us, would it kill you to be nice to his wife?"

I wasn't finished fighting, but I continued my battle covertly. "Okay, I'll meet Bryony. And I'll be suitably sycophantic to your boss's wife if that will make you happy. But I can't change my rehearsal schedule every time someone at the club snaps her fingers."

"Of course, darling. Whatever you say." George was delighted with my seeming acquiescence.

I put my book on the nightstand. "There's only one thing I need from you."

He sat up. "Tell me what you need. No problem."

"I can't go to these group golf lessons two or three times a week. Too much time, and I'm not getting the kind of attention a beginner like me needs."

George nodded seriously. "Do you want private lessons? That would be the best way to learn the game."

I smiled. "Exactly. I know it's pricey, but maybe I could withdraw from the group lessons and do one private lesson every week or so."

George wrapped his arms around me. "That's why I married you. You're the smartest woman I know."

Indeed.

*　*　*

46

Without explicitly lying to George, I allowed him to think I scheduled a private lesson before meeting with Bryony. In the hour I would have wasted on the practice range, I tracked down employees who might help exonerate Miguel.

He meant more to me than most of my former students. I encouraged him to apply to college and spent hours helping him with his essay. So many of his challenges mirrored mine when I was his age, and I wanted to help him in the same way one of my favorite high school teachers helped me. Despite Miguel's financial instability, deceased mother, and negligent father, he graduated at the top of his class in high school and was on a path to do the same at college. A kid like that deserved help. Bryony, and even George, doubted my knowledge of Miguel's character, but that was because they didn't understand how intimately teachers got to know their students.

I began by questioning the kitchen staff and the women who cleaned the bathrooms. They were kind, and they wanted to be helpful, but none of them was on duty the day Elliot Tumbleson was killed. Or at least that's what they told me.

I stole into the closet-sized room where the workers checked in and took a screenshot of their schedule. Even if it didn't establish an alibi for Miguel, it would let me know when to return to interview people who were present when the murder was committed. I headed toward the caddy shack next, taking an indirect route to avoid the driving range, where the usual lesson was in progress.

Carl Bagarosa, the ex-Marine who now commanded an army of landscapers, wasn't pleased to see me heading in his direction. I didn't blame him for his ungracious reaction. The last time we met, it was over Elliot's dead body.

Ignoring his obvious disinclination to talk to me, I said, "So nice to see you again, Carl."

Carl looked suspiciously at a square of grass that had failed to achieve the exact shade of green as the rest of the lawn. "I'm kind of busy right now."

I joined him in his perusal of the grass, hoping that a shared concern for lawn care would soften him. "Did you see Miguel on the day Elliot was killed? He's a former student, and I know he couldn't possibly be guilty of murder. I want to help him out if I can."

"I don't know anything about him. Don't have much to do with the waitstaff. Anyone is capable of murder, under the right circumstances." He turned his gaze from the grass to me and closed the gap between us. "Even you, Ms. Hopewell."

I stood my ground, although his nose was uncomfortably close to my forehead. "That sounds like an accusation. Or a threat. Which is it?"

He looked confused, so I clarified it for him. "I've heard people claim that anyone is capable of murder. But I don't think that's true. And even if it is, surely some people are more likely, or at least more willing, to murder than others. Unless the killer is a psychopath, he or she has to have a motive. And Miguel has no motive. Can you think of anyone who does?"

While Carl cleared his throat with stomach-churning thoroughness, I put enough distance between us to give any sick-making germs some room. He noisily breathed in, as if to expectorate, but at the last minute rethought the action, probably in deference to Club Rule #14A (No Spitting.)

He went into his cowboy act, drawling, "I don't know anything about motives, Ms. Hopewell. I take care of the golf course and don't stick my nose where it don't belong. None-a my business what goes on in those offices." He said the word "office" so derisively he might as well have said, "playground for whiny over-privileged nincompoops."

"You're an employee of this club, are you not?" A tiny bit of English teacher frost crept into my tone. I couldn't help it. It was in my bones.

Looking marginally less antagonistic, Carl said, "Well, yeah. But not my business."

"Tell me one thing, Carl, something that is your business. You were very close to Elliot when he was murdered." He looked startled, so I added, "I mean, you were physically close to him. Maybe fifteen, twenty yards away."

Carl's cheeks got redder, and his voice louder. "What are you saying? You think I did it?"

I sighed. Diplomacy wasn't my strong suit. "I'm not saying anything of the sort. But you were the first one to come when I yelled for help. Did you see anyone along the path?"

Carl grew restive. "The only person I saw was Mrs. Tumbleson."

I already knew Melinda Tumbleson had been walking along the path at about the time Elliot was killed, but I asked, just to be sure, "Which Mrs. Tumbleson? The first one or the second?"

He chuckled and raised his eyebrows. "The good-lookin' one."

I didn't let him see my excitement. "Of course, yes, Sonya. I was at a golf lesson with her. So…when did you see her? When she was on her way to the golf range? Or on her way back?"

Carl Bagarosa looked down at his feet. Cursing softly, he bent down and plucked a brave little dandelion from the edge of the grass. He held up the flower as if he held me personally responsible for its invasion. "She looked like she was heading to the parking lot."

I mentally mapped the route from the driving range to the crime scene to the parking lot. Why would Sonya have gone to the parking lot when she was supposed to be having a drink with her friends?

The time frame for the murder was narrow. I'd seen Elliot a scant hour before his death. "Carl, can you tell me what time you saw Sonya Tumbleson?"

With a cry of pain, he plucked another dandelion. "Can't talk, Ms. Hopewell. Got an emergency weed situation." He nodded curtly and headed to his office in the caddy shack.

I followed him, walking faster than he did so I could see his face. "It's a simple question. What time did you see her?"

"All I know is…" He paused for a moment and then redoubled his pace. "I don't know anything. I'm not even sure she's the one I saw." With a nasty smile, he added, "Good luck with your golf game."

After my sprint to the caddy shack, I walked more slowly to the clubhouse. I couldn't figure out if Carl Bagarosa was a suspect or a witness. Had he seen Sonya? Or was he implicating her to cover his actions? I longed to follow him, since he seemed on the verge of saying something interesting, but doing so would cut into the time I'd have with Bryony.

My reluctance to meet with her had been both childish and shortsighted.

Bryony was responsible, either directly or indirectly, for implicating Miguel in Elliot's murder. By her own admission, she knew very little about the staff, but no one was more knowledgeable about the private lives of the members. And she was sharp. Let others underestimate a beautiful, bored woman with impeccable taste in clothing. I wouldn't make that mistake.

Chapter Nine

Words are easy, like the wind...
—William Shakespeare / The Passionate Pilgrim

I arrived at our reserved table at the appointed hour, but Bryony didn't show up until fifteen more minutes elapsed. When she made her entrance, which she did with some flair, she waved at several friends before acknowledging my existence. She paused on her way to our table to chat with a group of three women whom I knew slightly. By the time she deigned to join me, my cheek muscles ached with the effort of keeping a fake smile in place.

Bryony sank gracefully into her chair, and two waiters, who had been chatting in a corner, sprang to her side.

The senior waiter asked, "The usual, Mrs. Aldridge?"

She nodded. "And bring my friend another of whatever she's having."

The waiters rushed off to do her bidding, and in the interim, she admired her diamond rings. They were quite lovely, if a bit large for her thin fingers. She yawned. "I can't talk until I have a drink. This day was too, too dull."

As Bryony settled into her martini, I covertly studied her from behind my Diet Coke.

"Can't I entice you to order a more interesting beverage?" Bryony's tone was amused.

"I'm afraid not," I apologized. "I have to be back at work soon. The first round of auditions for the school musical is tonight."

"I have no idea how you do it, though I guess teaching isn't too taxing. You do have the summers off."

I hate it when people say this. "I don't get paid in the summer. Like most people, I don't work unless I'm getting paid."

This statement of fact garnered a more positive reaction. "I know what you mean. I'm on two tennis teams, and honestly, it's like a job that costs you money instead of paying you. I'm constantly running around to lessons, practices, and matches. No time off at all. And, for freak's sake, the clothes! No one wants to be like Melinda Tumbleson, who wears the same pathetic outfits, week after week. Although I guess with her figure, it doesn't much matter what she wears. Not to be *too* catty, but facts are facts. Nothing is going to look good on her except a potato sack."

Overcome with her own wit, Bryony laughed immoderately, and I attempted an amused expression. It wasn't easy, because her assertion that her days on the tennis team were like my days in the classroom irked me. I wished, not for the first time, that I had a more glamorous job. No one hears "English teacher" and thinks: *Wow, that sounds interesting!*

I squeezed a wedge of lime into my soda and switched to a more serious topic. "Why did you want to meet with me? Does it have anything to do with Miguel?"

"I don't follow the trials and tribulations of the kitchen staff." She yawned again and surveyed the room as if looking for more stimulating company.

I pressed her. "And yet you told the police Miguel was skimming money from the club. Did Cooper ask you to forward that information to the cops?"

"My husband is the treasurer, and yours is the assistant treasurer. That's their business, not ours. I presume the police will investigate Miguel's motives. Why not ask them?"

I drained my soda with an unladylike gurgle. "Because I'm asking you. You're the one who reported Miguel. You must have some evidence to support the accusation."

Bryony swirled the dregs of colorless liquid in her glass and circled her hand around the rim to indicate her desire for another drink. "I was only guessing about the whole financial motive, because in the last few days, Elliot was constantly blathering to anyone who would listen to him about some big revelation. I'm sure your husband knows about it. Elliot wasn't the most popular guy at the club, and I thought he was looking for attention." She laughed. "Elliot could barely get anyone to play golf with him. He was so obnoxious."

Her attempts at humor induced a gag reflex that made swallowing difficult. But I wasn't so overcome that I missed her reference to George's knowledge of the financial dealings at the club. Why hadn't my husband told me? George knew my father was a grifter who supplemented his income with petty theft. Although I wasn't familiar with high-class embezzlement, I could have given him a few pointers on how cons get done. Like how the first rule of a successful con is misdirection.

Bryony might not know much about the missing money, but she was an expert at ferreting out more personal secrets. Trying not to sound too eager, I said, "Tell me about Elliot's relationship with Sonya. I already know his relationship with Melinda wasn't good."

She leaned her elbows on the table and rested her chin in her hands, which made me feel as if I was now part of her privileged circle. "You know, of course, the police were called to their house last week. Sonya said later it was all a mistake, but I saw her in the dressing room with these huge black and blue marks."

For someone who had no interest in Elliot, Sonya, or Melinda, she was remarkably well-informed. "I didn't know, and I'm so sorry to hear that." I felt a rush of pity for Sonya. "I suppose if the police hadn't taken Miguel into custody, they might have gone after Sonya."

The waiter placed a second martini on the table and brought me another Diet Coke. Bryony stirred her drink. "If Sonya did kill him, no one here would blame her."

"I didn't know about his abuse. Did she fear for her life?" Another thought struck me. "Did Elliot also abuse Melinda and Jack?"

She put down her glass. "I'm not saying Elliot deserved to die or that Sonya killed him. When things go south, anyone with half a brain gets a good divorce lawyer and takes her husband to the cleaners. I did that to my last two husbands. And believe you me, I have no regrets. You don't have to smash someone's head with a golf club to make them suffer."

Bryony's sentiment didn't shock me, but she seemed too young to have been divorced twice. "How did you know the police were at the Tumblesons' house? Did Sonya confide in you?"

"Sonya and I are country club friends, so we see each other quite a bit. I don't socialize with her outside Meadowfields, although she lives down the block from us, on Mountain View Avenue. Huge, ugly mansion. Looks like someone threw a bunch of concrete blocks together and then added a gas station on the side. I simply don't know what the Town Council was thinking, to allow them to build that monstrosity. Hideous taste. Of course, you've seen Elliot's wives. One is a dowdy slob. The other a total tart."

Bryony seemed more offended by the Tumblesons' architectural crimes than by Elliot's assault on his wife. I wondered, for the tenth time, what prompted Bryony's invitation. I was as dowdy as Melinda. Sadly, I lacked the personal charm that would have rendered me as tarty as Sonya.

I hadn't had time to change and was wearing my usual school uniform: stretchy skirt, sleeveless tee, and a long sweater that hid weekend indulgences in a few too many spoonfuls of ice cream. Bryony wore clothes that suited her but inspired no envy in me. She sported a pale pink shirt and pink floral skirt. A white sweater, made from some cloud-like material, lay carelessly across her shoulders. The picture of well-bred, upper-class innocence.

And yet, Bryony was anything but innocent. Without inflicting a single wrinkle to her brow or her clothes, she'd suggested potentially powerful motives in the murder of Elliot Tumbleson. It wasn't yet clear to me if those comments were artless or artful.

I didn't like her but felt morally compelled to warn her. "Someone in the club, or associated with the club, is a killer. Be careful, Bryony. You're wrong about Miguel, but you don't want the real murderer feeling threatened by you."

Bryony patted her mouth with a napkin. "I'm very discreet. You're not going to rat me out, are you?"

I promised to take her secrets to the grave and said, "Tell me about Carl

Bagarosa. He was nearby when Elliot was killed and has no alibi."

Bryony's mocking smile froze. "Why would you ask me about him? I'm not friends with the grounds crew any more than I'm friends with the kitchen staff."

"I've already told you why I'm interested in Carl."

She smoothed beads of condensation from her glass. "I wouldn't waste time talking to him. He's a woman-hater. Worse than Elliot."

I cautioned her again about discussing Elliot's murder, which, for some perverse reason, restored her usual aplomb. She gestured to the waiter and, over my protests, signed the check for both our drinks. Tossing back her hair, she smiled and said, "I have nothing to worry about, Liz. After all, who'd want to kill me?"

I could think of four people who might want to silence her acid tongue, not including me. Bryony claimed she saw Miguel at the scene of the crime. If she saw him, the killer may well have seen her, which would explain her shocked reaction when I told her Carl was a possible witness.

Chapter Ten

I'd strike the sun if it insulted me...
—Herman Melville / Moby Dick

By the time most kids get to high school, they understand that being popular isn't the same as being liked. Bryony Aldridge, however, must have led so charmed a life she never learned that extra-curricular lesson. Her nonchalant assumption, that no one would want to hurt her, had two possible justifications. Either she had an exceptionally shallow understanding of human nature, or she was the killer. Despite this enviable self-confidence, I'd bet the price of a Broadway ticket that Bryony's coterie of admirers would cheerfully soldier on if she moved to a Better Place. Not necessarily the afterlife, but perhaps the West Coast.

As unpleasant as my cocktail hour with Bryony was, I had the advantage of not being outnumbered. This wasn't the case at Valerian Hills High School, where an agitated crowd had me beat by a factor of eighty to one. Since I was a mere three minutes late in beginning the audition for *Grease*, I offered no apology and halved the opposition by telling the parents to leave.

The kids trooped into the auditorium and their mothers and fathers, with varying degrees of grudging acceptance, complied with my request. The only exception was Melinda Tumbleson. The president of the board of education accosted me as I fiddled with a baffling series of light switches inside the auditorium door.

"Ms. Hopewell! I must talk to you immediately about Jack." She regarded me with the approximate level of loathing Ahab had for the whale that bit off his leg.

I spoke more kindly than I would have if she and her son had not suffered through Elliot's harrowing death. "I'd be happy to have another conversation about Jack, but now's not a good time. The kids are waiting."

"The kids are waiting because you failed to show up on time, and this is urgent information you need to have about Jack. When he went to theater camp, all of the counselors said he was the most talented actor and singer they'd ever seen. And, no offense, of course, but I think these professionals know a tiny bit more about acting than you do."

Back in September, when the administration assigned me all of the Advanced Placement English classes, I was so grateful I agreed to direct the school play. If Melinda wanted to release me from the burden of rehearsing forty kids in a production of *Grease*, I was all in.

For once, I didn't have to weigh my words and had the luxury of complete honesty. "Those camp counselors are welcome to take over. As are you, given your expertise in spotting talent."

Melinda muttered something under her breath about my attitude and said, "No one is irreplaceable."

I limited my answer to inarguable facts. "Not a single other person who works in this school is willing to do the job. And speaking of school, can I assume that since Jack is at the audition, he will be back in class tomorrow? Because, technically, if you aren't in school you aren't allowed to attend extra-curricular activities. Which means I shouldn't allow him to audition at all."

"Fine. Don't let him audition. Give him the part without auditioning." Melinda peeled back her lips in an evil smile. "Great idea, Ms. Hopewell."

I closed the door, leaving her in the hallway and me in the auditorium. I walked slowly toward the kids, who were massed in front of the stage. There was a nervous buzz as they rehearsed their lines and the songs they'd prepared.

I was about to address the crowd when Brittany and Bethany, the perfectly perfect twin girls in my Advanced Placement English class, approached me. "Oh, Ms. Hopewell. We're just checking. You aren't going to have everyone in the auditorium, are you? Because that would be weird. We all usually wait outside and get auditioned one by one."

There's nothing as nerve-racking as learning on the job. Putting a good face on top of my chagrined one, I said, "Of course, Brittany. I, uh, I need to talk to everyone first."

They both smiled. The one who'd spoken up informed me, "That's great, Ms. Hopewell. But I'm Bethany."

Ugh. Would I ever learn to tell them apart? "I'm so sorry, Bethany. I wasn't paying attention."

The girls were too smart to fall for my lame excuse but too polite to indicate their disbelief. They simply nodded and rejoined their large pack of friends, all of whom had straight white teeth and long, shiny hair. It was a miracle I could tell any of them apart, let alone a pair of identical twins.

I promised my thespians dire consequences if they were late or absent for rehearsals, assigned them numbers, and dismissed them to wait their turn in the hallway. Thirty minutes into the audition process, I did the math. If I allotted more than five minutes per kid, we wouldn't finish until long after my usual bedtime.

With that thought in mind, I ruthlessly cut off, mid-speech, each member of my hopeful troupe of actors. Even so, it was a three-hour slog to get through the lot of them. By the end of the audition I'd heard so many off-key renditions of "Beauty School Dropout" I regretted not becoming a beautician myself.

Jack sang like a sick moose and had the stage presence of an overcooked noodle. His competition, however, wasn't much better. Very few of the boys got to the end of "Greased Lightning" without forgetting the words.

Many of the girls demonstrated real talent, which made casting the lead female roles difficult. Brittany and Bethany presented a unique challenge. One of them sang and acted better than her sister, but I had no idea which one it was. I made a list of the most promising girls, added all the boys' names, and decided on a second round of auditions for the major roles.

After dismissing the kids, I checked my phone, dawdling inside until the fiercest and most motivated stage parents drove off. When the parking lot was nearly deserted, I exited the building. Picking my way across the dark path, I nearly had a heart attack when Melinda Tumbleson stepped out from the shadows. "Ms. Hopewell! A moment, please!"

It took me a moment to recover the use of my voice. "You scared me half to death, Melinda." I looked around her and behind her. "Where is Jack?"

"Jack left with a friend." She spoke in an aggrieved tone, as if it was my fault she was stalking me. "Since you were too busy to talk earlier, I decided to come back. My son is busy doing the unreasonable amount of homework you assigned him, despite the fact that the kids had to prepare for the audition. Bad planning, Ms. Hopewell."

Although she was taller by a good six inches, I refused to give her the satisfaction of looking up to her and delivered the classic teenage retort *Whatever* to her neck. Ignoring her glare, I unlocked my car.

With a move that was bold, even for her, she parked her rear end against the car door. "I am aware of your involvement on the day my husband, er, my ex-husband, was murdered. Trust me, Ms. Hopewell, you do not want me as your enemy."

I was sick of letting this woman bully me. Instead of backing away from her, I got closer. "Are you threatening me the way you did Elliot? Is that the reason he wanted to take out a restraining order against you?"

"I-I don't know what you're talking about. Y-you're playing some kind of sick game. Bluffing. Trying to make yourself out to be more important than you are." She clenched and unclenched her hands as if unsure what to do with them.

Melinda's nervous response was scarier than her angry one, but the words that came out of my mouth weren't well-suited to de-escalating the situation. "If you're innocent, you have nothing to worry about, do you?"

Her eyes widened, and she grabbed my wrist. She must have been working out, or perhaps endless hours on the tennis court made her strong. Her grip was astonishingly painful. "Tell me what you said to the police."

Having grown up on the rough streets of pre-gentrified Brooklyn, I feared and detested physical violence. But that same childhood taught me how to deal with it when I had to. I jerked my elbow up and toward her, and she released my arm. Had I completed the move, the president of the Valerian Hills Board of Education would have ended up with a broken nose. She backed off, and I swung open the car door. I'm a peaceful sort of woman and, therefore, didn't use the door to bruise her prominent hip.

I peeled out of the parking lot, an unnecessarily dramatic maneuver since Melinda knew where I lived and didn't have to tail me to hunt me down. Her behavior was alarming. Over the years, she'd made many teachers miserable, but she'd never before given any indication she was capable of physical violence. This tall, strong, evil-tempered woman was now my prime suspect for the murder of her ex-husband.

* * *

The drive home was uneventful. I poured myself a glass of wine and scrolled through my messages. George had texted twice, having forgotten about the audition. I was long past the stage when I expected him to remember things I'd told him dozens of times and that were marked on a calendar tacked to the refrigerator. His messages, along with a series of friendly reminders from the chimney cleaner, the rug cleaner, and the lawn service, got deleted.

Without listening to Susan's voicemail, I called her back. Her tone was glacial.

"What was so important that you couldn't get back to me? Did you even listen to my messages? It's a good thing one of us is on the case!"

With the memory of Melinda's threats and Elliot's murder fresh in my mind, I was temporarily at a loss. "It's too late for guessing games. And how could you possibly investigate Elliot Tumbleson's death from New York?"

Susan noisily sighed into the phone. "I'm talking about the murder of our mother. Have you forgotten your promise to me?"

Goosebumps popped out on my arms. "We don't know for sure she was murdered, because we don't yet know enough about Mom's life, let alone her death."

"Thanks to me, we've got our first break in the case. You're not the only one who can be a detective."

Sibling rivalry rarely divided us, but it did emerge from time to time. Susan sounded as pleased with herself as when she won first place in the Brighton Beach Junior Miss Beauty Queen Contest.

I was too tired to defend myself. "Susan, I've had a long, hard day, and I'm not staying on the phone for this. Either tell me what you've been up to or hang up."

She answered in a marginally less smug tone. "I've tracked down where Lousy went after he abandoned us."

She gave me time to praise her, but I waited without speaking.

After a dramatic pause, she continued, "About five years after Mom died, Dear Old Dad got a job in an insurance company and relocated to a town in upstate New York. But of course, when he got there, the first thing he did was to hook up with the local small-time crooks. He did some time in the local lockup and, when he got out, moved to a cabin in the woods. He seems to have died a short time later if the obituary column in the local paper can be trusted. The article had less information about him than it did about a pie-eating contest at the state fair."

Thinking about my father made me nervous enough to pour another glass of wine. "This is great stuff, Susan. I wonder what he was doing and where he was, between the time of Mom's funeral and his move to upstate New York. Do you know how he died?"

"The obituary stated that he died in a boating accident." She sharply exhaled. "Now for the interesting part. The body was never found. A local family found a beat-up motorboat with two empty bottles of whiskey inside. No Lousy Bastard."

I tabulated all the ways this story didn't add up. "Lousy wasn't a drinker. He might have a whiskey sour at a wedding, but that's it. He was no more likely to have drunk two bottles of whiskey than Mom was to have loaded up on pills and alcohol. And he hated the water. I'm not even sure he knew how to swim. We might be looking at two possible murders, maybe by a single killer."

Susan's words came slowly. "There are a few other similarities to Mom's death. Both were in a vehicle that crashed. Both deaths appeared to have been accidents."

A migraine took root behind my eyes. "The major difference between the two deaths is that Lousy might not be dead."

"Don't say that!" Susan sounded out of breath. "I don't know what to think now. Or how to feel. What kind of person is disappointed to find out her father might not be dead?"

"The kind of person who suffered a traumatic childhood, thanks to her terrible father. But let's not get ahead of ourselves. You should be patting yourself on the back, not blaming yourself. I'm so proud of you. How did you find out about...er...about him? Did you hire a detective?"

Susan's composure returned. "I didn't hire a detective. I *was* the detective. I'm tempted to trumpet my investigative skills, but to be honest, the information wasn't hard to come by. The first thing I did was find Alan Goldfarb, which took all of ten seconds, since he's on Instagram and Facebook. I would have tracked down his sister also, but it wasn't until I friended Alan that I remembered her name."

Despite Susan's protestations, I was impressed. "Nice work. How's Alan? I don't think I've seen him since his bar mitzvah."

"Don't let us get sidetracked," Susan chided. "Let me finish telling you how amazing I am. Alan told me his family moved out of their apartment in Brooklyn and relocated to a house on Long Island. His parents are now living in a retirement community not far from their old place. Alan doesn't know much about Lousy, because his parents never talked about him."

I felt a familiar twinge of shame. "They probably got sick of giving him money."

Our father mostly consorted with crooks, but he also had a few friends of the non-criminal variety. He borrowed money from them as often as he could, as I knew quite well from personal experience. He liked to take me with him when he pleaded his case, because he knew the presence of a child made decent people sympathetic. No wonder the Goldfarbs shunned him.

Susan didn't feel the same humiliation I did, probably because she was younger and her memories of that time were less vivid. She said, "We have an appointment to see the Goldfarbs this weekend. They might tell us stuff they kept from their kids."

I hesitated. "This weekend is kind of busy. It's my turn to carpool. And the house is a wreck."

From across the Hudson River, her disdain was palpable. "Whatever you say, *mon amie*. But I'm going to see them, with you or without you. I was hoping to avoid the Long Island Railroad, but if you don't want to be part of this investigation, I can live with commuting for one day. Although the weekend schedule is impossible. The trains leave every two hours. I don't know how you've survived ten years in Oak Ridge."

I dreaded another fight with George. "I'll, um, I'll get back to you."

Susan's tone changed from combative to wheedling. "I'm looking forward to seeing Ira and Arlene. I always liked them."

I also had fond memories of the Goldfarbs. When I was a kid, their kindness seemed odd and wonderful. After I became a parent, I understood them much better. And my father, much less.

I made up my mind. "No need to brave the LIRR. Come here on Friday night, and we'll drive in together on Saturday." I took a final gulp of vinegary wine. "I'm almost afraid of what we might learn."

Pleased, she quoted our favorite detective. "Where there is no imagination, there is no horror."

I winced. "Not the most apropos Sherlock Holmes quotation. But I suppose it will have to do."

My sister answered more seriously than was her wont. "Where the Lousy Bastard is concerned, horror is a given."

Chapter Eleven

Love is not love, which alters when it alteration finds.
—William Shakespeare / Sonnet 116

"Spaghetti with ketchup. It scarred me for life." Susan began her catalog of grievances against the Goldfarbs at the toll booth entrance to the Garden State Parkway and picked up speed when we hit the Long Island Expressway. "Do you remember those bowls of tuna fish that looked like cat food? I'll never forget the look on Lousy's face when Ira and Arlene served us the supermarket brand of mushy hot dogs. He asked them if they saved their more expensive food for a better class of guest."

My sister put her feet on the dashboard and began painting her toenails. I opened two windows and said, "Maybe the Goldfarbs were tired of us freeloading all the time. And speaking of things that stink, that nail polish you're using is making me sick."

She sniffed. "Now you know how I felt, watching your son drown his eggs in an ocean of ketchup."

I didn't answer Susan immediately, because navigating an unfamiliar route made me nervous. I lacked the self-assurance of drivers who first got behind the wheel when they were teenagers, at a time when they believed they were invincible and immortal.

"I regret you were so traumatized by lunch with the Goldfarb family. I'm not as willing to ding them for stinginess, because with the money they saved not buying gourmet tomato sauce and boutique tuna, they bought a house and sent their kids to college."

Susan yelped as we hit a pothole, "Hey! Take it easy. I'm trying not to smear the polish on your upholstery." She dabbed at her toes. "Your favorite childhood meal was a mayonnaise sandwich. I, at least, have some standards." She leaned over to check the speedometer. "On the topic of standards, do you think you could speed things up a bit?"

At three miles above the speed limit, cars were passing us with the ferocity of starving cheetahs. Brushing aside Susan's critique about my driving, I reverted to the topic of food. "I doubt Arlene will be serving either ketchup spaghetti or cheap tuna today. I'm hoping for a cup of coffee and some pertinent information."

Chastened, Susan said, "*Oui, ma chère.*"

No one can irritate me as thoroughly as my sister. "If you speak French to Ira and Arlene, they may take their revenge by answering our questions in Yiddish."

"I think you're jealous, which is understandable. I lead an exciting life filled with interesting people, and you've become a Stepford Wife." She blew on her toenails to hasten the drying process.

"Nicole Kidman played the lead role in the movie version of *The Stepford Wives*. So, I accept the compliment. If things keep going the way they are now, I will end up thin and gorgeous, with red hair and perfect skin."

A flurry of text messages boinged through my sister's phone. With an aggravated snap of her fingers, she said, "My date for tomorrow night just canceled. Something about his kid. Remind me not to hook up with anyone dumb enough to become a parent."

Susan was childless by choice, and although she was a doting and excellent aunt to Ellie and Zach, no one would ever mistake her for the maternal type. "I thought your sophisticated Georges didn't have kids."

"This is a new guy. Who's now an ex without us ever meeting." She held up her phone to show me his picture before deleting it.

"I'll make you a deal. You speak English, and I'll scrub all references to children, my own included. In the meantime, keep your eyes peeled for the exit. Everyone around me is doing ninety miles an hour, and I'm a little stressed."

"I think it's the prospect of seeing the Goldfarbs that's stressing you. When was the last time we saw them? Could it have been at Alan's bar mitzvah?"

"No. It was at Mom's funeral." Susan's confusion was understandable. The two gatherings had a similar guest list.

"Yeah. I remember now." She gazed out the window, but not, I suspected, to check for the exit sign.

In the past, I'd shut down memories of both events, but it was time to face them. "The bar mitzvah was the first time I realized people felt sorry for us and were whispering about us behind our backs. I wonder how many people knew about Lousy's other family and never told Mom."

Susan pressed her hands to her chest. "The same thing happened at the funeral. We were kids, so it makes sense we didn't understand. We thought it was normal to have a father we hardly ever saw. But how is it possible Mom didn't suspect anything?"

The words hurt, but I said them anyway. "Maybe she did know, and that's the reason she loaded up on downers and vodka before wrapping her car around a tree."

The authoritative voice of my car's navigation system interrupted our conversation, and I took the next exit. Five miles off the expressway, we followed a long private road to the Peace And Love Active Adult Association. All the streets had otherworldly names, like Astral Avenue and Dream Drive. The single-story aluminum-sided houses looked like those in a thousand other retirement communities, although the backyards sported an unusual number of teepees and yurts.

I pulled into a guest parking spot on Imagine Street at the corner of Lennon Lane. "Let's open with a few leading questions and then let them talk. We may learn something we haven't anticipated."

She slid her feet into open shoes and swore when the polish on her big toe smudged. "Did you learn this technique on one of your detective shows? Maybe you should expand your horizons a bit. Instead of tame British shows where old ladies do the detecting, you should watch a few NYPD cop shows or some of those dark Norwegian mysteries. I say we hit them with everything we've got."

"Are you suggesting we tie them up and beat them with a rubber hose? They're law-abiding senior citizens, not drug kingpins."

The door to the Goldfarbs' house opened before we rang the bell. Ira and Arlene were ten years older than my parents would have been had Mom or Lousy survived. I expected to see two wizened, elderly people, but they looked much younger than their biological age. Arlene wore an intricately embroidered peasant blouse and skirt. Long silver earrings dangled from multiple ear piercings, and her hair cascaded past her shoulders in a mass of gray and black curls. Ira was in bell-bottomed jeans and a fringed vest, which he wore over a tie-dyed tee shirt. Tanned, relaxed, and slim, they looked healthier and happier than I did. Their clothes were circa 1969, but they wore them with hipster ease, if not hipster irony.

"Come in, come in! We were so happy and excited to hear from you. You girls haven't changed a bit." Arlene instructed us to remove our shoes and ushered us into the living room, which was heavily perfumed with patchouli. Cushions covered in batik prints dotted two long, low sofas. In the middle of the room, a large coffee table held three sticks of incense and a score of family photographs. Two desks with bubble-letter nameplates in a groovy psychedelic print identified one surface as Ira's and the other as Arlene's.

Arlene offered us herbal tea and hemp cookies, which we politely declined. Ira stood a bit stiffly in the foyer, but, at his wife's urging, sat in a chair opposite us. We weren't expecting to see their children, but Alan and Alina entered from the kitchen and hugged us in that awkward way people do when they're not sure how to greet former friends.

Alina said, with a self-conscious laugh, "As you can see, Mom and Dad have embraced their inner hippie."

Susan took in the pillows and the incense. "Cool."

She, like I, was a bit dazed by the fidelity with which Arlene and Ira had recreated the Summer of Love.

Arlene explained, "We wanted to downsize, but we didn't want to move to the typical retirement community. We heard about this place and immediately felt at home. It's like the name. Nothing but peace and love and good vibes."

Ira added, as if to reassure us that he hadn't completely lost touch with the current century, "The Peace and Love Community also has great dining options and a championship golf course. Everything is organic. No pesticides, and a lot of the food they serve is locally sourced."

Alan muttered, with a wink at his sister, "Don't forget the pot. There's a virtual haze over the place."

Ira perked up. "You want to see my plants? Totally medicinal."

Arlene waved him off. "The girls didn't drive all this way to look at your garden." She extracted a photo album from a stack on Ira's desk and grew misty-eyed as she paged through her kids' meticulously documented lives.

Ira was almost as twitchy as Susan, and when Arlene paused at a bar mitzvah photo, he snatched the album from her and said, "Oh, Arlene, the girls don't want to see those."

I thought he wanted to spare us the agony of more pictures, but after grabbing the album she was holding, he put it at the bottom of the stack and replaced it with one that was indistinguishable from the original.

My sister, after mumbling a few lukewarm compliments, gave up her pretense of interest. In a staccato tone, she said, "This is all very interesting, but it's not why we're here. We want to know what happened the day my mother died."

Ira froze. Scarlet-faced, Arlene stammered before answering. "We loved you girls like family, but, well, you know how it is. We moved out of the old neighborhood and lost touch with your parents." A clock that had been inaudible suddenly made its presence known with appallingly loud ticks.

Alina, who was as lovely and gentle now as she was at twelve, proved herself a true Goldfarb. She papered over the uncomfortable silence by whipping out her cell phone to show us pictures of every vacation she'd taken with her photogenic husband and two perfect children.

Susan pressed her lips together. Before she could open them and potentially end all hope of getting information from the Goldfarbs, I intervened. "Beautiful photos, Alina. I'd love to see them another time, but we're here because we need information. We know so little about our father and mother. And now they're dead. That's why we turned to your parents for help."

Ira was inexplicably angry. "Why do you need to know anything more than you do? It would be hurtful to all concerned."

This was one argument I was prepared to rebut. "That excuse silenced me as a kid. It's not going to work now. If we don't get the answers we want from you, we'll get them from someone else."

Talking to the Goldfarbs transported me back to some of the most painful episodes from my childhood. With startling clarity, I had a vision of myself as a young and confused kid. A deep desire to defend and protect that vanished girl, who existed in the past, or perhaps only in my imagination, possessed me. In the days and weeks that followed our mother's death, grief numbed me. It wasn't until I became a parent that I recognized how The Lousy Bastard manipulated us. Susan and I lost our mother, and with her death, the cardboard façade of the life and family we thought we had collapsed, leaving us doubly bereft.

Unlike Lousy, Ira and Arlene were decent people, good parents, and bad liars. I settled in for a nice, long visit.

Chapter Twelve

And, after all, what is a lie? 'Tis but the truth in masquerade.
—Lord Byron / Don Juan

Without asking the Goldfarbs for permission, Susan moved the burning incense sticks to the kitchen. Relieved of the noxious fumes, I concentrated on defusing Ira's anger and engaging his sympathy. "After Mom died, our father took everything that wasn't nailed down and walked out, leaving no forwarding address. If you think about it like that, you might find it easier to tell us what we want to know."

Ira walked over to the window, and Susan followed him. She said to his back, "There's no story you can tell me about our father that I can't top."

Again, the clock ticked against the silence. Arlene picked up a hemp cookie but didn't eat it. Ira made the kind of gestures people engage in when they're talking, although no words came out of his mouth.

Alan stood near the door, as if ready to bolt at a moment's notice. "Mom. Dad. Tell her whatever you know."

Ira looked worriedly at his wife and half-turned to face Susan. "On the day she died, your mother went to see That Woman. You, uh, you know about her? She lived near our old apartment, maybe half a mile from you. Don't know why your mother drove there or where she was going after she left."

Susan and I exchanged glances. We knew Lousy had another wife and two sons, because he told us about them before he left us. We didn't know their home was our mother's destination on the day she died. It seemed like a cruel joke that our half-siblings lived in Brooklyn, not far from us. I suppose if you're going to lead a double life, you have to weigh convenience against secrecy. My father, of course, was a betting man, but one with extraordinarily bad luck and instincts.

Ira went back to gazing at a house across the street that was an exact double of his. I said to the nape of his brick-red neck, "How did Mom find out about her? Did his other wife contact her?"

He wiped his eyes and nose with a paisley-printed handkerchief. "Your mother found a picture of him with her and his other kids. She called your grandparents, who told her the whole story."

I wondered if one of those pictures had made it into the photo album Ira didn't want us to see. I shut my eyes to better focus on the past, and a few missing pieces of the puzzle fell into place. "Mom discovered her in-laws already knew about this other family. And then she realized everyone knew. How humiliating for her." I was so detached, I felt as if I were talking about a minor character in a book I read a long time ago.

Susan was lividly pale, except for a bright pink spot on each cheek. She breathed deeply, struggling to control herself, but the tears fell anyway, making wavy black mascara marks on her cheeks. "What did he tell Mom on the nights he didn't come home?"

Ira couldn't meet her tearful eyes. "Your father never could hold down a steady job. Half the time, he really was driving a gypsy cab. He used to hang out at the airports, picking up passengers who didn't want to pay the standard cab fare."

This was true. Lousy often took me with him on these trips, because the tips were better when I rode shotgun. I would do my homework in the front seat while he bragged about how smart I was to the passengers in the rear.

"What happened after Mom went to see That Woman?" Susan was too emotional to draw the obvious conclusion, or maybe she couldn't face it. I understood, for the first time, why no one questioned our mother's car crash. They assumed her broken heart and spirit had made her reckless, maybe even suicidal. Except what was obvious to everyone else wasn't as obvious to me.

Underneath her tan, Arlene's face was gray. "I don't know what your mother was trying to accomplish. Maybe she thought That Woman would give up your father if she knew he was married."

Blood pounded in my ears. "And did the other woman know about us?"

Ira barked out a mirthless laugh. "Damned straight she did. And didn't care who she hurt. Not you, not your mother, not even her own kids. She always said she knew what she wanted and knew how to get it."

Arlene glared at him. "When did she tell you that?"

He sat next to her and said, "I met her. Just the one time, though."

Ira's protest reminded me of Bryony's declarations of ignorance. Neither rang true. "I see. And yet you know quite a bit about her for only meeting her one time."

In a too-quiet voice, Arlene said, "Liz makes a valid point. Are you sure you only met her once? You never told me you did. Any other secrets you've been hiding? Any other women you were seeing behind my back?" She shoved the stack of photo albums at him.

With all four Goldfarbs otherwise engaged, I retrieved the album Ira had placed at the bottom of the pile. A thin envelope slipped out of the back cover and fell to the floor.

Ira put his arm around his wife and said, "I didn't want to upset you."

She broke his embrace and said, "You never told me you met her. Why, Ira? Since when do you lie to me?"

He stammered, "I-I-I didn't lie to you. She, uh, she contacted me a few times."

Arlene stood up, hands on her hips. "You never told me you knew That Woman. You lied by omission."

Alan sprang to his feet. Although the younger Goldfarb clearly would choose to swim the English Channel in January before suffering through a repeat of the last fifteen minutes, he said, "We should do this again real soon, but Alina and I have to go."

He hooked his sister's arm in his. "Come on, Alina. Don't forget, we have to, uh, take care of that, that thing." Alan waved, and Alina blew a half-hearted kiss before they escaped out the door.

Ira tapped a quantity of pot into a rolling paper, licked the edge to seal it, and lit up. He pointed the glowing end at me. "Are you happy now? Did you get what you wanted?"

I waved away the smoke. "No. I need her name and address. And the names of her kids."

"I, um, I don't recall. It was such a long time ago. Water under the bridge and all that." He tapped his foot on the floor with arrhythmic intensity, inhaling deeply and waiting for the pot to restore the Active Adult Peace and Love Community vibe that Susan and I had obliterated.

With growing anger, I said, "Save your lies for your wife. Give me the names, and we'll leave you alone. You can forget you ever knew our parents. Or us."

Arlene grabbed the joint but didn't smoke it. "Tell them. I know you know."

Perspiring and red-faced, Ira said, "Her first name is Velma. I don't remember her last name. And I don't know the kids' names. Two boys. Don't know anything more about her." He pleaded with Arlene, "I swear, I only saw her the one time."

I stood up. "And where is she now?"

Ira choked and said, "She's dead. Died years ago."

My students were much better liars. "Try again, Ira. She's not dead. When did you see her last? Is she still in Brooklyn?"

"Maybe. And anyway, she *could* be dead." He eyed me suspiciously. "Why do you need to know where she lives?"

"We're going to track her down." I didn't understand his fear, but it pleased me for reasons I didn't bother to analyze until later.

"I advise you to leave well enough alone. She was like your father. It's why they got along so well."

Arlene clutched my arm. "You cannot go see That Woman. Please, Liz. Don't do this. It can only hurt you."

I uncurled her fingers. "What could possibly hurt me more than what I already know? It's not knowing that's painful. And I have two half-brothers I've never met. I'm going to find them."

"They're not your brothers. They might share some genetic material with you and Susan. And that's only if your father was the actual father. It's like Ira says, That Woman can't be trusted." She swung her head from side to side so vigorously her long earrings slapped her cheek.

Susan disregarded Arlene's distress. "We're not girls anymore. We deserve the truth. As do our half-brothers. Tell me, at least, if you've heard from our father."

Ira cut off his wife's response with a sharp gesture. "He's dead. Died years ago. Sorry about that. Velma's probably dead, too."

Arlene picked up the plate of cookies as if weighing its potential as a missile. We let ourselves out of the house. As we walked towards the car, we heard the sound of broken glass. Arlene screamed, "They're not the only ones who need to know the truth. I always suspected you had a girlfriend. Ira, how could you?"

Susan reversed course and put her ear against the door, although their argument was audible not only to us but to everyone on Imagine Street.

Arlene continued to yell. "You're a liar and a cheat. What hold does That Woman have over you?"

Her husband said, "You don't want to know."

We heard nothing more until a grinding sound from the adjacent garage door sent us scurrying. I fumbled for my key, which delayed our departure long enough for us to witness Ira peel out in a red sports car. The opening notes from the Beatles' song, "A Hard Day's Night," were audible as he raced down the block.

Our to-do list now included an investigation of our two long-lost half-brothers, their homewrecker mother, Ira Goldfarb, and the Lousy Bastard who united us.

Chapter Thirteen

The past is never where you think you left it.
—Katherine Anne Porter / Ship of Fools: A Novel

I drove, far faster than I usually did, down Peace Path and onto the road that would take us to the highway.

Susan grabbed my arm. "I can't believe I'm saying this, but you have to slow down. How will you explain a speeding ticket to your doting husband?"

"If you don't keep your hands off me, we're going to get in an accident. And don't make snarky remarks about my husband."

She was immediately contrite. "I apologize. But please take it easy. That visit was enough of a disaster for one day. Let's talk calmly and pretend we didn't wreck the Goldfarbs' one hundred-year-long marriage."

I eased back on the accelerator and then sped up again as we merged onto the express lane to the highway. "I don't care about them or their marriage. Or that godawful incense and pot smoke that's glued my sinuses shut. Unlike Ira and Arlene, I care about us. And about Mom. We're trying to investigate a murder that no one else thinks happened, and we don't need two elderly stoners slowing us down."

Susan peeled two drops of spilled nail polish from the dashboard. "They may be slightly overfond of weed, but we did get some information from them. We don't have a lot of other options. How are you going to interest the cops in an ancient murder case without any evidence that a crime was committed?"

"Don't be so negative. We start by finding out the names of the police officers who were at the scene when Mom died. They're probably retired by now and might be willing to talk. At the same time, we'll begin our search for Velma. Ugh—horrid name."

"How are we going to find Lousy's other wife if she's not in Brooklyn? I grant you, it's a rather uncommon first name, but we have our work cut out for us without a last name to go with it."

I breathed deeply to clear my brain and my lungs. "That's where you're wrong. You've spent too much time on the Upper East Side. Don't you remember what it was like when we were kids? Every neighborhood in Brooklyn is its own little world. It's like Oak Ridge. If you were looking for someone who lived in my town and you stopped five random people, you'd find someone who knows them. Less than six degrees of separation in most neighborhoods."

Susan waved at the horizon. "I may have spent too much time on the Upper East Side, but you've spent too much time in New Jersey. Brooklyn has changed a lot since we were kids. Neither of us could afford to live there now. You wouldn't believe the prices in neighborhoods that used to be war zones. Shoe repair shops are now wine bars. Old-fashioned delis have gone the way of the dinosaur, and if you want a restaurant meal, you have to mortgage your house."

"That didn't happen where we grew up. You're thinking Williamsburg or Bed-Stuy, but I visited the old neighborhood a few years ago, and nothing has changed. The same junky stores line the avenues, except now they're owned by a new generation of immigrants."

"You went there without me?"

Typical Susan. She bypassed the informative part of what I told her and zoomed in on the nonessential emotional backstory. For reasons I didn't explore, even to myself, I made occasional pilgrimages to the scenes of my childhood.

I regretted telling her about my solo trips into our shared past. "Don't get sidetracked. The important part of what I told you is that there are plenty of old-timers who haven't left. People who live in rent-controlled apartments don't move out until they die. If Velma's in Brooklyn, we'll find her. And if she moved, we'll find someone who knows where she went, including if it was to a cemetery." I jerked my thumb at the backseat of the car. "You always make fun of me for carrying a big bag, but as I've told you many times, it can come in handy."

Susan reached behind. "It's one thing to carry a large handbag. It's another to equip yourself with enough supplies to survive the aftermath of a nuclear winter, which is what—" She stopped talking when she found the packet of photos in my bag. "How did you manage to sneak these out of their house without anyone, including me, seeing you?"

"It struck me as odd that Ira would take the album Arlene was showing us and replace it with one that was so similar. When they started arguing, I grabbed the one he didn't want us to see. The envelope fell out of the back cover."

My sister flipped through the photos. "I don't recognize most of these people, but I'm sure we can figure out who they are."

I made her put them away. "No fair. You have to wait for me. I won't be able to resist looking at them."

Susan groaned but didn't argue the point. "I wish we had Velma's last name. If we weren't so close to Oak Ridge, I'd make you turn around and go back."

We passed the Garden State Parkway sign that said, *Welcome to New Jersey!* That made me feel better. Almost home. "I have a feeling we're not going to need Ira to get Velma's last name. I think I already know it."

Irritated, Susan said, "Since I don't have a crystal ball, maybe you could share your extra sensory insight with me."

"I have a dreadful feeling that Velma's last name is the same as ours. Even if Lousy didn't officially marry her, she might have taken his name."

My sister looked as if she might faint. "I hope you're not right."

"Me too. But I think I am. I'm pretty sure Lousy married her at some point." I thought about the irony of us looking for someone who shared our last name, a name neither Susan nor I kept for long. We both married young, although Susan's first marriage didn't last a year. Neither did her second or third.

I said, "In a weird way, what we're really searching for is ourselves. So finding people with our name will be a good place to start, metaphorically, if not literally."

Immersed in a Google search for Velma, she didn't answer. After a quarter-hour of scrolling, she said, "Nothing so far. We can do a deeper dive when we get back to your place."

We drove the rest of the way in silence, each of us wrapped in our private thoughts and fears.

George bounded down the stairs the second we entered the house. "Where have you been? Have you any idea what time it is?"

I got a bottle of wine from the fridge. "If you're worried about dinner, let me put your mind at rest. We're ordering in." Although I was on fire to examine the photos, I didn't want to explain to my husband where I got them.

George wrested the wine from me and said, "We're not ordering in. And don't drink any wine. I'm sure I told you we're going to a wine tasting and dinner at the club. Might as well wait and drink the stuff I've already paid an arm and a leg for."

"And I'm equally sure that you didn't tell me we're having dinner at the club." The second the words were out of my mouth, I did have a dim memory of him blathering something about an executive board meeting and a dinner afterward. I didn't admit this lapse, because he routinely forgot important things I told him. For once, he was on the receiving end of indifference.

George went into the bathroom and emerged with my bottle of Excedrin. His tense expression made me suspect he was looking forward to the evening's events as much as I was, which was to say, with all the happy anticipation of a visit to the New Jersey Department of Motor Vehicles. He shook out two pills and said, "We don't have time to argue the point. Get ready and wear something nice."

"My clothes are perfect for an evening with Susan. I refuse to ditch her to spend time with your country club chums."

Susan took possession of the wine. "Don't worry about me. I'll order some pizza and hang out with the kids."

"Don't be ridiculous. The kids don't need a babysitter. They're either going out with their friends, or they're babysitting for somebody else's kids. You'd be here all by yourself." Against my better judgment, I offered George a compromise. "If Susan can come with us, I'll go."

My husband squinted his eyes and pressed his lips into a thin line of disapproval. "I have to get there early to attend the pre-dinner meeting. And now, of course, to purchase another ticket to the wine tasting." He looked darkly at Susan. "Don't be late."

Happy to be rid of his toe-tapping impatience, I told him we'd be early. Susan and I got dressed, made up, and ready to go in under an hour, which gave us time to examine the photos I'd swiped from the Goldfarbs.

We flipped past images of people we didn't recognize and concentrated on four that were taken on the Boardwalk at Coney Island. The sparking waters of the Atlantic Ocean were in the background of some; in others, I could make out the steeplechase and iconic Cyclone roller coaster. Lousy and Ira must have taken turns snapping them, for the third person with them appeared in all the photos. She was small and slight, with dark brown hair and a sharp chin. Her face teased my memory.

"I guess that's Velma." Susan put her face in her hands.

My eyes were dry. "Yes. And Susan? I've met her. I didn't know who she was, or that she had any connection to Lousy or Ira, but I know I've seen her before."

She examined her stricken face in the mirror. "I'm not going to the club. I can't."

I pulled her away from the mirror. "Tom Harriman hasn't returned my phone call, and I'm worried about Miguel. We can't lose sight of that other murder we're investigating. Mom's death was in the past. Elliot Tumbleson's murder matters right now."

She put the photos in the envelope and, with a weak smile, said, "As my favorite English teacher would say, 'Once more into the fray.'"

Chapter Fourteen

Of my state, I will make no boast
—Geoffrey Chaucer/ The Wife of Bath

Susan's disdain for the Meadowfields Country Club vanished when she saw the luxurious lobby and elegant dining room. Backlit by the New York City skyline and haloed by antique globe lamps overhead, sommeliers staffed four tables filled with expensive wines. As we examined booklets that described each selection, one of the waiters offered "a well-balanced Sancerre containing hints of grass and citrus."

After spending the day with the Goldfarbs and finding pictures of our father's other wife in Ira's possession, we were more interested in the calming effects of alcohol than where it lived and worked. Nonetheless, we sniffed, swirled, and agreed that the floral notes didn't overpower the underlying nuances.

Not everyone was there for the wine. Orders for martinis, straight shots of hard liquor, and pitchers of frozen drinks kept the bartenders at the opposite side of the room busy. Shouts of laughter and loud conversations from the bar broke through to the more decorous atmosphere at the wine tasting.

Ryan Walker, whose day job was as the golf pro, often functioned as a de facto social director. He offered golf tips and inside jokes to the crowd at the bar and knowledgeable advice to the winetasters. My sister picked up his accent from the opposite end of a table that featured rosés from Provence.

Susan put her mouth to my ear. "Who is the gorgeous Aussie? You must introduce me immediately. And then get out of my way."

I shouldn't have been surprised. "What happened to Georges, the newest and most Frenchified love of your life?"

Without bitterness, she said, "It didn't work out. I thought my Georges was better than your George. Turns out he's worse. A lot worse."

I guided her into the line for Bordeaux. "That was a quick reversal. Was he a serial killer? Or poor?"

She shrugged. "He's married, with six kids, and lives in Queens."

I nearly spit out a mouthful of wine. "What about those box seats to the opera? Did he spend his kids' college tuition on three hundred dollar tickets to *La Traviata*?"

"He works part-time as an usher at the Metropolitan Opera House and is first in line for freebies when the season ticket holders cancel." She patted me on the shoulder. "Don't worry about me. Georges did seem too good to be true. The worst part of this sad story is that he's not French. He *teaches* French. In a middle school."

I drank the rest of my thimbleful of wine without further mishaps. "Is his name Georges?"

Susan tried to frown but ended up laughing. "Nope. His name is Sidney Appelbaum. Needless to say, I'm now back in the dating game, though not with the creep who canceled on me this afternoon."

She removed a tiny compact from her bag and inspected her face. Satisfied, she clicked the case shut. "You can do your part by hooking me up with that blue-eyed guy from Down Under. Do so, and I promise to love you forever."

"You can't seriously be interested in Ryan Walker. He's not your type." Susan had married and divorced a penniless indie filmmaker, a best-selling author of pop psychology books, and a high-powered lawyer. I couldn't imagine her swapping nights at the opera for days on the golf course. She had worse hand-eye coordination than I did.

With admirable finesse, Susan finagled two glasses of Bordeaux ahead of a heavy-set man and two elderly ladies. "Why wouldn't I be interested in a hot golf pro? Other than him, it's slim pickings here."

The answer was self-evident to me. "I can't think of two people who have less in common than you and Ryan. What will you talk about?"

Susan raised one eyebrow. "I don't plan on doing too much talking."

"Wait! I know exactly what you should talk about." I made sure no one was close enough to hear and then whispered, "Question him about the murder. Ask Ryan what he was doing when Elliot was killed."

"That's tempting, but at the moment, I have something more interesting than death on my mind." She eyed the crowd.

"Silly me. I was worried about an innocent young guy who's been unjustly accused of murder. But if that doesn't move you, how about the fact that there's a killer on the loose?"

I stalked off ahead of her, but she pulled me back. "You underestimate me, dear sister. If you introduce me to Ryan, I promise to find out all I can about Miguel and Elliot. Two birds. One stone."

"That's more like it. Please remember, though, that everyone is guilty until proven innocent."

Ryan, who was talking to Cooper Aldridge, rendered any move on our part unnecessary when he joined us. "What can I get for my best and most elusive golf student?"

I gazed into the golf pro's glittering blue eyes and wanted to kick myself for not capitalizing on previous opportunities to question him. My golf swing was unlikely to improve, given my utter lack of talent, but lessons with him would have given me an excuse to learn more about possible suspects in the murder of Elliot Tumbleson.

I acknowledged the truth of his gentle reproof and said, "I've been meaning to call you. This week, we'll do a lesson without fail."

Ryan gave me a dazzlingly white smile and said, "If you introduce me to this charming lady, whom I am sure is your sister, then all is forgiven."

Susan smiled and, more subtly this time, raised one eyebrow. I introduced them and then left, ostensibly to find George.

I circled the growing crowd and found my husband in an alcove, talking to Bryony Aldridge. She was attired in a very brief black cocktail dress with insets of black lace. Dangling from her wrist was a beaded evening bag adorned with a large pink satin bow. She looked, with scornful eyes, at my long stretchy skirt that masked last week's pizza and at the plain black leather handbag I took to school. I wished I'd dressed with more care, but I needn't have worried about what George thought. He barely noticed me.

Bryony drawled, "So lovely to see you, Liz. I missed you at our last golf lessons. If you'd only practice more, there's a chance you could someday make one of the low-level golf teams." Her smile was edged in malice. "Having seen you in action, I don't think the A team is in your future. Which doesn't mean you couldn't enjoy the competition. But you have to be serious about it. For a lot of us, it's like our job."

Having heard Bryony and her friends express similar sentiments, I was prepared. "Unless you're playing for the LPGA, what you do is a game, not a job."

Bryony didn't acknowledge the implied insult, which was more annoying than if she'd responded with another catty remark. She simply laughed and said, "How quaint! What are we going to do with her, George?"

My husband looked at her with a fatuous expression that made me want to puke. Before I could frame the angry words that came to mind, Cooper, Ryan, and my sister joined us. Cooper clapped George on the back and said, "Great to have you on board! The executive council needed some new blood."

Ryan raised his glass. "Yes, mate, I hope you can help us get to the bottom of this financial mess. Bad karma and all that. Even without the murder."

George rubbed his forehead. "It is a bad business. And the books are a mess. It'll take time to figure it all out, and I'm no expert."

Bryony edged closer to him. "I'm sure if anyone can figure it out, you can." Her honeyed words turned his complexion the color of an undercooked salmon fillet.

My husband's admiration of her elicited emotions more complicated than simple jealousy. I almost felt sorry for George. Not that I was such a prize, but Bryony? The woman had the depth of a Wikipedia entry.

Cooper frowned. It wasn't clear to me if his displeasure was a function of Bryony's cooing praise of my husband or the perilous financial situation of the club. He signaled impatiently for a waiter to bring him another drink.

"We'll see what we can do, but I suspect untangling what happened may be beyond even George's superpowers. I won't speak ill of the dead, but for a CPA, Elliot made a hash of the financial records and—"

A shrill voice, slurred with too much alcohol, cut him off. "If you don't want to speak of the dead, then don't." Melinda Tumbleson jostled her way into our circle and leaned so far forward I worried she would tip over and fall on her face. She pointed to Cooper with her glass. He brushed aside her arm, and she stumbled, spilling red wine on Bryony's pink evening bag.

Bryony furiously blotted at the drooping bow. "You're drunk. I'll have the doorman get you a cab before you do any further damage."

"Don't need a stinking cab. Need justice. P'lice all over me." Melinda appealed to Cooper. "You tell 'em. Tell 'em I'm innocent. Sonya killed poor Elliot. Poor slob. All she wanted from him was his money." She wiped her eyes.

Angry at the ruin of her beautiful handbag, Bryony said coldly, "Poor Elliot screwed up the financial records. Poor Elliot beat Sonya black and blue. Poor Elliot was a loser."

Ryan tried to defuse the situation with a bland remark about everyone coming together for the upcoming golf tournament, but he couldn't stop Melinda.

She got out from under the golf pro's restraining hand and switched her attention to him. "You think you know everything! But I know a few things about you that might surprise your bosses."

He pried the wineglass from her fingers and handed it to one of the servers. Bundling her in a tight grip he half-walked, half-carried Melinda to the front entrance. The man holding Melinda's glass left it on a table and followed them from a discreet distance.

Bryony said, "I'm beginning to think that Michael didn't kill Elliot, even though he was on the scene at the right time. Melinda is a lot scarier than he is. Maybe the waiter is innocent, and the ex-wife did it."

Susan looked puzzled. "Who is Michael?"

The floral and grass notes in my wine turned bitter. "Michael is Miguel. At the country club, he's known as Michael, for embarrassing reasons that don't bear discussing right now."

I was certain my explanation would invite an angry pushback, but Cooper carelessly agreed with me. "Yes, we don't want to look as if we're hiring illegal immigrants."

A headache bloomed in the center of my forehead and spread tentacles behind my eyes. "Miguel is an American citizen and always has been. Him and his whole family."

Bryony tittered. "Michael, er, *Miguel* was Liz's student. Which makes him innocent, of course. Unless he flunked English? Or maybe, since he's so American, he flunked Spanish?"

Cooper laughed. Susan looked stunned. The waiter who was poised to refill our glasses had no expression at all.

I popped two aspirins with a wine chaser and said to Bryony, "I don't understand how you made such a serious accusation against him without knowing anything about him."

Bryony placed an index finger on her temple as if remembering events from the recent past was proving difficult. "I already told you why I suspected him. Elliot and Miguel were together shortly before Elliot was killed."

She stepped back to make room for Ryan, who'd returned after escorting Melinda outside. I hoped he'd put her in a cab and hadn't allowed her to drive.

Placing a delicate hand on Ryan's muscled bicep, Bryony said, "You remember, don't you? You said Miguel had been stealing from the club."

The golf pro's smile lost some of its dazzle. "Did I? You might be confusing me with someone a lot more important."

I wondered if that more important someone was Cooper. Or Bryony herself. For a brief, disloyal moment, I even suspected George, although he could never involve himself in anything illegal. "Is there any proof Miguel was the one who stole money? He was hardly in a position to do so unless someone much higher up was helping him."

Susan narrowed her eyes at Bryony. "Are you sure the person you saw was Miguel? Maybe he was some random guy in a white shirt and black pants.

85

No one notices the help."

Least of all Bryony, I silently added.

Ryan resisted the grim mood that infected the rest of us. "This is all beyond me." With an appreciative nod in Susan's direction, he said, "Liz, your sister is meeting me tomorrow for a golf lesson. I hope you'll join us. Two for the price of one. You can't resist."

I didn't resist. Each time the discussion turned toward murder, Ryan introduced a neutral topic to distract us. Although I doubted he was guilty of killing Elliot, I suspected he was hiding something. Susan and I would have a better chance of extracting information by double-teaming him.

George winked at Ryan. "Save yourself. The last thing you want to do is take Liz's sister out on the course. Liz is a big enough challenge."

Ryan was undeterred. "I'll take good care of both of them." He clinked his glass against Susan's. "To the great game of golf!"

Cooper and Bryony silently toasted each other. I hit George's glass. The resultant sound was hollow.

Chapter Fifteen

A people without the knowledge of their past history, origin and culture is like a tree without roots.
—Marcus Garvey

T he morning after the wine tasting I woke to the unpleasant fact that I'd agreed to attend a golf lesson with Susan. To mitigate the effects of a late night, an unaccustomed amount of alcohol, and an emotionally draining day, I brewed an extra-strong pot of coffee. While Susan applied makeup at the kitchen table, I recharged my brain by seeking advice from a few favorite sources.

The ancient Greeks knew plenty about homicidal revenge. Thinking of Melinda Tumbleson, Elliot's rejected first wife, I consulted my old friend Euripides. In his play, *Medea*, the title character kills her faithless husband's girlfriend. Not content with the death of the girl, Medea kills her own kids as well. It's complicated.

Susan lost interest halfway through my retelling of the story. "I'm not buying it. Medea sounds like a better match for our other murder investigation. Velma had a great motive to kill our mother. Our father, too, now that I think of it. Find another Greek drama queen to solve Elliot's murder."

I brought a pile of books from the den and spread them across the table. "What about Clytemnestra? She kills her husband after he sacrifices their daughter, goes off to war, and comes back with a beautiful girlfriend. Melinda accused Elliot of neglecting Jack for his new son, and she was jealous of his sexy new wife."

"That setup works better. Both are jealous wives and protective mothers." She began a painstaking application of mascara. "I know how you like to get all English-teacher in times of stress, but you might be barking up the wrong bookshelf. From everything you've told me, and everything I've seen for myself, the Tumbleson family problems sound more like a reality show slugfest than an epic Greek tragedy."

"Those gods and heroes could put reality shows to shame." Despite my argument, I didn't dismiss Susan's criticism, and I returned to the bookcase in search of a better match. If Elliot physically abused Sonya, as Bryony claimed, he probably did the same to Melinda. Perhaps his violence, and not his infidelities, had led to their divorce. On the other hand, if Melinda wanted to kill her ex-husband, she would have done so years ago. She divorced him instead, which was the course of action Bryony recommended for a spouse who'd outlived his usefulness.

Susan interrupted my reverie. "You told me Melinda's fight with Elliot was about money. I think that's a better motive."

"You're right. That was her main concern, and he shut her down." I shelved the books and grabbed the car keys.

Susan surveyed my outfit. "You're going like that? Don't you have anything better to wear?"

I was wearing a collared shirt and yoga pants. Susan, however, looked like an ad for Vogue Golf. She wore a smartly tailored, short blue skirt and a thin, clingy, white shirt. She also sported a straw sun visor and a set of bracelets made of tiny blue, green, and gold beads. Humbled by her mastery of country club chic, I swiped a bit of makeup on my face while she put last-minute touches to her hair in the bathroom.

George joined me in the kitchen. He drummed his fingers on the counter and said, in a low tone, "I'm paying extra for this double lesson, so take advantage of it. Don't let your sister hog Ryan's attention. He's supposed to be teaching you golf."

"Ryan said he'd only charge us for one lesson. And anyway, as you may have already guessed, I'm hopeless at golf. With or without my sister, paying for golf lessons is a waste of money."

For a moment, I experienced a twinge of regret. Golf had become so important to George. I felt as if I were letting him down. There wasn't much we had in common anymore, other than our kids. Maybe golf was his attempt at bringing us closer together.

He clapped me on the back, perhaps mistaking me for one of his country club buddies. I glared at him, and he hugged me, finally recognizing that I was his wife and not part of a weekend foursome. "Don't give up. Believe me, I know how you feel. Golf is difficult and frustrating."

"Then why do it? If you want us to spend more time together, we should do something we both enjoy. I wish I could understand you."

He poured milk and sugar into his coffee. "It's not about the game. Hanging out at the club will help me business-wise. Cooper has big plans for expanding into other parts of New Jersey. And now I'm in on every single meeting."

"Unless you're getting more money than you're telling me, I don't know how we can afford the membership." George and I had separate checking accounts, one joint account for paying bills, and a college fund for the kids. In money, as in so much else, there wasn't a whole lot of transparency in our marriage.

He banged a cereal box, bowl, and spoon on the countertop. "Cooper handled the membership discount. Don't worry about it."

I tossed a notebook in my handbag. "You've framed this as a business decision, but that's not the whole story. There's something more to it than that."

George splashed milk into his cereal. "Chalk it up to a mid-life crisis. Even though I'm not good at golf, I love the game. Never had the money or the time to pursue it before."

Given the fact that we were facing two college tuitions in the next few years, his assertion of financial security was laughable. "We don't have the money or the time now."

"Try to be positive, for my sake, if not for yours. I'm off to meet Cooper and some potential clients. Luckily, they're even worse at golf than I am."

He exited as Susan returned to the kitchen, carrying with her a cloud of expensive perfume.

She opened the back door and trilled to George, *"Bonne journée!"*

He acknowledged her with a half-hearted wave. Ellie and Zach drifted into the kitchen, which prevented us from further discussions about murders past and present. Zach poured the remaining cereal into a bowl and drowned it in a gallon of milk. He didn't say much, because his teenaged body doesn't work until he's put ten thousand calories in it.

Ellie, whose dearest wish was to be a professional dancer, was more health conscious. Her breakfast consisted of sliced strawberries and plain yogurt. She looked at my sister and said admiringly, "Aunt Susan, you look amazing! I love that shirt."

Susan kissed her. "It's yours, my dear. I'll leave it in your room before I go."

Ellie and I protested, but Susan was firm. "It's too young for me. But perfect for Ellie. So no more arguments." She brushed a final coat of gloss on her lips and said, "Ready, sis?"

I observed that I had been ready for over an hour. Susan was an excellent mimic, and she perfectly aped my disapproving expression and posture, which tickled Zach and Ellie.

As we backed out of the driveway, she said appreciatively, "Nice kids. Especially now that they're older. You've improved as well. It's a pleasure to spend time together without listening to you blab on and on about babysitters and playdates." She thought for a moment and added, "Although you obsess over them to an unhealthy degree."

I slowed down as we approached a large oak tree, which was so close to the driveway its roots were pulling up the expensively repaved surface. "Life will get even easier when Zach gets his driving license."

Thinking of my son behind the wheel made me so nervous I narrowly missed dinging the car on the tree trunk, although no one was likely to notice. Both the car and the tree had plenty of miles on them.

* * *

At the club, Susan breathed in the scent of mown grass and said, "I must say this place was a pleasant surprise. It's not going to win any awards for creativity, as it's a trifle too corporate America for me, but I will admit it's tasteful. And the restaurant had surprisingly sophisticated food and wine."

Jokingly, I asked, "Are you thinking of joining?"

"Perhaps I'll marry someone who's a member. It's been two years since my last divorce. I think I could get used to this." She walked through a high gate to the pool. Although it wouldn't open until Memorial Day, the borders were banked with spring flowers, and the outdoor patio was bright with gaily striped umbrellas. "I could see myself lounging by the pool, being served iced drinks by attractive young waiters."

"How do you plan to seduce young waiters while being married to an old golfer?"

Susan curled the end of her ponytail around her fingers. "I'm sure I wouldn't be the first one to double dip."

I squinted at the cloudless sky and handed her a bottle of sunscreen. "You won't get far if you end up with sunstroke."

We slathered our post-winter, sun-starved skin, which in Susan's case constituted considerably more square inches, and headed to the driving range. I slowed down as we passed the clump of bushes where Elliot Tumbleson died. "I haven't been able to pin down precisely when Bryony saw someone dressed in a waiter's uniform who looked like Miguel. The time frame is so narrow. I saw Elliot before the golf lesson, Bryony saw him during the lesson, and I found him right afterward. Carl Bagarosa, the groundskeeper, said he saw Sonya Tumbleson walking this way at about the time of the murder, but he couldn't or wouldn't give me any more specific details."

We both got distracted at the sight of George and Cooper with the same two women they'd played golf with on the day Elliot was murdered. My heart lurched. Were these women the real reason George was so eager to play golf?

I badly wanted to discuss my fears with Susan but said nothing. Some things were too personal to discuss with anyone, even a sister.

Susan had no similar compunctions. "No wonder George wants to play golf all the time. Who are the two babes with him?"

"They're clients." I acted as if I didn't care, but my sister wasn't fooled.

She kicked a loose pebble in their direction. "I've been around the block a few times. And I don't like what I see."

Under my breath, I told her to shut up, and so we walked without speaking down the path to the range. It was a beautiful day, and the place was packed. Carl eyed Jack Tumbleson and Kevin Sugarman, who were hacking away on the putting green. Convulsed with laughter, the kids were unaware that they were annoying the Sergeant of the Sod. After Jack took out a chunk of grass with a heavy-handed swipe of his club, Carl cruised toward them with the grim determination of Admiral Nimitz at the Battle of Midway.

At the driving range, the usual group of fanatics practiced their golf swings with both conviction and passionate intensity. Bryony slammed her club over and over again, quickly diminishing the number of balls in her extra-large bucket. I wondered if she too was keeping an eye on her husband and his pretty clients.

The only person we didn't see was Ryan. In no great hurry, I strolled to the snack bar, thinking that perhaps our popular golf pro had taken a break between lessons. Behind the small window, a familiar face greeted me.

Chapter Sixteen

But some women only require an emergency to make them fit for one.
—Thomas Hardy / Far From the Madding Crowd

M iguel was wearing Ian's nametag and a baseball cap with the club logo pulled low on his forehead. He put a finger to his lips to warn me to be quiet. I stepped aside to let two women order lunch. They took an unconscionable amount of time deciding between kale salad and Cobb salad. I was on the cusp of offering my vote for the Cobb salad when, in a burst of creative problem-solving, they decided to order both salads and share. They sat on the patio to await their order.

As soon as they were out of earshot, I returned to the counter and said, "What happened with the police? Have they eliminated you as a suspect? Did the club reinstate you?"

With stagey casualness, Miguel said, "Ms. Hopewell, your order will be ready in a few minutes. You can pick it up in the back."

I opened a side gate, and Miguel met me halfway. He wiped his hands on his apron. "I don't have much time before I have to get back to work. I'm subbing for my cousin today, but I do have some good news. Mr. Aldridge recommended me for a job at one of his buildings. When that goes through, I'm never coming back to this place."

I wondered if Bryony knew about her husband's kind offer and regretted misjudging Cooper. While I'd merely sympathized with Miguel's plight, George's boss had actively worked to help him.

I congratulated him on his new job and said, "I hope this also means you're no longer a suspect."

He swallowed hard and said, "I didn't get arrested, but I'm not in the clear. My cousin got me a lawyer, and the detectives let me go, but I'm still freaked out. Somebody told the cops they saw me with Mr. Tumbleson right before he was killed. They said I was the last person to see him alive." He kept his head down and his voice low, but the tension behind those stoic words was unmistakable.

My hands curled in sympathetic worry. "Is that the only evidence they have?"

He burst out, "Look, it was like this: I had a flat tire. So Ian clocked me in. If you're one minute late, they dock you a half hour. And I didn't want him to get into trouble for signing me in when I wasn't here. No one could have seen me with Mr. Tumbleson, because I didn't get to the club until right before the police cars and ambulance came. I snuck in through the back way."

Maybe I'd been worrying unnecessarily. "Surely, by now, the police would have reviewed the CC cameras."

His shoulders slumped. "No cameras along the back. It's a dirt road. But I swear I didn't kill Mr. Tumbleson."

As I suspected, Bryony saw someone dressed as a waiter and leaped to the conclusion it was Miguel. "This is easy. The witness who identified you made an honest mistake. It happens all the time. Tell your cousin to go to the police and explain what happened. He can testify that you weren't here when Elliot was murdered. You'll be off the hook."

"I can't do it, Ms. Hopewell. Ian will get into trouble, and he can't afford to lose this job. He got accused of stealing at his last restaurant." He wiped his eyes with his sleeve. "I trusted you. Promise me you won't tell."

There was no diplomatic way to say what was on my mind. "I'm sorry to have to ask this question, but did your cousin have any reason to kill Elliot Tumbleson? Maybe Elliot found out what happened at Ian's last job and was going to fire him."

Miguel stiffened. "Ian swore to me he didn't know Mr. Tumbleson, except by sight. None of us in the kitchen knew him, except as a customer. My cousin may have had some run-ins with the law, but nothing like this. And anyway, that was years ago."

"I appreciate your loyalty, but this goes way beyond what's reasonable. Your cousin wouldn't want you to be accused of murder." I took out my notebook and added Ian's name to my list of suspects.

He bent over my shoulder to see what I'd written. "If the police had charged me, Ian would have come forward."

"Is there anyone besides Ian who looks enough like you that someone would mistake you for him?"

"No one pays attention to the waiters. We're here to work, not to make friends." With greater heat, he said, "Do you know who fingered me? I have to find out, so I can defend myself."

His priorities, like his loyalties, struck me as misplaced. "That unreliable witness isn't your biggest problem. I'm more worried about your cousin's role and his failure to come forward."

He crossed his arms and tilted his head to one side. "Ian is family. I trust him with my life."

I gave up, for the moment, trying to persuade Miguel that his cousin might not have his best interests at heart. "Here's my cell number. Call me tomorrow, and we'll figure something out."

Miguel returned to the snack bar, and I went back to the driving range. George would be furious if he found out I let Susan hog the entire lesson.

But Susan wasn't with Ryan. At first, I didn't see her, but clouds of smoke from behind a large oak tree tipped me off. She sat on a stone bench, puffing on a cigarette, which, according to Club Rule #6A, was strictly forbidden outside the designated areas. I grabbed the butt from her fingers and hid it in a pansy-filled urn.

She was without remorse. "No one saw me. But enough about me. What about you? Where have you been? Did you find Ryan? I'm bored."

I wheeled the golf bag back to the range, where we found Ryan slapping golf balls. He said he'd been looking for us, but his eyes restlessly scanned the surrounding area, as if he were searching for someone else.

Susan struck a seductive pose, leaning into one hip. "We must have been circling each other. I was looking for you."

Although Ryan was a master of both the innuendo and double entendre, he dropped the conversational ball Susan so temptingly offered. He appeared distracted, looking right and left, but not at us.

My sister refused to give up without a fight. "I'm currently available. Let's do it now."

Ryan gestured to the driving range. "After you, ladies."

For about fifteen minutes, he seemed like his old self. He demonstrated how we should stand and showed us how to hold the golf club. I theoretically knew this already and let my mind wander to Miguel's plight.

Ryan decided Susan needed a more hands-on approach, and he positioned himself behind her, taking several practice swings with her. When he deemed her ready to take a swing by herself she demurred, and he once again cocooned her, this time without leaving any space between his front and her rear.

While they were folded in each other's arms, I continued to whiff at the ball. And then, to my surprise, I hit three solid shots. This minor accomplishment wasn't as gratifying as getting an A in metaphysical poetry, but there was no denying the pleasure it gave me.

Flushed with success in one endeavor, I renewed my efforts toward a more important goal. I turned to the golf pro, who'd missed all three of my adequate swings. "When did you last see Elliot? Was he alone?"

Ryan didn't appear to hear my questions. He whipped his phone from his pocket and said, "So sorry, ladies, but I have to take this call. Carry on, and I'll be right back."

Susan watched him walk toward the snack bar. "If I want to get stood up by a conceited jerk, I can do that in New York. I don't have to travel to the ends of the earth for the privilege."

"Oak Ridge is not beyond the pale of human civilization, and I think it's a perfectly fine place to get stood up. Your love life, however, is getting in the way of our investigation. Ryan is a possible witness and is also on my list of suspects. I want to see more talking and less body language."

"There's no evidence he's guilty." She swung at a golf ball. "It figures the first attractive guy I meet in weeks you suspect is a killer."

I grew uneasy as the minutes ticked by. Susan complained, "I'm tired. And hot. And I've lost interest in golf. Let's bag it for the day. We can sit on the veranda and get a cool drink, preferably something with gin in it."

"I'll text Ryan, so we can reschedule the rest of the lesson. I'm surprised at him. He might be a killer, an accomplice, or a witness, but it's not like him to be so rude." I tapped out a message but there was no answering text.

Susan took out her phone. "I'm not leaving without giving that Down Under Don Juan a piece of my mind."

"Please don't. You don't have to come back here. I do." In truth, I didn't try all that hard to stop her. I also was peeved at the waste of time.

She darted out of my reach and completed the call but gave up when it went to voicemail. With a resigned shrug, she said, "You win. Buy me a drink, and all is forgiven."

We returned to the snack bar, where a woman had taken Miguel's place behind the counter. As we waited at a table for our drinks, Carl Bagarosa rushed past us. His usual florid complexion was an unhealthy purple, and I figured his beloved grass had been violated by a novice golfer or an insufficiently reverential group of kids.

Carl's hasty run ended at the far end of the parking lot, and I stood up to get a better look. Susan craned her neck. "What's all the fuss?"

A growing crowd converged around the groundskeeper. George, Cooper, and their clients weren't among them. They were across the fairway. Relieved to see my husband was safe, I stopped worrying about him and said, "Let's find out."

We got close enough to see the president of Meadowfields support a weeping Sonya Tumbleson. Susan pulled me back. "I don't like the looks of this. Let's get out of here while we still can."

I was spared having to argue with her when cop cars and an ambulance cut off the exits. One person managed to elude them by speeding down a dirt road through half-closed gates at the end of the parking lot.

My sister gave an exasperated groan. "It's too late. We're stuck."

With a sick dread mounting inside me, I called Ryan Walker one last time.

The opening notes of "Born to Run," Springsteen's iconic call to freedom, emerged from the bushes next to Carl.

At the sound of Ryan's ringtone, Sonya fainted. It took every ounce of self-control not to follow her example.

Chapter Seventeen

That we shall die we know; 'tis but the time
And drawing days out, that men stand upon.
—William Shakespeare / Julius Caesar

After white-suited crime scene techs removed a body bag containing the remains of Ryan Walker, the police wrapped crime tape around a wide perimeter that stretched from the edge of the parking lot to the edge of the path. Most people retreated to the lawn, which allowed them to observe the police without getting personally involved in the tragedy. Susan, after some initial reluctance, allowed me to draw her closer to the action.

When Sonya emerged from her swoon, her voice was hoarse. "What kind of sick individual could have done this to Ryan? Everyone loved him."

Sonya's words pulled me out of a horrified silence. I leaned close to my sister and said, "She makes a good point. Ryan, unlike Elliot, was well-liked. I've never heard a word against him. Women adore him, and men want to be him."

Passing clouds dimmed the sun, and the temperature dropped, as if in sympathy with this new tragedy. Susan spoke through chattering teeth. "Even if that were true, which I highly doubt, people don't get killed because they're unpopular. The motive, at least in detective novels, is always either love or money. And he appears to have been quite the player. I imagine he left a trail of broken hearts."

"That's too simplistic an explanation for a death that occurred so soon after Elliot's murder. There must be some connection between them. Ryan must have posed a danger to the killer, either knowingly or unknowingly." I clung to facts, because if I let emotion overpower me, I wouldn't be able to stave off a complete breakdown.

Susan dropped onto the grass and hugged her knees to her chest. "Ryan was late to meet us, distracted during the golf lesson, and then ditched us without explanation. I wonder if he knew he was in danger."

I sat next to her as my legs, like hers, were feeling the strain. "I agree he was inattentive, which isn't—wasn't—like him. But Ryan didn't look scared. More like he was waiting for something or someone." From behind large sunglasses, I watched Detective Sorkin interview Sonya Tumbleson and wondered if she was the person Ryan was waiting to meet. Her distress seemed quite real but could have been the regret of a killer and not the shock of an innocent witness to a crime.

The shadow of an approaching figure brought me out of my reverie and onto my feet. Appalled to find Miguel so close to the scene of the crime, I said, "Go away! Get back to the snack bar, or wherever it was you came from."

He looked confused. "Don't worry about me. I'm on my break. Magda, one of my friends, said there had been an accident, and I wanted to make sure you were okay." He knelt next to Susan, who sat, white-lipped and wobbly, at the edge of the path. "Do you need a doctor?"

I answered for my stunned sister. "Get back to the kitchen. Or the snack bar. Or wherever it was, you came from. Talk to the other waiters. Make sure you have witnesses who can account for your time from the minute you arrived at the club until right now. Ryan Walker didn't have an accident. He was murdered. I don't yet know how, but it looks as if he met the same fate as Elliot Tumbleson."

Miguel turned and fled, not toward the kitchen, but to the far end of the parking lot.

"No!" I ran after him. "The cops have blocked off the driveway, and the worst thing you could do is run away."

He said, over his shoulder, "That's what you think. As far as any of the members know, I was never here."

Miguel soon outstripped me. From a distance, I saw him jump into a battered car and speed down a dirt road that ended in a narrow opening in the greenery. This jogged a memory of someone else leaving by the same route, but I couldn't recall the type of car. The harder I tried to remember, the further away the memory receded.

As news of Ryan's death spread, a brigade of golf carts left the fairways and converged closer to the scene of the crime. When George saw us, he leaped out of the cart and looked wildly from me to Susan. "What's happening? What's wrong with Susan? Is she sick?"

Cooper, with less agility, followed George's lead. The two women who formed the balance of the foursome clung to each other before finding steadier support in the form of my husband and his boss.

I approached the one who'd attached herself to George and extended my hand. "I regret we had to meet under these circumstances. I'm Liz Hopewell."

She didn't relinquish her grasp on him. "This is terrible. Were you the one who found him?" She pointed to the bushes and then buried her face in George's shoulder.

I used our handshake to yank her away since my husband seemed disinclined to do so himself. "No. I was on the veranda when I saw Carl Bagarosa and Sonya Tumbleson in obvious distress. I hope it wasn't a jealous wife who committed this murder." I fixed her with a hard look. "Because if it was me, I'd have gone after the girlfriend instead."

My phone alarm went off, startling all of us with its insistent ring. I'd set it to remind myself to drive Ellie home from her ballet rehearsal.

When I told George he'd have to go to the ballet studio, he looked bewildered. "Ellie? Ballet?"

"Yes, Ellie. Our daughter." I spoke loudly enough for his clingy golf partner to hear.

George was too enmeshed in either the horror of Ryan's murder or the pleasure of his pretty companion to process what I told him. "What does Ellie have to do with any of this?"

"Nothing. She needs a ride, and I can't leave." I pressed a hand against my chest to slow the quaking inside. "I don't want Ellie to worry. Be-be-because she needs a ride home. And I'm too upset to get behind the wheel."

I couldn't explain to my husband, because I didn't analyze my feelings until much later, that I felt out of control and needed to find some way to tame that sense of helplessness. Stumbling upon Elliot's dead body was shocking and terrible, but knowing Ryan had met the same fate was worse.

The effect wasn't simply cumulative. I knew Ryan. Liked him. In the same way that a single death of someone you know is more devastating than a tragedy affecting dozens you don't, I grieved for him.

George appeared similarly moved. "There's nothing I'd like more than to escape this horror show, but neither of us is going anywhere. The police have roped off the exits."

I texted Ellie and, without explaining why I was delayed, told her to ask a friend for a ride home. She messaged back a happy face, three hearts, and the message, **No worries, Ma!**

My husband, with a sick look on his face, gestured to the bushes. "What happened? I got five texts that said five different things."

My throat and tongue were thick in my mouth. "Someone killed Ryan. Brutally killed him."

He stuttered, "Is he—are you sure it was—"

Trembling, I nodded an affirmative answer to both implied questions. "Susan and I didn't see what happened, but we saw the cops take him away in a body bag. And we heard Sonya's statement to the police." Cooper, who stood behind George, cursed softly.

It was déjà vu all over again. The ambulance. The police. The persistent questions and the staring faces. Detectives Sorkin and Harriman, when they finished taking statements from Sonya, Carl, and two others close to the scene, signaled to us that it was our turn.

Sorkin pinned me with a sharp look. His first question, after listening to my halting summary, was about my former student. "Was Miguel here today when Mr. Walker was killed?"

I figured he already knew the answer to the question and wondered if this was some kind of test. "He, er, he was here earlier to help out at the snack bar. So, he couldn't have had anything to do with this attack. I, um, he's already gone. Finished his shift."

He pulled at his tie to loosen it. "We've got a dozen witnesses who saw Mr. Walker go to the snack bar where Miguel was working despite the fact that he was fired."

Chills ran down my back. "He wasn't fired. He got a better job offer but came back to cover his cousin's shift. Only an innocent man would return to the scene of the crime."

Sorkin squinted as if trying to bring my face into focus. "It's a guilty man who returns to the scene of the crime."

His correction irritated me. "That's what people say. I don't happen to think it's true."

Tom came up from behind me and said, "Criminals often return to the scene of the crime, for many reasons."

I whirled around. "Whose side are you on?"

"I'm not on anyone's side. Ben and I need to find a killer, and we don't let personal feelings get in the way of our investigation."

George grabbed my arm and drew me to him. There was no tenderness in the proprietary gesture. He acted more like a traveler grabbing his suitcase from an airport conveyor belt than a loving husband protecting his wife. His words, however, were more supportive than his body language. "Liz is right. This is the last place Miguel would want to be seen if he was guilty of Elliot's murder."

Ben was even less impressed with this argument after hearing it from George. "Not if he was plotting another murder. This is exactly where he'd want to be, and he'd have the added bonus of setting Liz up to confirm an alibi. He knows she's prejudiced in his favor."

A white-suited scene-of-crime investigator emerged from the bushes and beckoned to the detectives. When they returned, Ben was holding a plastic bag with half of a gold-plated nametag inside. He held it up to my face. "Have you seen Ian?"

I could see from his expression he already knew Miguel had been wearing his cousin's nametag. The same cousin whose shift Miguel had covered.

Ben said, with more sympathy than I expected, "Ms. Hopewell, I need you to trust me. We can't get to the bottom of this without a full account from you. You're a smart woman. You don't want to be the next victim." He put a hand on Tom's shoulder. "Detective Harriman here will finish taking your statement."

It was at this point that George decided he'd had enough of the police. "Detective Sorkin, stop harassing my wife. She's told you everything she knows and has been through enough for one day."

The detective's answer was devoid of emotion. "Liz has more guts than any civilian I know. I feel sorry for anyone who gets in her way."

I considered Ben's words as something of a compliment, but George was not equally pleased. "Forget about her guts and respect her brains. If Liz says Miguel is innocent, he is."

I would have kissed George if he hadn't glanced in Heather's direction, as if checking to see that his chest-thumping impressed her.

Ben said, "It's up to Liz. You, however, will give Detective Harriman your statement now."

I repeated to Tom everything I'd already told Ben. When he ended the interview, I told George I was leaving and grabbed Susan.

"Get a grip. We have work to do."

Chapter Eighteen

Literature is eavesdropping.
—Ralph Waldo Emerson

Susan was unenthusiastic about any plan that would delay her departure from the Meadowfields Country Club. "What do you need me for? I'm sorry, Liz, but I'm taking the next train back to the city. I can't wait to get out of the suburbs and back to New York, where I don't have to worry about violent crime."

"Two men are dead. An innocent man is suspected of murder. And you're worried about getting the next train home?"

Susan stuck out her bottom lip. "Don't cross your arms at me like some snooty headmistress. The police are responsible for finding the killer. Not me and not you."

The logical side of my brain agreed with her, but every other part resisted. "If someone came forward to help us when Mom died, that would have changed everything. It's why I can't now turn my back and walk away. You're scared and upset. But this isn't about you, Susan."

"That is the meanest thing you've ever said to me. And the most untrue. All I do is think about other people. I never put myself first." Her eyes reddened with a fresh wash of tears.

I elected not to remind her of dozens of episodes that belied her assertion. If we started exhuming resentments from the past, we'd never get anything done. Instead of arguing, I kissed her. "We cannot fight each other. Two men are dead. Miguel is still a suspect. We have to stand together."

She managed a weak smile. "Yeah. That's what I meant to say. So, what's next?"

"Let's try the kitchen first. I didn't think we'd be able to get there ahead of the police, but they don't look like they'll be done with the golfers any time soon."

We entered the clubhouse, and the incongruity of our surroundings hit both of us. Outdoors, cop cars loomed, lights flashed, and a man lay dead. Inside, plush carpeting, velvet sofas, and vases filled with fragrant flowers masked the ugliness beneath the surface.

Susan's face was pale and tear-streaked. "How about a visit to the bathroom first? We can do a quick washup before we start asking questions."

The men's bathroom was on the first floor, but the women's was at the top of a long curving staircase. My sister moved slowly, using my arm and the banister for support, but perked up when we entered the softly lit lounge. Crystal bowls brimming with candy and an array of packaged snacks sat on low tables. Susan unwrapped a few chocolate mints, and I poured two cups of coffee from a silver urn.

We sat in an alcove, which was fitted out with marble sinks, adjustable chairs, and an array of sweet-smelling toiletries. With short, efficient strokes, we raked our hair and cleaned off smeared makeup. In the adjacent locker room, two women talked over the rush of water.

A high-pitched voice said, "Well, that was a lousy end to a very promising day."

The shower muffled the next part of their conversation, but when they turned off the water, their voices rang with startling clarity.

Her companion said, "Just be happy that we were among the first the cops talked to. I wish they'd finish with George and Cooper so we could wrap up this deal and move on."

"The delay might be a blessing in disguise, though not, of course, for the golf pro. I've got my eye on George. And Cooper is definitely interested in seeing more of you."

"Both of them are married. So the best we can hope for is free meals, free golf, and sex in a crappy motel. I think we stick with the original plan."

Breathless, I tapped Susan's arm. She nodded, a grim look on her face. I hadn't exchanged many words with George's golf partners but was able to distinguish Amanda's voice from Heather's.

Amanda said, "Cooper has more money, but George is better looking. Too bad he has kids."

Heather sighed loud enough for us to hear. "I agree. I'd need a lot more money than either one of them has before committing to a suburban lifestyle with a divorced dad. If that's what you're after, there are plenty of guys here in a more attractive tax bracket. And the last thing I want is to get stuck with someone else's kids on the weekend."

Both women made gagging sounds. Through gales of laughter, Amanda continued, "George's wife seems like the motherly type. Definitely would insist on custody. Bryony, on the other hand, would probably force Cooper to take the kid."

The other woman's voice was thoughtful. "Bryony doesn't have any kids. Cooper's got a son with his first wife, but he's grown, which does simplify things. I think George's brats are in high school. So no matter what, they'll be out of the house soon."

I shot Susan a warning glance to keep her quiet and listened as the two women plotted the breakup of my marriage and the disposal of my children. My self-control paid off as Heather and Amanda discussed their more practical plans for my husband and his clueless boss.

Heather said, "Let's not forget the primary reason we're here. We need to dump the Pemberton building, and Cooper seems willing to buy it. He's also offered to manage our other properties for a lot less money than what we're paying now. I think we can negotiate a decent price and get out from under the worst of our money pits."

Amanda's answer sent stabbing pains through my heart. "Cooper isn't the problem. It's George we need to convince. And I hate to break it to you, but I think he's more interested in Bryony than in either one of us."

"I disagree. Cooper's the boss, and I get the distinct feeling he can be, well, persuaded. As for Bryony, she doesn't strike me as the kind of woman who's in any relationship for the long haul."

Heather's smug assertion drained the last dregs of my patience. I marched into the dressing area with Susan close behind me. "Get out, before I throw you out."

They were as shocked as if a team of paratroopers had been the ones to intrude upon their privacy. Heather recovered first. "What kind of creep are you to listen in on our private conversation?"

Confrontation wasn't my strong suit, but they tapped into an unplumbed level of rage I hadn't known I possessed. "You don't get to be the injured party here. It's my marriage and my kids you're planning on blowing up. So get dressed, ladies. I'm giving you ten minutes before I call security and report you for theft."

Amanda tried to brazen it out. "You're crazy. We're guests of your husband and Cooper, and we haven't stolen anything."

"Your word against mine. I'd say the odds are in my favor." I pointed to her gym bag, which had two plush towels with the Meadowfields Country Club logo tucked inside. "What are you going to do next? Empty the candy dish?"

Heather gave me a wide-eyed, innocent look. "Listen, you're taking this way too seriously. We were kidding. And anyway, we didn't know you were listening. So you can't hold it against us."

Susan took a picture of her gym bag and towels. "She can and she will."

Amanda snapped, "Don't get yourself worked up over nothing. Like Heather said, it's business."

My sister put her hand on the doorknob. "I changed my mind. Take all the time you want. I'll be downstairs, telling Cooper everything you said about that crappy building you're hoping to offload on him."

Susan's poise suffered a blow when the door she was leaning against opened unexpectedly. Sonya Tumbleson, after helping my sister regain her footing, stared at Heather and Amanda with the kind of well-bred chill I would kill to possess.

She greeted me with unexpected warmth. "Liz, we need to talk. This is such a tragedy. I'm absolutely shattered."

Amanda pulled a spandex dress over her head. "Yes, Liz, why don't you talk with your little friend, so that Heather and I can have some privacy here? Or do you get your kicks from watching?"

They were no match for Sonya. She eyed them as if they belonged to a uniquely repulsive species of dung beetle. "You ladies are not members. And you are not welcome. If you don't pack up your discount makeup and your knockoff clothes, I'll ask someone on staff to help you to the exit."

Magda, one of the waitresses, put a temporary end to hostilities. She knocked on the door and opened it a crack. "Mrs. Tumbleson, Mr. Felician is ready to take you home."

Sonya's face immediately transformed. The amused and malicious look she'd trained on Heather and Amanda changed to an expression of heartfelt grief. Even her body looked different. One moment, she was all wiry intensity. The next, she was a fragile figure, barely able to stay upright. With a curl of her lip, Magda offered Sonya an arm and escorted her out of the room.

The interruption helped me attain a more rational perspective. Heather and Amanda might be shallow and conniving, but they also were potential sources of information. I settled back into one of the chairs and said, "What time did you arrive at the club? And where were you before you met George and Cooper?"

Heather dumped the stolen towels and zipped her bag with a vicious yank. "Where was I? Where were you? You're the one who keeps finding dead bodies."

Technically, I'd only found one dead body, but I didn't correct her. Susan stepped between us and said, "You probably don't know how closely Liz works with the police. Failing to answer her questions will not go well."

Amanda was tight-lipped. "Don't say a word, Heather. We'll do our talking to the cops."

I beckoned to Susan. "Let's not waste any more time here." My sister followed me as I walked heavily in the direction of the staircase and then tiptoed back. I pressed my ear against the door, but all I heard was the sound of muffled laughter.

For all of my bluster, the encounter wounded me far more than it could

Heather or Amanda. They wouldn't have spoken as they did if George hadn't given them a reason to think he was interested.

Susan rubbed her head. "Let's go. I've had enough drama for one day."

"Don't let those two homewreckers dictate our actions. We came here to interview the kitchen staff, and that's what we're going to do." I led her down the stairs and toward the Employees Only door, but Susan held back. I took her hand. "Let's go," I urged. "We might as well get something positive done. I promise we'll go home right after."

Her foot-dragging was understandable. Despite the expensive furnishings, the elegant floral arrangements, and the flattering lighting, the atmosphere at Meadowfields Country Club felt poisonous.

* * *

The lobby was crowded and much noisier than usual. Ben Sorkin was talking to Carl Bagarosa, who looked as if he'd rather seed the grass with dandelions than continue the conversation. At the bar, anxious members whiled away the time with expensive drinks and free peanuts.

Susan looked longingly at the drinkers. "We need sustenance, or we'll faint."

"Good thinking. The bartenders probably know more about the goings on at the club than the servers." All the seats were taken, but we squeezed into a space next to the computer station, where the waiters entered their drink orders. I motioned to one of the bartenders, and after requesting two sodas, asked, "Have the police interviewed you yet?"

He swiped the sticky surface with a cloth and said, "Not yet. Mr. Aldridge wanted the cops to talk to all the members first."

I leaned over the bar. "What have you heard from the staff? Do they have any idea who did it?"

He slapped a bowl of nuts in front of us. "It wasn't one of us, if that's what you're thinking. We all liked Ryan. He was good for business and an all-around nice guy."

"That leaves the members. Any ideas about who might have had it in for him? Or Elliot?"

The bartender's strained smile remained fixed on his face. "That's way above my pay grade. Your guess is as good as mine. Probably a lot better."

His answer was similar to Carl's. Although the bartender was more polite than the groundskeeper, both men suggested the killer was someone in a position of power. With a pang, I remembered that Ryan had said nearly the same thing, in nearly the same words.

Susan and I emptied our glasses and then, at my urging, crossed the room and entered a narrow corridor that led to the kitchen.

I pushed open the swinging door. Ignoring the surprised looks from the staff, I said, "Did anyone here see Miguel today?"

A young man planted himself in front of me. "Sorry, ma'am. He doesn't work here anymore. We haven't seen him in days."

Chapter Nineteen

The nature of bad news infects the teller
—William Shakespeare / Antony and Cleopatra

T he guy who blocked me from entering the kitchen lied with such skill that if I hadn't spoken to Miguel a few hours earlier, I would have believed him. He insisted Miguel hadn't been at the snack bar that day and acted surprised when I challenged him. Without actually patting me on the back, he motioned somewhere above my shoulder to indicate his sympathy for my mistake.

I adjusted my response to match his determination. "Don't gaslight me. You're trying to protect Miguel, but lying isn't going to help him. He was working the snack bar. I saw him and talked to him. What are you hiding?"

"I'm sorry to upset you, Ms. Hopewell. Maybe you don't remember me? I'm Ian, Miguel's cousin. I can assure you he hasn't been here. Sorry for your trouble." Ian smiled slightly and shifted his gaze toward a dark-haired, dark-eyed waiter who stood next to him. "Perhaps you confused him with someone else?"

"I am—I was—Miguel's English teacher. And I can assure you that I did not mistake him for anyone else, although he was wearing your nametag."

Magda, the sweet-voiced waitress who escorted Sonya out of the bathroom, intervened. "Ian meant no disrespect. But you must be mistaken. Now, why don't you two ladies come with me to the dining room? I'll get you a nice drink and something to—"

The chef stepped away from the stove. "What's the holdup? We've got a houseful of people here waiting to be fed. Get a move on!" Without waiting for an answer, he dashed back to the flaming pans.

Magda said, pleading, "Please, Ms. Hopewell. Please leave us. We must get back to work."

As if to punctuate Magda's words, one of the line cooks began calling out dishes waiting to be served. "Kale salad, dressing on the side! Two burgers, medium rare! BLT! Side of fries and side of rings!" He clapped his hands. "C'mon, people! Move, move, move!"

Magda piled four heavy plates on a tray and balanced it on her shoulder. I held the door open for her. As she passed through she blinked slowly and then tilted her head towards the back exit. I needed no further invitation.

While we waited for Magda, Susan smoked behind a tree, and I paced. Through the plate glass windows, we watched the servers move about the room with purposeful grace. I lost sight of Magda until I saw a flash of her white shirt as she descended the stone steps. She scanned the immediate vicinity, and without acknowledging us, she strode behind the snack bar to the same deserted area where I'd spoken with Miguel.

When we caught up to her, she breathlessly whispered, "I know you mean well. But please, leave us alone. You're making everything worse. Worse for Miguel and worse for all of us. Ian is Miguel's cousin. He knows what he's doing. He's trying to help him."

Susan stubbed out her cigarette. "How is Liz making things worse? Miguel is already a murder suspect. And I don't care what lies Ian is spreading about not seeing Miguel. Liz talked to him today. At the snack bar where he was working. Ian is making things better for Ian. Not Miguel."

Nervously craning her neck from side to side, Magda answered, "We can take care of our own. No offense, but the members don't make friends with us, and we don't make friends with them. Leave us be."

I forestalled Susan's impatient response and assured Magda, "We'll do as you say, but only up to a point. Maybe you don't want me to interfere. But Miguel does. And I owe it to him to do so. He's the one who's in danger, and he's the one who concerns me the most."

"You think we're not concerned, too? The kitchen workers are like family."

She stared at the horizon as if to emphasize the distance between us. "And Miguel is Ian's actual family."

I didn't trust her any more than I trusted Ian. "Whose side are you on? You claim to be Miguel's friend, but it sounds to me like you're covering for Ian."

She bit her lip. "You got some nerve, accusing me."

"What other explanation is there?" I handed her a scrap of paper with my phone number. "Call me. If you're working tomorrow, I can be here as early as 3:30, but we don't have to meet at the club. You pick the place. I'll make it my business to be there."

Magda took the paper and punched the number into her cell phone. She returned to the kitchen, and we walked through the lobby and past a line of people waiting to be interviewed.

Ben frowned at us. "I thought you left an hour ago. What have you been up to?"

Susan put the back of her hand against her forehead and gave every impression of a woman about to faint or become hysterical. "Oh, Detective Sorkin. I'm so dizzy. Is it at all possible for you to talk with Liz tomorrow? I have to lie down before I fall down."

He succumbed to her plea, and I drove her to the train station. There was much we could have said, but a surfeit of emotion rendered both of us silent. I waited with her until the melancholy sound of the approaching train woke us from our reveries.

She rummaged in her bag and handed me a gold earring. "You dropped this in the grass. I almost forgot to give it to you."

"It's not mine. Where did you find it?" The earring had gold swirls and a tiny diamond in the center.

"It was in a crack between the path and the grass." Her mouth opened slightly. "Do you think it's a clue?"

"I hope so. I'll give it to Detective Sorkin tomorrow. It might help clear Miguel's name, although we don't know how long it's been there."

"I wouldn't be too quick to make a judgment." Susan paused as the train roared into the station. "To me, Miguel is looking more suspicious, not less."

I watched the train recede into the distance. When I got home, I closed the curtains and crawled into bed, but my brain refused to cooperate by similarly shutting down. The day unspooled in my mind's eye in an unstoppable loop of random images.

Melinda and Sonya were playing tennis, though not with each other. The two Mrs. Tumblesons could barely bring themselves to share the planet, let alone a tennis court. Cooper was playing golf with George and their scheming clients. Bryony was hitting golf balls. Carl was obsessively guarding the grass. I wondered what time Ian arrived at the club and if it was before or after Ryan was killed.

And Miguel? He had his cousin's nametag pinned to his shirt when I saw him at the snack bar, but I couldn't remember if he was wearing it when he arrived at the crime scene. I wanted to believe the nametag the police bagged had been there for days, but the cheap gold paint would have dulled had it been left outside for any length of time. Ryan's murder, like Elliot's, didn't appear to be premeditated. And yet, someone had planted the nametag at the murder scene. Ian's nametag, however, wasn't the only piece of evidence. The earring Susan found might be another.

The door slammed, indicating George's arrival. I went to the kitchen, where he was pouring himself a large shot of bourbon.

I picked up the nearly empty bottle. "Since when do you drink so much? I'm surprised that after spending all afternoon with Cooper and the good-time girls, you're not already sloshed."

Perhaps that wasn't the most diplomatic of openings, but the memory of how Amanda and Heather assessed George's potential as a future partner irked me. The only person upon whom I could vent my frustration was George.

He swallowed all of the amber liquid and poured more bourbon into his glass. "What good-time girls are you talking about?"

"Don't make me repeat myself when you know what I'm talking about. We had a very interesting conversation this afternoon."

He perked up. "Who? What? Uh, what did Heather and Amanda say? Anything about me?"

I felt sick to my stomach, talking to my husband as if we were in the sixth grade, and he was asking me if one of the popular girls liked him. Like, *like* liked him.

I rarely drank hard liquor, but since drinking bourbon was an essential skill for hardboiled detectives, I emptied the bottle into a glass. After a single, scorching swallow, I added ice and club soda. Perhaps I'd be a soft-boiled detective first.

I collapsed into a chair. "The good news is that Amanda and Heather don't think you're as dumb as Cooper. The bad news is you don't have enough money to seriously interest them. I guess you're stuck with me. Oh, wait a minute. They did also mention that you were more interested in Bryony than in them or me."

George fumbled with the now-empty bottle. "Did you discuss our marriage with our business associates?"

"No. I overheard them talking about you and Cooper while in the bathroom at the club." I watched him from the corner of my eye. "They weren't complimentary."

He tried to talk over me, so I talked louder. "I didn't go there to eavesdrop, and I certainly didn't want to hear what they said, but you might want to find a tactful way to tell Cooper they're hoping to dump a worthless property on him, even if it means stringing him along like a pathetic puppy."

George stalked out of the kitchen, returned with a new bottle of bourbon, and snapped it open. "Cooper is a smart businessman. No one's putting anything over on him, and by the time we're finished negotiating, he'll have that property for ten percent under its market value. Is there anything else? Or are we done here?"

"I'm not remotely close to being done. Are you having an affair with Bryony? Amanda and Heather seemed to think so." My hand shook so badly, the ice in my drink rattled.

He twisted the glass away from me. "There is something seriously wrong with you. Do you think I would have an affair with my boss's wife?"

"Is the fact that Bryony is your boss's wife the only reason you're not having an affair with her?"

I knew, even before the words left my mouth, that there was a better way to communicate my fears to George. But I couldn't explain to him, or fully admit to myself, how much it would pain me if the one trait my husband shared with my father was infidelity. Was there no escaping that legacy of betrayal?

His hot temper turned cold. "I'm trying to get ahead, and you're dragging me back. Everything I do is a means to an end."

It didn't escape my notice that he failed to answer the question. Instead of addressing his evasion, I told him, "You're not the only one who's changed. I'm not the same credulous housewife I used to be."

Of all the things I said in anger, this was the truest. Because the woman he married, the one who ran from her past and feared the future, was ready to take on a killer. More than one, if necessary.

Chapter Twenty

Alone, alone, all, all alone / Alone on a wide, wide sea
—*Samuel Taylor Coleridge / The Rime of the Ancient Mariner*

After the fight with George, I fell into a tortured slumber filled with anxious nightmares. My dream self visited the country club, Valerian Hills High School, and the Brooklyn apartment house of my childhood, where I pounded on a door that refused to open. In all three places, I frantically searched for keys. As an English teacher, I found my subconscious embarrassingly bereft of subtle metaphors. A marginally competent therapist would be bored stiff with the obvious symbolism.

In the morning, I dug through the mess in my closet to find the black skirt and sweater that made me look thin. I took pains with my makeup, telling myself that meeting Detective Ben Sorkin had nothing to do with the early-morning beauty routine.

Ellie approved. "Not bad, Ma. You look like you're going to a funeral, but a super nice one. Who are you trying to impress?"

George looked up when Ellie commented on my appearance. Other than that brief moment, he dedicated himself to reading the newspaper. We didn't argue in front of the kids, which in the last few weeks left us with little to say to each other when they were around.

Heavy rain and gusty winds slowed my commute to Valerian Hills High School. An additional delay ensued when I found a Mercedes SUV that looked suspiciously like Melinda Tumbleson's parked in the space that belonged to me. Annoyed and impatient, I drove to the visitor's lot. As I made my way down the driveway, I noticed the cars that should have been parked next to mine were missing. In place of Bill's battered Nissan Altima, a BMW roadster preened. In the spot reserved for the librarian's ancient Ford Focus, a Lexus rested at an awkward angle.

My miniature umbrella lost its battle with the wind, and I was soaked when I arrived at the main office. Timmy was behind his desk and stroking, with inappropriate fondness, a football-themed tie. Most days, I avoided him, a favor he willingly returned to me and all staff members who didn't coach a team. (The school play didn't count in his estimation of value.)

Timmy had trained his secretary to bar uninvited visitors, but she was in the supply closet and emerged too late to stop me.

The principal swiveled in his chair so he didn't have to look at me while he spoke with male-bonding good cheer into the phone. "Awesome, dude. Really awesome. See you tomorrow." Timmy ended the call and gave me a double thumbs-up. "I was talking to our new English teacher. He's an amazing guy. Going to be a great addition to the wrestling team."

Although I was bubbling with annoyance over the parking situation, Timmy's unexpected news distracted me. "A teacher on the wrestling team? What are you talking about?"

He clamped his lips together to prevent a smile from breaking through his sad expression. "Bill is going to be out of commission for the rest of the year. A health thing. Kind of a shame, of course, but he's no spring chicken. The good news is that Evan Carlsson, one of my former students who is now an English teacher, is willing to leave his old district to come to us. When he was in high school, he won us the state championship in wrestling, and on top of that, he was one heck of a tight end."

Nearly everything that came out of his mouth was a mystery. "We're getting a tight end to teach English?"

Timmy examined his tie as if he needed a pictorial reminder to assist his brain function. "Football term. What did you think I meant?"

"Honestly, nothing rational came to mind. I'm sorry to hear that Bill is in such bad health. What happened?" I held the dripping skeleton of my umbrella in both hands, which gave my fists something to do, other than bang them on his desk.

"This has been in the works for a few weeks. Bill gets a break from school, and we get a fantastic coach for the football and wrestling team." He was fairly humming with excitement.

"And the English department," I reminded him.

"Absolutely. He's very good in English too. You guys are going to love working with him. We need more young teachers to liven the place up."

Timmy said this without blushing. Perhaps he was unaware that the entire school knew about his affair with Ashlee Becker, the youngest member of the English department and a former student at the school. Of course, with Timmy, you never knew. Maybe he also had forgotten about Ashlee.

The warning bell rang, but I stood my ground. "I have a rather time-sensitive problem, which is that someone, probably Melinda Tumbleson, has parked in my spot."

"Okay, so I know I'm going to get a little flack for this, but I think in the end, we can all agree that the parking situation needs improvement." He pointed to the clock. "You're going to be late."

Last year, I would have apologetically left the office. But dealing with murder had made me less timid. "Timmy, if I'm late, it's going to be because someone took my parking spot and because you haven't answered my question."

After ten revolting seconds of sputtering and coughing, he realized I wasn't leaving until he answered me. "From now on, the spots reserved for the English department, the Art department, and the librarian are going to students. Jack Tumbleson has been assigned your parking spot. So it's Melinda's car but Jack's assigned place."

My Brooklyn past roared back to life. With difficulty, I refrained from using the words that first came to mind. "The teachers will not put up with it. I know I won't."

Timmy was defiant. "Not my call. Melinda Tumbleson insisted. She doesn't want Jack to have to cross the parking lot. It's dangerous in the morning, with all that traffic. Don't take everything so personally. This isn't about you, Liz. It's about student safety. You can't be against student safety!"

If I stayed, I'd probably be arrested by the Valerian Hills equivalent of the House Un-American Activities Committee. I walked, in no particular hurry, up the stairs and down the empty corridor. Emily was standing in the hallway between our two classrooms, wringing her hands. With obvious relief, she whispered, "I'm glad you got here. I texted you, but you didn't answer. I didn't want Timmy to find out you were late."

I stuck my head in the classroom and told the students to begin reading *The Rime of the Ancient Mariner*. "No worries. I was with Timmy."

"Did you talk to him about the parking situation? I got an email late last night from Mrs. Tumbleson. So did Ashlee." She twitched as the door to the English office opened. Caroline strode past us without talking, and I surmised from her pinched expression that she, too, had gotten evicted from her parking spot.

I tossed my useless umbrella in the garbage. "I don't check my school email when I'm at home. If I knew at ten o'clock at night that Jack was getting my parking spot I wouldn't have gotten any sleep at all."

"The administration doesn't want the kids to have to cross the parking lot after a late practice." Emily apologized for this statement, not because she was guilty of any transgression, but because unwarranted regret was an essential part of her personality. She was the opposite of Melinda Tumbleson.

I wasn't a violent person, but if I had Melinda in front of me at that moment, I would have been tempted to take a swing at her jutting jaw. The massive chip on her shoulder was another target that begged for attention.

Emily checked her watch with another nervous twitch. "There's an English department meeting after school tomorrow. Maybe we can talk about it then."

"Not a good idea. We're getting a new English teacher to replace Bill, someone Timmy handpicked. I wouldn't say anything in front of the new guy until we know we can trust him."

At that moment, we caught sight of Timmy, who was executing his daily rounds. Our principal spent the first hour of each day making sure the teachers on hall duty didn't take illicit bathroom breaks or chat with other teachers who were supposed to be explicating the tragic implications of *The Rime of the Ancient Mariner.*

Emily scurried down the hall. I entered my classroom, where I found the kids texting and chatting. Jack Tumbleson and his best friend, Kevin Sugarman, were entertaining themselves by balling up wads of paper and tossing them into the recycling bucket. A few students were reading, but not many.

I dumped my bookbag on the desk and said, "I told you to begin reading *The Rime of the Ancient Mariner.* You're an AP class, and you're supposed to be more mature than this."

Jack stuck out his lower lip. "You didn't tell us the page number. It's your fault we didn't do it."

Kevin turned his book upside down and shook it. "Yeah! How were we supposed to find it?"

After a sleepless night of mourning Ryan's tragic death, my nerves were scraped raw, and what might have amused me on another day sorely tested my patience. "Allow me to introduce you once again to the table of contents. Maybe you could remember to use it if you thought of it as a GPS for readers."

The GPS metaphor reminded me of driving, which reminded me of parking, which made me angrier than I would have been if Jack's mother hadn't enacted a hostile takeover of my parking spot during a monsoon.

Jack flicked the pages without looking at them. "And maybe you should pick something that isn't so boring."

"Next class, you and Kevin can read *The Cat in the Hat,* unless you think that's also too big a stretch."

I regretted the words as soon as they were out of my mouth. Rarely did I resort to sarcasm with my students, but I occasionally made an exception for Jack and Kevin, who often worked in tandem to disrupt the class. The boys were popular and, at the same time, widely disliked, broadly courted by their less aggressive classmates but in possession of very few friends.

I chose several volunteers to act out the story, but Jack grew restless when he wasn't the center of attention. "Hey, Ms. Hopewell! It says in the intro that the guy who wrote this was a drug addict. Are you sure we should be reading it? It's like you're telling us to do drugs."

Kevin, taking his lead from Jack, said, "This thing was written, like, two hundred-something years ago."

From the corner of my eye, I saw Kevin and Jack grin at each other before simultaneously knocking their books and their metal water bottles off their desk. The loud crash startled the other students, who began laughing when the two boys, with exaggerated politeness, apologized. "Oh, Ms. Hopewell, so sorry, we didn't mean to disturb you. We love poetry, especially these old, boring ones. We're really, really sorry."

I gave them the choice of cooperating with me or going to the principal's office. To my surprise, they settled down, even though they knew that Timmy dealt with misbehaving athletes by blaming the teacher for her inability to control the class. After listening to the kids' side of the story, he'll commiserate with them before moving on to a discussion about any upcoming games.

After a slow start, the kids, almost against their will, got caught up in the narrative. We reached the point in the poem when the Mariner shoots the albatross. None of the students had ever heard the expression of an albatross around one's neck. After I explained the meaning of the term, an impromptu debate about modern-day burdens overtook the discussion I'd planned. Several kids volunteered to share their albatrosses, which included bratty siblings and French homework. Very quickly, though, the discussion became more serious and more personal. One girl railed against her new stepfather, and the new kid in the class, with some difficulty, talked about how hard it had been to change schools. Jack, who'd zoned out when the discussion began, suddenly perked up. He made a move to raise his hand, a rarity for him, but when I called on him, he reconsidered.

I was sympathetic to his dilemma. Revealing one's albatross is a deeply personal matter. I suspected Jack's tragic burden wasn't the death of his father but having Melinda Tumbleson as his mother.

He wasn't alone. I'd carried the albatross of my mother's death for many years and had yet to break free from the guilt and the shame, not from anything I did, but for all the things I didn't do.

With a mock-serious expression, Jack said, "This class is like an albatross around my neck."

I acknowledged Jack's complaint and pivoted to a topic with fewer potential landmines. "How many people have eaten chicken in the last week?" The class laughed at the non sequitur, and most of them raised their hands.

I raised my hand with them and said, "So, we all ate a dead bird, and we didn't feel guilty about it. What sin did the Mariner commit? After all, he killed a bird. And a chicken is also a bird. What's the big deal?"

Brittany and Bethany, my star AP students, both raised their hands. I chose one of them, though I wasn't sure which. We were sitting in a circle, and unless those identical twins were in their assigned seats, I couldn't tell one from the other.

She said, "Because it's not only a bird. It's, like, more important than your average bird."

I was pleased. "So what happens when something seems to mean more than its literal definition?"

Her sister chimed in. "It's, y'know, a symbol. The Mariner killed a good thing, so he had to suffer."

When the bell rang, the sisters invited the new kid to eat lunch with them. Sometimes, I just love teaching.

Chapter Twenty-One

The past is always tense, the future perfect.
—Zadie Smith

At the end of the school day, Emily stopped by my classroom to bemoan the results of her performance review. She pointed to the "Needs Improvement" section where Timmy accused her, among other crimes, of acting like "a sage on the stage instead of a guide by the side." Despite the catchy rhyme, which formed the centerpiece of a recent workshop, the comment cemented my belief that Timmy was the educational equivalent of a stegosaurus: big body, small brain, and ultimately doomed to extinction. It was equally possible, however, that he represented the future of education, and I was the one who wouldn't survive.

Emily was uninterested in my metaphor. "This is so unfair," she wailed.

On any other day, I would have continued to console her, but Ben Sorkin and Tom Harriman were due to arrive within minutes. There was one sure method to get Emily to leave without hurting her feelings. With every appearance of interest, I asked, "What's Mavis doing this afternoon?"

Emily snapped to attention at the mention of her teenage daughter. "I almost forgot about her test tomorrow! Sorry, Liz, I have to go home and help her study. We got an A- in chem, and we need to pull that grade up before the end of the marking period."

In the few minutes left before the detectives arrived, I reapplied lipstick and neatened my desk. Compared to my clothes closet, which was badly in need of a professional organizer, my workspace was relatively tidy. No teacher wanted the nightmare of looking for a misplaced assignment.

The more elusive things I was trying to find—answers to the mystery surrounding my mother's death, the identity of the country club killer, the key to a happy marriage—they all remained out of reach. But at least I wouldn't have to waste time sifting through a stack of essays on *A Midsummer Night's Dream* to locate Jack's (late, as usual) essay on *1984*. Yes, I still hadn't finished those.

I did a last-minute check of my school email, where I found messages from Jack's mother, Kevin's mother, and Timmy. Unusually, the first was the mildest. In it, Melinda congratulated me on obeying her order to cast Jack as the lead for our production of *Grease*. I gnashed my teeth over that one. Jack could neither sing nor act, and he was a terrible dancer. However, he was the only available kid whose voice could reach the back of the theater. Also, his father had been murdered. Melinda assumed my decision was in deference to her heavy-handed threats, and there was a smug and insulting tone to her email: *I knew even you would realize what I've told you all along...*

Ms. Sugarman's email was far sterner. It said, in part: *You violated the HIB school policy regarding harassment, intimidation, and bullying. I have spoken to my good friend Melinda Tumbleson, and she is bringing this matter to the board for a disciplinary review.*

Telling Kevin Sugarman his next assignment would be *The Cat in the Hat* instead of *The Rime of the Ancient Mariner* had been foolish. I didn't think, however, that it met objective standards for psychological cruelty and child abuse.

The third email was from Timmy: *It has come to my attention that your attitude in class is not conducive to a productive learning environment and that you have negatively impacted student safety. You have been scheduled for a disciplinary review. This is a serious matter, and you should consider bringing union representation.* He signed off with a cheery *Have a nice day!* which was Melinda Tumbleson's favorite parting shot when she'd done everything in her power to ensure the opposite. Stupid tears, the result of too little sleep and too much stress, pricked my eyes.

Ben Sorkin and Tom Harriman walked in, and I hurriedly wiped my face.

Tom spoke first. "What's wrong? Are you okay?"

I delivered an abbreviated version of my woes. Tom gave me a lopsided smile and said, "What could Melinda Tumbleson do? Put a black mark on your permanent record card? You're a great teacher. Look, you got even me to read Jane Austen. Even though it was a total chick book, I liked it."

I blew my nose and considered his words. "There are a million ways to make my life miserable. They could put me on an action plan and begin the process of withholding my salary increment. They could put me on perpetual cafeteria duty. They could move me to the middle school."

Tom was skeptical. "Sounds a little extreme to me. Maybe they'll give you a wrist slap."

"My wrists are very sensitive." I circled the room, looking at the posters on the walls, the books on the shelves, and the smiling photos of my students, and tried to imagine doing something else with my life. "Maybe it's time to change careers while I still can. I could become a private detective and solve crimes using my talent for literary criticism."

Tom folded himself into one of the kid's desks. "Sounds like a plan. You can corner the market on English department murders."

Ben, who had been silent up to that point, followed me to the bookshelf. "We're here to talk about murder. Not literary criticism. I have a few questions about the statement you gave us yesterday."

I waved at the tightly packed shelves. "Pick any book, and I'll prove the answers are in literature as much as in witness statements."

After some deliberation, he chose *The Age of Innocence*. "How about this one? Will it help me find the killer?"

I opened the book to a page marked with a sticky note and read *It was the old New York way...the people who dreaded scandal more than disease, who placed decency above courage, and who considered that nothing was more ill-bred than scenes.*

Ben leaned closer to read over my shoulder. I stepped back, uncomfortable with being so near to him. His fingers tightened as he regarded me with blue eyes so dark they were almost black.

He swallowed with visible effort, but his tone remained cool. "Those words sound good, but they're not much help in a murder investigation."

"I disagree. That's a perfect description of the social scene at the Meadowfields Country Club. People are more upset about the club garnering a bad reputation than they are about the murders. It wouldn't surprise me a bit if the killer was motivated by fear of a scandal." I flipped through the pages for more examples. "There's a lot in here about unhappy marriages, but we already know Elliot's relationships were far from ideal. And Ryan Walker may have had something to do with that. The latest gossip tagged him as sleeping with both Mrs. Tumblesons."

Ben reacted to the mention of marriage by removing from his case a copy of the statement I'd given him. I answered the detective's questions but didn't share with him my growing suspicions about Ian or my upcoming meeting with Magda. If Miguel's coworker told me anything relevant to the case, I'd inform the police after the fact.

I limited my commentary to more general conclusions. "The murders were so gruesome and bloody it's easy to assume they were crimes of jealousy or passion. If that was true, it makes sense that Ryan Walker was a target. But I don't think that was it. Around the country club, money is sexier than actual sex."

Ben looked away from his notebook and stared out the window at the traffic jam below. "If money was the motive, Elliot's two wives remain strong suspects. His life insurance policy will make Sonya a wealthy woman. And while Melinda won't personally benefit as much as Sonya, her son Jack most definitely will."

Thinking of the many emails the board of education president had sent me, I said, "That would be more than enough motivation for Melinda. Her whole life is wrapped around Jack, though not always in a good way."

Tom studied a lineup of class photos, which hung on a wall in the back of the classroom. "You said that after having Miguel in your class for two years, you knew him well enough to be sure he couldn't be the killer. What about Jack? He's been in your class since September. Can you say the same about him?"

Shocked, I immediately rejected the idea. "Jack is a kid."

Ben wasn't moved by this argument. "Kids his age often commit violent crimes. You told me that on the day of the murder, Melinda was yelling at Elliot because he was ignoring Jack in favor of the son he fathered with Sonya. The boy could be carrying a lot of anger and resentment."

Tom said, "Jack is a football player and stronger than most men. He could have killed Elliot without breaking a sweat. And he had plenty of motivation to do so. Revenge and money. Same as any adult."

I couldn't deny Jack was a bully and used his physical strength and size to intimidate other students, but there was a big leap between shoving kids in the hallway and murder. "I'm not as certain of his innocence as I am of Miguel's. But I can't completely discount the possibility. There are rumors that Elliot abused Sonya. He could have done the same to Melinda and Jack."

Neither detective wrote this down, which suggested they already knew of Elliot's violence toward his wife. Tom spoke slowly, thinking through this latest possibility. "Kids who have been abused are more likely to become abusers. If there is even a remote possibility he did it, then you need to be careful. You can't be here after hours. Too risky."

If only life were that easy. "Great idea, if I weren't directing the school play. I've scheduled late rehearsals until opening night, and Jack's got the lead role."

Tom shook his head. "You'll have to change the schedule. Do you want a repeat of last year?"

"Jack is a jerk, not a psychopath."

Ben looked up from his notes. "This is taking longer than I thought. Tom, you get started with the next interview. I'll let you know when I'm done here."

Tom didn't look pleased at the division of labor. "Um, okay. Unless you'd rather switch?"

"No. Mrs. Tumbleson is more likely to confide in you than me. We didn't hit it off too well. See if you can pin her down regarding Jack's whereabouts yesterday." He waited until Tom was out of the room before continuing. "Miguel has as good a motive as either of Elliot's wives. Maybe better. According to the new club treasurer, Miguel was implicated in a kickback scheme."

My pulse quickened, thinking of George's boss. Cooper was at the top of my list of suspects until I found out he offered Miguel a job. "Talk to him again. I think he's changed his mind about that. Have you made any headway in untangling the club finances?"

"We've got a forensics accountant working on piecing together the missing records, but we share those resources with the rest of the county, and it's going to take a while. In the meantime, Cooper Aldridge is helping fill in the blanks. I expect Mr. Hopewell can also assist us."

I didn't relish the idea of George getting involved. "My husband didn't have access until after Elliot died when Cooper nominated him the assistant treasurer. Was there anyone Elliot trusted? Anyone who might have been his confidante?"

"If there's one thing I know for sure, it's that there was no love lost between Elliot Tumbleson and Cooper Aldridge." Ben thumbed through his notebook. "Make that no love lost between Elliot Tumbleson and anyone. He seems to have been universally hated."

George had already told me how unpopular Elliot was. "Like father, like son. The other students don't like Jack, but they all let him bully them. They laugh at his jokes and excuse his behavior." I wished I could stay longer, but I didn't want to be late for my meeting with Magda. "I have to go. But let's meet again in a day or so. I might have more information for you then."

Ben snapped his notebook shut. "I don't want you talking to any of the suspects, including Miguel. If he's guilty and thinks you have information that could hurt him, he'll go after you next. And if he tries to contact you I want to know about it. You think you know him. But I'm not sure you do."

I locked the windows and closed the blinds. "I can't avoid talking to the suspects. It wasn't my choice to join the Meadowfields Country Club, but now that I'm a member, discussions about murder are inevitable. I can be your inside source. It's not unprecedented. Police use informants all the time."

"There's a difference between reporting information and pursuing it. I'm trying to protect you." He slid *The Age of Innocence* to its proper place on the bookshelf. When I told him he could borrow it, he declined. "I saw the movie. If memory serves, it was all about missed opportunities, which means it's not a great source of inspiration for a cop." A hint of an amused smile softened the corners of his mouth.

Hot prickles ran down my back. Was he laughing at me? "Maybe I could change your mind about the book, if not about letting me help your investigation."

"I'm open to persuasion about literature. But not about you taking an active role as an informant." He held open the door and followed me down the hall. "I'll walk you to your car, and you can tell me more about your literary method of deduction."

"We'll have plenty of time to talk. My car is now in Siberia. Although, on the plus side, the rain has stopped."

A muddy puddle forced us to walk single file. He said, "I don't like this. It's bad enough you have to leave school after hours. Whose idea was it to move you?"

"Melinda Tumbleson." I didn't trust myself to add any editorial comments.

When I stopped at my car, he turned to leave, then splashed back through the mud. "I forgot to ask one other question. How close is your husband to Cooper and Bryony Aldridge?"

"Cooper is George's boss. Why the interest?" My throat went dry. Was Ben trying to catch me off guard by pretending the question was an afterthought? Surely, the detective didn't, couldn't, wouldn't suspect my husband of any wrongdoing.

"No reason. A couple of people mentioned George's name in connection with them. Means nothing, but anything you or he can tell me about the Aldridges would help."

"What are people saying?" I immediately regretted the question. I had a pretty good idea of what people were saying about George and his boss's wife.

Ben held out his hands. "Nothing much. Tying up one or two loose ends."

Did he think George was implicated in the embezzlement scheme? Or was he referring to a rumored affair between George and Bryony? Horrified at either possibility, I stuck my hands in my pockets, where I found the earring my sister gave me. I explained how Susan found it and offered it to him.

Ben's impassive exterior made me so nervous, I dropped the bag that held the earring. We bent to retrieve it at the same time, and he put a steadying hand on my bare arm.

Detective Ben Sorkin's cool demeanor cracked. He rubbed one palm against the other as if my skin had burned him.

I was a woman of many words, and there was a lot more I wanted to say, but we parted in silence.

Chapter Twenty-Two

He that dies pays all debts
—William Shakespeare / The Tempest

I drove from Valerian Hills High School to the Meadowfields Country Club on winding, rain-slicked roads. The tennis courts and golf course were empty, but the glassed-in patio revealed a crowd of people enjoying the foggy view. Following Magda's directions, I drove past the cluster of cars and parked near the pool, which wouldn't open for several more weeks. Densely planted arborvitae bushes bordered all four sides, and behind the bushes, tall pine trees loomed. A high wooden gate, which was the only access to the pool area, hung ajar.

I closed the gate behind me and made my way past a grove of ornamental pear trees. Lacking the blithe confidence of fictional heroines, the rustle of leaves and deepening shadows scared me, and I wished Magda and I were meeting in a well-lit diner. When her head popped up from behind a rhododendron, I didn't faint, but the last time I shrieked that loudly, a squirrel had gotten into the basement laundry basket.

Magda opened the conversation with admirable economy. "Tell me what you want, and then, please, go away."

I reached into my purse and removed a notebook and pen. "Why did the club threaten to fire Miguel? Did it have anything to do with the missing funds?"

She peered over the hedge before answering, as if to assure herself we were alone. "He wasn't fired. After the police took him in for questioning,

Ian gave him a heads-up that his job was on the line. Mr. Aldridge offered him a job right away, so Miguel could quit and wouldn't have a black mark on his employment record. Yesterday, when Ian couldn't make it to the snack bar on time, he asked Miguel to fill in. It's the kind of thing we do for each other all the time. It's totally innocent and none of your business."

Magda confirmed what Miguel told me, but I sensed there was more to the story. "If everything was above board, why the secrecy? Miguel may not have been officially terminated, but he also didn't get the chance to clear his name."

"You say you're Miguel's friend, and you want to help him. But you're on their side. If I have to take advice from someone, it's going to be Ian, not you." She again looked over the hedge. "Did anyone follow you here?"

"No." Honestly required a more precise answer. "I don't think so. I can't be sure."

Her wariness was understandable. From Magda's perspective, I was a nosy country club member, perhaps one of those overly friendly people who demanded deference and gratitude in exchange for an inherently unequal relationship.

More important than Magda's attitude was Ian's behavior, which smacked of the kind of scams my father used to pull. Lousy was an expert at getting someone else to hold the bag at just the right time. I suspected Ian was using Miguel as a fall guy and not for something as innocent as a late arrival. Another mark against Ian was that he was in charge of the waitstaff and in a much better position to skim money from the club coffers than my former student. This also gave Ian an excellent motive for killing Elliot.

I wondered how far Magda would go to protect Ian. "What advice did Ian give you, aside from telling you not to talk to me?"

She thrust chapped hands into her jacket and hunched her shoulders. "You're like all the rest. Don't you see I'm in a better position to help my friends than you are?"

"You said you hadn't seen Miguel. Why did you do that? Were you following Ian's orders? You lied to me and the police. Miguel might need you for an alibi, which you now can't provide since you claimed you never saw him."

"It's all for the best. Nothing for you to worry about." She spoke in tones that were overly kind and patient, like a mother trying to convince her kids that their dead goldfish was in Goldfish Heaven, feasting on ice cream and swimming at a special goldfish water park.

It was Magda's bad luck that I didn't have the gullibility of a three-year-old. "Lying to the police is a risky business, especially since so many people are involved in the lie. Someone, not me, already told them Miguel was here at the time of the murder. At the time of both murders. As for Cooper Aldridge, I thought he was the one who brought charges against Miguel. What changed his mind?"

She edged toward the gate as if preparing to make a run for it. "Mr. Aldridge found out Miguel wasn't guilty of stealing, and he promised to take care of it. Is that clear enough for you?"

"No. It's not clear at all. Can you give me details about the initial allegations against Miguel? How was he implicated? At the country club, the waiters don't handle cash or credit cards. Everything goes on the members' tabs."

Nothing Magda said explained why the staff conspired to lie about Miguel's presence when Ryan was murdered. It would have been easier, and better for Miguel, if they'd provided him with an alibi, proving they were with him when Ryan was attacked. Ian, for reasons I didn't yet understand, had orchestrated this effort.

Dark clouds moved swiftly overhead, and a few drops of rain fell. A bolt of lightning lit up the sky, and a crack of thunder immediately followed. Magda removed a folded umbrella from her bag, opened it, and ran across the lawn. Over her shoulder, she said, "You better go now. It's dangerous to stand under trees in a thunderstorm."

I followed her, heedless of the deluge. "This is no good, Magda! I need answers, and I'm not giving up until I get them."

She stopped short. "Listen, lady, I think your friends know what happened. Talk to them."

She was the fourth employee to offer this opinion. Did Carl, Magda, Ryan, and the bartender know something I didn't? Or were all four repeating a made-up story to protect each other?

Magda resumed her dash toward the clubhouse. I kept up the unequal race, even as the distance between us grew longer. "Have you spoken to Miguel? I've tried getting in touch with him, but he hasn't gotten back to me."

Without breaking her stride, she said, "I'm late for work, and I don't know where Miguel is. If he's smart, he'll stay far away from you."

Soaked with rain, freezing cold, and wearing heeled shoes, I couldn't overtake Magda, who was wearing rubber-soled boots. She disappeared into the employees' entrance of the clubhouse.

I opened the door to find Ian blocking the way. He looked down at me with eyes that were Miguel's shape and color, but lacked his cousin's warmth. I tried to get past him, but with a murmured apology, he closed the door and locked it.

I sprinted to the front entrance and headed for the dining room. A group of women, dressed as if ready to play a round of golf despite the filthy weather, sat at a large table overlooking the course. Sonya Tumbleson pretended she didn't see me, but Bryony acknowledged my presence with a languid wave of her hand.

A staff member stopped me from entering the kitchen. With a tight smile, he said, "I'm sorry, madam, but club rules don't allow guests into employee-only areas. Perhaps you'd like to sit in the dining room or at the bar."

I saved myself the humiliation of arguing with him and went home. Neither Magda nor Miguel answered my calls.

* * *

The following morning, George informed me that he had an emergency meeting at the club and wouldn't be home for dinner. He scrolled through a series of messages before answering my question about the reason for his meeting.

"There's been an accident at the club. One of the kitchen staff was hit by a falling branch in a freak accident. She's in the hospital."

Dread made me queasy. "Who was it?"

"Magda Hoffman. I'm meeting with the other members of the board to discuss liability."

I followed him into the bathroom. "Liability? A woman is injured and in the hospital, and you're worried about money?"

"I'm sorry about Ms. Hoffman's accident, but I can't ignore my responsibility for dealing with it." George gave the sort of longsuffering sigh that made me wonder if any vestige of the guy I married was lurking inside the corporate suit who'd taken his place.

I weaseled out of him the name of the hospital where Magda had been admitted and went there after school. The hospital staff said she didn't want visitors. I hoped to run into Miguel, but if he was there, I didn't see him.

George wasn't in the mood to talk when he came home. But he knew, as well as I did, that the list of crimes that occurred at the club now included theft, two murders, and one suspicious accident. I had no proof Magda was attacked because the killer saw her talking to me, but the timing of her injury strongly suggested a causal relationship.

Any club member sitting on the enclosed patio could have seen me pursue Magda. Any member of the waitstaff could have heard me try to gain entry to the kitchen. But only one person knew with certainty that we'd met in secret.

Ian was now my prime suspect.

Chapter Twenty-Three

Whereof what's past is prologue, what to come/In yours and my discharge
—William Shakespeare / The Tempest

The Meadowfields Country Club sent an email to its members, explaining, in oblique language, why a section of the golf course would be closed for the day. At a loss for how to proceed with one investigation, I focused on the second. The Goldfarbs had given me plenty to think about.

My grandparents were dead, and my parents had no siblings. Other than the photos I swiped from the Goldfarbs, I had few pictures and no personal belongings from my childhood. My mother's mania for cleanliness and order, a trait neither I nor my sister inherited, was partly to blame.

I couldn't remember if she had any friends, other than Arlene Goldfarb. My family's isolation was exacerbated by the nomadic life we led, with frequent trips out of state when things got too hot for Lousy. During flush times, our home functioned as a storage unit for stolen televisions and the like, which, Lousy explained, "Fell off the back of a truck." As a child, I was constantly on the lookout for things to fall out of a truck until an older kid explained the facts of criminal life to me.

I called my mother's Brooklyn high school and learned they had copies of yearbooks dating back to when the school opened. In a graduating class of over two thousand students, it would be difficult to figure out who her friends were, but one of the few facts I knew about my mother was that she was a cheerleader for her school's football team, which had won a total of six games in the four years she was there. Those failed athletic efforts were good preparation for her self-imposed burden of supporting Lousy, another perennial loser.

My father, unlike Mom, had a large circle of contacts, and the small-time crooks with whom he consorted were the only constant in my childhood. An online search revealed that two of them, Mel Weinstock and Phil Fleishman, hadn't left Brooklyn. I wasn't surprised. New Yorkers of modest means tended to hold onto their rent-controlled apartments until death forced a relocation.

* * *

Despite the gloomy nature of my quest, I looked forward to seeing the old neighborhood. This sentimental anticipation evaporated as Susan and I neared Mel Weinstock's address. The streets were rougher, more rundown, and noisier than I remembered. Avenues that once sported an unbroken lineup of mom-and-pop stores were now pockmarked with abandoned properties, and boarded-up windows were a sad testament to the area's decline. While much of Brooklyn had been gentrified to within an inch of its brownstoned life, these streets were mean.

A group of kids followed Susan and me from the car to Mel Weinstock's apartment building. They ranged themselves on the stoop when we entered the vestibule. I pressed the buzzer for apartment 3F. A loud burst of static issued from the intercom, but we couldn't hear anything else. I shouted into the rusty grid as the jittery kids watched from outside a rickety door with a cracked window.

I armed myself with a keyring, holding it so that each key protruded from between my fingers. The boys were young, no more than fourteen, but I didn't underestimate them. They were cocky, nervous, and quite capable of stealing our belongings and leaving our beat-up bodies in a dumpster. Susan pressed one hand against the inner door, ready to burst through as soon as we were buzzed in. In her other hand, she held a can of mace. We may have looked like pushovers to the predators who roamed this block, but we grew up there, and if a fight came to us, we'd be ready.

The kids huddled together and, after a brief discussion, clapped each other on the back. If we were their targets, they hesitated a fraction of a minute too long. When the ringleader tried to open the outer door, I slammed it back in his face. Startled, he stepped back to save his fingers, and the rest of the gang retreated with him. Susan pressed every intercom button, and someone buzzed us in before they could regroup. Their shouts and curses followed us, but unless they wanted to try their hands at breaking and entering, we were safe.

The stairway smelled of boiled cabbage and cigar smoke. For other people, the sounds and smells of childhood were pleasant and soothing, but not for my sister and me. Despite growing anxiety, I pressed the Weinstock's doorbell. The door opened three inches, which was as far as the security chain allowed.

Mrs. Weinstock checked us out from behind thick glasses. With a curt nod, she let us in and yelled into the adjacent bedroom, "Mel! The girls are here."

We entered a room frozen in time. Susan whispered, "What do you think? Circa 1974?"

Unlike the Goldfarbs' home, which was a self-conscious re-creation of the nineteen sixties, the Weinstocks' apartment was a genuine time capsule of the following decade. White furniture with plastic-covered lime green upholstery lined three walls of the room, and a burnt orange shag rug with threadbare patches covered most of the floor. The curtains were printed with a faded geometric pattern of orange and yellow and were held back with neon green plastic rings. Only the large screen television, bolted to the wall, intruded a twenty-first-century aesthetic.

Mrs. Weinstock was dressed to match her décor in a blousy orange dress with lime green pockets. Mel wore white pants, white shoes, a white belt, and a shirt so blindingly yellow it hurt my eyes to look at it.

Neither host invited us to sit down. Mel said, "What's the occasion? We ain't heard hide nor hair from you two for as long as I can remember."

His wife put one gnarled finger on Susan's face and said, "You look like your mother." To me, she said, "You're more like your father." It wasn't a compliment.

Mel's eyes were cold. "So what can I do for you? Kind of busy right now."

I continued to hold my keyring in a defensive mode. "Tell us about my father's second wife, a woman by the name of Velma. Does she still live here?"

Mrs. Weinstock's hand shook slightly. "That Velma's no good. And her kids ain't no better. What do you want with her?"

Susan sat on the sofa, which made soft puckering noises when she moved her legs on the yellowing plastic. "No matter how Velma's kids turned out, they're our half-brothers. We were interested in meeting them, maybe getting to know them."

Mrs. Weinstock's voice trembled. "Bad things happen to people who get on the wrong side of Velma and her no-good kids. Their cars get keyed. Their houses get trashed. Their dogs get run over." She looked nervously at her husband. "Or worse."

I remained standing, ready to grab Susan and run if things got ugly. The elderly couple looked harmless, but underneath the wrinkles and gray hair was a core of cold anger.

In a honeyed tone, Susan addressed Mel. "Oh, Mr. Weinstock, I remember my father saying you knew everyone in the neighborhood. He said you were the king of the track and king of The Club. A real legend. But that was a long time ago."

My sister was understandably selective in what she told them. A less abridged version would have included Lousy's assertion that Mel was a two-bit loser who would turn in his grandmother if he could make ten cents doing so. However, as usual, Susan's flattery worked better than candor. And as much as Mrs. Weinstock's inadvertent admission regarding Velma intrigued me, changing the subject was probably the best way to avoid being thrown out of their house.

Mel breathed in deeply, puffing out his chest. "Well, little lady, I guess you could say that. Everyone in the neighborhood knows who I am."

Susan crossed the room as if to admire the faded curtains, but I suspected she was checking to see if the gang of kids who'd tailed us were lurking outside. "I suppose you've lost touch with the guys you and my father hung out with. A lot of time has passed. People move on."

He cupped his right hand around his ear and admonished my sister, "Don't hear so good from this ear. What's that you say?"

Susan retraced her steps and spoke louder. Mel scowled. "I'm still connected and we still got The Club. There's plenty of the old gang who stayed. But Velma moved outta the neighborhood years ago." He dropped his hand and leaned back, uninterested in hearing more.

Mrs. Weinstock edged toward the door. She didn't tell us to leave, but she stood with an expectant air as if waiting for us to take the hint.

I ignored the implicit request for us to go. "We came here to find out more about our past. I think you know more than you're telling us. Do you know where Velma is now? And where are her kids?" Silently, I added, *And what happened to our mother?*

"Why not take the girls to The Club? There's people there that can tell them what they want to know." Mrs. Weinstock sent her husband a look I couldn't decipher. "And they can't get in without your help."

Mel considered this suggestion, and after a few moments, he rose to his feet. "Not to put too fine a point on it, but your father owes me. Let's say an even thousand."

Susan blurted, "You want us to pay you?"

Mrs. Weinstock clicked her tongue. "You come here asking for a favor. The way we see it, you already owe us plenty. Nobody went after you when your father skipped town with cash that didn't belong to him, and there was plenty of talk about shaking you down." She smiled with her mouth. "I'll tell you what. We'll take five hundred. That's more than fair. And it ain't half of what your father owes us. But seeing as it wasn't your fault, we won't ask for it all."

Her words transported me back to the haggling flea markets of my youth, and I realized this was a game, albeit one with grim stakes. "It wasn't from the goodness of your heart that you and the scum you hang with didn't go after us. You left us alone because it wouldn't have done any good. Whacking our kneecaps or dumping our bodies in the landfill wouldn't earn you a dime from our father. Hell, he'd have done it himself if it netted him an extra dollar. So I don't owe you anything. But for old time's sake, we'll give you one hundred bucks."

Her voice turned flinty. "Two fifty or nothing. You're not getting inside The Club without Mel's help, and he don't work for nothing. And you ain't only paying to get in. Mel will make sure you get out." She fingered the hem of Susan's silk shirt. "You can afford it."

Susan snatched her shirt from Mrs. Weinstock's roughened fingers and got into the spirit of this bitter bargain. "One fifty."

When they didn't answer, my sister and I walked to the door. We were nearly at the staircase when Mr. Weinstock called me back. "I'm being a real softy here, but I'll do it. For old times' sake. But it's a private club. You can come as my guest, but don't try to get in without me. We don't like strangers messing in our business."

Mrs. Weinstock said, "We're not the only ones who got cheated by your father. He left behind a lotta bad debts. People don't forget, no matter how much time goes by."

I'd watched my father bluff his way through many a poker game, and although I wasn't up to his level of skill, I decided to go all in. "Where is he?"

The five-second pause before they answered with a faltering *huh? what?* confirmed what I already suspected was true. Like me, the Weinstocks knew, or suspected, that the Lousy Bastard wasn't dead.

Chapter Twenty-Four

Woe, destruction, ruin, and decay;
The worst is death, and death will have his day
—William Shakespeare / Richard II

After Susan offered Mel Weinstock one hundred fifty bucks in exchange for entry to The Club, he hurried to seal the deal. He wanted his payment in cash, and after shooing the gang of kids on the stoop by swinging his cane at their heads, the three of us walked to a nearby ATM. I blocked his view of Susan's fingers as she keyed in her passcode. Mel had years of experience as a small-time crook, and I didn't put it past him to hire one of the kids to grab my sister's purse and use her card to extract the other eight hundred and fifty extra dollars he thought we owed him.

Susan shared my misgivings. Using the whirring noise of the machine as cover, she said, "Maybe this wasn't such a good idea. I don't trust Mel or his wife."

The sense that we were getting closer to uncovering the mystery behind our mother's death overcame caution. "We might as well get our money's worth. It's too late to back out now."

After the requisite number of bills spit out of the machine, Mel held out his hand. I stopped Susan from giving him the wad of money.

"Not so fast, Mel. Forty bucks now, and the rest after you take us to The Club. No offense, but for all we know, this is another one of your cons. I don't want to get there, and the only members still alive can't remember their names, let alone any details about my parents."

He glared but didn't argue. When we stopped at a traffic light, Susan said, "We don't belong here. We worked like hell to get out of this crappy place." She shivered, although the day was warm. "Ever since we arrived, I've had a creeping sense of doom. I had nightmares after we met with the Goldfarbs, and the Weinstocks are worse. It's brought back our whole miserable childhood. Even if we found out that Mom was murdered, even if we found out who killed her, it would make no difference."

I knew how she felt, but I'd come to a different conclusion. It would have been easy to give up. To say goodbye to Mel and return to our lives. It wasn't as if he'd be disappointed to get rid of us. He'll still be up by forty bucks.

My answer was as much an attempt to convince myself as it was to convince Susan. "You heard what Mrs. Weinstock said about Velma. No one would have been higher on Velma's hit list than Mom. If she murdered our mother, I will spend the rest of my life tracking her down and making sure she is punished for what she did."

What I told her was true but incomplete. "I should have done more to protect Mom. And to protect you. I wish, just once, I'd hit him back, but I was too scared." I wondered if that was how Jack Tumbleson felt about his father.

The light changed, and we continued the trek toward our past. Susan said, "You have nothing to feel guilty about. But I see what you mean. Even if we don't get any information about how Mom died, maybe we'll learn something about how she lived and how she dealt with Lousy. What she knew and didn't know." Shamefaced, she added, "Sometimes I hate her as much as I hate him. She could have rescued us. Given us a different life. But she picked him over us. Why didn't she leave him?"

She knew the answer as well as I did but perhaps had a harder time facing it. "Mom stayed with Lousy because she loved him more than she loved us. About that, there is no mystery. What we need to know is if she paid for that loyalty with her life."

I forgot how old I was when I discovered other kids didn't have to hide bruises, pick open locks, or break into their apartments through the fire escape. Our family secrets set us apart from others. Instead of friends, I grew up with Francie Nolan of *A Tree Grows in Brooklyn* and later with Oliver Twist, Nicholas Nickleby, Jane Eyre, and Elizabeth Bennet. The feeling of displacement, that I was living in the wrong location and time, followed me into adulthood. In Oak Ridge, as in Brooklyn, I was a stranger in a strange land.

Lousy drilled one idea into our heads: *You only trust your family.* He did this because he feared we might spill secrets to other kids, or teachers, or to any of the nosy social service workers who showed up at our house after too many visits to the emergency room. The bitterest irony of all was that he was the one who betrayed us.

How deep did that betrayal go? Was his story a stereotypical tale of a cheating and abusive husband? Or did his treachery reach further than that? I'd never allowed myself to fully explore the possibility that he'd had a hand in my mother's death. Those days were over.

* * *

We entered a grimy luncheonette, one I recognized from my childhood. MarVel's Coffee Shoppe was as little changed as the Weinstock's living room. On the left was a soda fountain with a long counter and stools that had the same cracked red leatherette tops I remembered from when I was a kid. On the right, a candy counter with glass-fronted shelves held delicacies I used to dream of. My grandmother, who contributed to the family fortune by becoming a card shark, used to sweeten her opponents' losses with MarVel's bridge mix, chocolate truffles, and the occasional box of Barton's candy.

In the rear of the dusty room, booths with sagging upholstery sat empty. They were reserved for those with enough money to buy a meal. People who could only afford ice cream or coffee had to sit at the counter. Tucked into a corner was a defunct telephone booth that belonged in the Smithsonian.

Mel nodded to the counterman before unlocking a door marked Private and ushering us into The Club. Smoke from many cigars and cigarettes hung in wreaths above a dozen beat-up wooden tables. Each table held a center stand with decks of cards and plastic poker chips.

Susan, with a swift intake of breath, said, "I know this place! We used to come here with Nana."

I nodded and didn't answer. Mel pulled out a chair for himself at one of the tables. There was no room for us to sit. The cardplayers, all men, fell silent when they saw Susan and me. I sensed that others in the room were looking at us, and I didn't blame them. We couldn't have been more out of place. The Club was still a men's club, although women were allowed in on weekend nights, which was when my grandmother made her money.

Mel said, "These two are—"

An unpleasant-looking man in a brown shirt that matched his teeth said, "We know who they are. Your missus phoned us. What do they want? Ain't seen the lousy bastard since I can't remember when."

Susan nudged me. We thought the name we used for our father was our invention. But maybe we chose that title because we'd heard it before.

For the second time in less than an hour, I aped my father's poker face, wondering if my expressionless pose was why Mrs. Weinstock said I looked like him. "We're here to find Velma. Our father's second wife."

The men around the table placed their cards face down. The gang of kids outside Mel's apartment building looked like innocent puppy dogs compared to the tough, leathery faces that eyed us. Those kids were amateurs. The men at The Club were pros.

There was a low rumble around the table. A thin man with glasses that made his eyes look cartoonishly huge said, "Now what do you fine ladies want with Velma? Back in the day, she was no friend of your Ma. Or of you."

Out of nowhere, his name popped into my head. "It's no problem if you're afraid to talk, Mr. Fleishman. I did hear that people are scared of her and her kids."

Phil Fleishman didn't take the bait. "Your old man owes me money. Maybe you wanna make good on his debt before you start asking for favors."

I may be terrified of rodents and high places and clowns, but I knew how to handle two-bit, over-the-hill thugs. Using the Brooklyn accent that I'd erased from my voice years ago, I said, "You gotta be kidding me. That

Lousy Bastard owes me a hell of a lot more than he owes you." After a brief moment of surprise, the men laughed.

The tight band of tension around my head eased, and I said, "Velma's got my dead mother's wedding ring and my grandma's pearl necklace. That a good enough reason for me to want to shake her down?"

Mr. Fleishman, like the rest, believed me. He said, "You're not gonna want to hear this, but it's not worth it. Leave it be."

I turned to Susan. "They don't know anything. We're wasting our time." To the cardplayers, I said, "Nice meeting you, gentlemen. It's been a real pleasure."

Mr. Brown Shirt called me back. "Velma disappeared a few years after your Ma passed. I heard she married an Irisher and moved to Bay Ridge. Or maybe Bensonhurst. Some bum from the force. Velma had two kids with your pa. Two boys."

Susan asked, too eagerly, "Where are they now?"

They answered with another ripple of laughter. My sister nervously extracted a cigarette and flicked a lighter. The men seemed to feel this gesture conveyed common ground, for after she blew smoke out of the corner of her mouth, Mr. Fleishman said, "One of 'em is easy enough to find. Ralphie's at Rikers."

Lovely. One of my half-brothers followed my father into the family business, right into the notorious men's prison. I asked what Ralphie was in for, but no one volunteered an answer, and I hazarded a question about my other half-brother. "Where can I find the other kid?"

The thin, large-eyed man took over. "You ain't far from him. He's at the precinct around the corner. Ask for Leo."

I thanked the men and turned to leave, figuring we could try our luck at the police station, when Brown Shirt said, "Leo's due to come by here any minute." There was no laughter this time. Mel said, "Leo's coming for his donation."

I wasn't surprised to hear that the brother who became a cop padded his income with kickbacks, presumably in exchange for protection. I wondered what Ralphie did to get himself locked up. It couldn't have been bookmaking or gambling, or Leo would have protected him. Probably not drugs either, unless Ralphie was a bigger player than most people in this part of Brooklyn. I wondered if he was in prison for murder. And if so, whose?

Chapter Twenty-Five

Blood and revenge are hammering in my head.
—William Shakespeare / Titus Andronicus

A wiry guy with nicotine-stained fingers swept up the playing cards and rapped them on the table. This seemed to be the group's agreed-upon signal to resume play. Mel rubbed his thumb against his fingers in a mute request for the balance of the money we'd promised him. "You girls can see yourself out."

Susan gave him the cash, and we thanked him. Although he and his surly companions treated my sister and me with barely disguised contempt, I was grateful for the information they'd given us. Mel could have told us everything we learned from his cronies at the club, and I wondered if he, like Ira Goldfarb, didn't want to admit to his spouse a continuing connection with my shady relatives. Susan and I exited the smoke-filled room, sat at the lunch counter, and waited for Leo.

My sister's hand shook as she fingered a plastic menu. "We knew Lousy had another family, but to find them after all these years seems surreal. And given what we now know about them, really scary."

"I didn't think we'd get this far." In a lighter tone, I said, "Are you sure you want to stay? If we leave now, we can quit stalking Brooklyn felons and go back to our investigation of suburban crime."

She shushed me, although an elderly man seated on a low stool behind the counter was the only other occupant. Susan interrupted his perusal of *The Daily Racing Form* to ask, "Do you know Ralphie? Leo's brother?"

Through tight lips, he said *yes*, before retreating behind the paper.

Susan persevered. "What's he in for? How long has he been at Rikers?"

The counterman didn't answer.

Susan gave him her most winning smile, which didn't help her case, since he didn't look at her. She leaned over the counter. "What about Leo? Can you tell us anything about him?"

He rattled his paper. "Nope. Don't know nothing about him neither."

I tried a less direct approach. "How long have you been working here? We used to come here when we were kids."

This got his attention. "I knew your old man. And his old man." With that, he went back to his study of *The Racing Form*.

I rolled my eyes at Susan and didn't bother to lower my voice. "Just our luck. We get a guy who outdoes Hemingway in his brevity."

The counterman offered his first bit of unsolicited information. "*The Old Man and the Sea.*"

Startled, it took me a minute to realize he was responding to my Hemingway reference.

He looked smug. "I read *The Old Man and the Sea*. It wasn't bad. Except for the ending. That stunk."

If discussing the final chapters of Hemingway's novel would engage this laconic critic of American literature, I was game. "The only thing our father had in common with the hero of *The Old Man and the Sea* was his love of baseball. How well did you know him? My father, I mean. Not Santiago."

"Enough to keep my distance. He didn't owe me nothing, because I never gave him nothing. Not like others I could name but won't."

I nodded. "Smart move. He owes me plenty."

He raised bushy eyebrows that met in a single line over his nose. "What else is new?"

"What's new is that my sister and I are waiting for Leo, who's our half-brother. Will you give us a sign when he comes in?"

Returning to his former brusqueness, the counterman said, "He'll be the one in uniform."

Susan frowned. "What if he's not wearing a uniform? Not that I'm too worried about identifying him. It doesn't appear as if we'll have to pick him out of a crowd. You're not exactly turning people away."

"Listen, girlie, he's always in uniform." The counterman gazed at her as if all the world knew this except for her.

I peered at the sidewalk through a dirty window. The street traffic was heavy, but the tables remained empty. "How do the owners get by? The only people here are in The Club."

"You just answered your own question." He placed two thick mugs of coffee in front of us and said, "Drink up. It's on the house."

With some trepidation, I sipped the murky brew. I tapped Susan's cup. "I know it looks more like mud than coffee, but honestly, it's very good. Try some."

She took a cautious sip. "It's delicious. Maybe they need to get the word out to the rest of Brooklyn. Let people know what they're missing."

"That's probably the last thing the owners want. I don't think coffee is how they make their money."

Susan was thoughtful. "You could be right. It wasn't coffee those guys were drinking."

I gripped the edge of the counter, mildly nauseated by a flood of repressed memories. "Correct. Running an unlicensed bar and gambling den probably nets them a lot more than selling great coffee ever could."

The tinkle of a bell interrupted us. The door swung open, and a ghost walked in, dressed in NYPD blue. We didn't need the uniform or the guy behind the counter to identify Leo. He was, without question, a son of The Lousy Bastard.

The most unnerving aspect of seeing this reincarnation of our father was that Leo was older than I expected. I put my hand in front of my mouth so the apparition couldn't hear me. "I thought Lousy married Velma after he married Mom."

My sister splashed hot coffee onto my fingers and the counter. "What if Mom was the other woman?"

Transfixed by Leo's resemblance to the man who'd haunted us for so long, I held onto my cup as if it were a life preserver. He walked around the candy counter and helped himself to a Milky Way candy bar. I was as scared of him as I'd been of my father. Although he wore a genial smile, he carried with him an air of coiled violence.

Coming to the old neighborhood had been a mistake. I put a few bills on the counter and prepared to leave. Susan dug her nails into my skin to stop me. Fearful of attracting Leo's attention, I sat back down.

Leo saluted the old man behind the counter. "Hey, Solly. Pick us a winner, will ya?"

Solly rose to his feet. "Yes, sir! Will do."

We didn't make the same impression on Leo as he did on us. He looked at us and through us, pausing only to check some messages that beeped his phone.

He was nearly at the entrance to The Club when Susan called his name. "Leo, I'm—my name is Susan. And this is Liz. We're your half-sisters."

He walked back to the counter. "I wondered if you'd show up someday."

I wasn't sure what I was expecting, but I did anticipate a bit more drama. Maybe not a two-armed bear hug, but something more emotional than the cool way he studied our faces. He wasn't even surprised. Maybe someone at The Club tipped him off, and his nonchalance was an act.

I modulated my tone to match his. "Leo, we've come here to see you. To, er, to get to know you."

"If you came here to see me, then it's because you want something from me. So yeah, go ahead, knock yourself out." Scorn was his only visible sign of emotion.

Susan bristled. "Are you angry about something? Did we do something to make you mad?"

Leo tore open the candy bar wrapper, bit off a large chunk of chocolate, and chewed. "Do something? Nah. It took you long enough to look me up. But you're here now, so like I say, shoot."

My heart was pounding. Memories of our father flooded my brain, and I was as scared as if I were ten years old and the target of his rage. Some kids might grow up calloused to Lousy's brand of intimidation, but it had made me quite fearful of physical assault. I still trembled when anyone touched my head, which was where Lousy preferred to land his blows, because those didn't leave a visible mark. As an adult, I hated going to the hairdresser and, for many years, cut my own hair.

I held onto the counter to keep myself steady. "I'm sorry you feel that way. We didn't find out where you were until today."

My sister said, in a choked voice, "If you knew about us, why didn't you try to find us?" She, like me, reverted to a Brooklyn accent and, in coarse tones, challenged him. "If anyone should be pissed off, it's me."

I saw the wheels slowly turn in Leo's head as he mulled Susan's accusation. "My ma told me you wouldn't want to see me. Cause of Dad leaving you to come back to us. She hated all of you."

For many years, Susan and I believed our father left us to marry Velma. But the timeline was wrong. Dear Old Dad had taken up with Leo's mother first.

Tempting as it was to continue this jaunt down memory lane, I adopted Susan's sharp tone. "We understand if you're not interested in a sentimental family reunion. But I think you knew our father better than we did. We came here to find out more about him."

Leo didn't answer. I said, as if the thought had just come to me, "If you don't mind my asking, where is your mother? Can we see her?"

He looked at me as if estimating my worth for an upcoming sale of used sisters. "Wanna go right now?"

I assumed Leo would refuse access to his mother or claim, as others had done, that she was dead. His acquiescence surprised and alarmed me, and I was tempted to refuse his invitation. I could go home and forget this day ever happened. Go back to grading papers and chauffeuring my kids and, from a safe distance, making sure my former student didn't get arrested for a crime he didn't commit.

Leo interpreted my silence as assent. "I'll take you. But first, I gotta pick up a few important messages from my friends at The Club."

I put my arm around Susan, who looked frozen with fear. "Drink your coffee, Sis. And pull yourself together. We're going to meet Velma."

"I can't believe those words just came out of your mouth." She blotted a line of sweat on her upper lip. "There is so much I wanted to say to the woman who stole our father and our lives. But I'm not sure I'll be able to speak without throwing up. Which might put a crimp in the conversation."

The sound of breaking glass filtered through to the counter where Susan and I sat. Solly muttered under his breath and got a broom and dustpan from a narrow closet. He didn't immediately approach the back room, however. Another crash followed, and then I heard what sounded like a table being overturned. I looked at Solly and said, "Uh, what's happening back there?" I didn't suggest he call the police, since NYPD's Finest, in the form of my half-brother, Leo, was already there.

Solly moved his shoulders a fraction of an inch. "Nothing. Nothing's going on."

Susan was impatient. "Of course, something's going on. We can hear it. Don't you want to see?"

Solly leaned on the broom handle. "No."

Susan and I stared at the door. She turned to me and said, "Do you want…"

"Are you crazy? No, I do not want. What could we do? Call the cops?"

My sister started laughing. After a moment, I joined her. In this world, luncheonettes were gambling joints, and the cops' function was to provide cheaper protection than the local gangs and rackets.

Leo emerged a few minutes later, slightly out of breath but smiling. He cracked his knuckles, swung behind the candy counter to filch a few more chocolate bars, and beckoned to us. "Right this way."

We followed him down streets I'd never traverse alone. Tiny, weed-choked patches of grass alternated with stretches of cracked concrete, and many of the buildings were scarred by graffiti. We stopped at an apartment house that was similar to the one the Weinstocks inhabited, but it was on a block made more desolate by the empty lot next to it.

Velma lived one flight up from the ground floor, which was a relief, given the groaning noises that issued from the elevator. Leo unlocked the door, and we walked inside a foul-smelling apartment. Cigarette stubs littered three overflowing ashtrays, and the odorous remains of a box of fried chicken mixed with the smell of dirty laundry.

I looked around. "Uh, where's your...where's Velma?"

Leo cocked his gun at my head. "I guess she couldn't make it after all."

Chapter Twenty-Six

There is nothing so confining as the prisons of our own perceptions.
—William Shakespeare / Hamlet

With Leo's gun pointed at my head, it wasn't easy to maintain a brave front, but I smiled as if this was all a bad joke. As a kid, I'd been beaten up by gangs of girls, and the worst thing, the most dangerous thing, was to let them see how scared you were. At his command to sit, Susan dropped immediately to the sofa, but I inspected it first, brushing a few crumbs from the fabric to the floor before following his direction. I said nothing. I was afraid my voice would betray my terror.

Leo's face was dark with anger. "Why don't you tell me the real reason you're here? Is this about Ralphie? Or is it the money you're after?"

Susan's lips trembled as she spoke. "We don't know anything about Ralphie. Just like we don't know anything about you. We want, that is, we wanted to know more about our past. Leo, please, you don't have to threaten us. If you don't want to tell us about our father, that's okay. We'll go, and we won't come back."

Leo removed a pack of cigarettes from his back pocket and used his teeth to extract one. He lit it with a silver lighter I recognized as our mother's. It was one of the few gifts Lousy had ever given her, and it held pride of place in each of the miserable apartments we called home, even when the home in question was a roach-infested motel on the edge of a highway. Rage overcame fear as I remembered her slim fingers flicking the wheel on the lighter.

I forced myself to look at Leo and not at Susan, who I feared would dissolve into tears or faint. Our half-brother was unlikely to be moved by either reaction, and it might make him more inclined to torment us for the pleasure it brought him. The resemblance between him and our father was quite remarkable.

I motioned to the pack of cigarettes. "Even a guy on death row gets a last smoke. Pass one over, brother." I gave the last word a sarcastic emphasis.

He narrowed his eyes, but, surprisingly, complied. He put the pack of cigarettes on the floor and kicked it toward us. I extracted two and motioned for the lighter. He tossed me a book of matches instead. Susan and I both reached for the matches, and they fell to the floor. Susan got to them first and lit both our cigarettes. The gun Leo held never wavered.

I leaned back and blew out a stream of smoke. This pose was slightly undermined by a fit of choking that accompanied my first draw on the cigarette. I rarely smoked and was unused to the high-octane brand Leo favored.

He watched me with unblinking, lizard eyes. "Why did you ask about Ralphie?"

Although wary of setting him off, I said, "We didn't mention Ralphie. You did. Susan and I wanted to meet your mother. We thought she might tell us about our father. We haven't seen him since we were kids. Have you?"

"I ain't seen him in years. Not interested. And if you know what's good for you, you won't go looking for him. The old man is dead, or as good as dead. He got on the bad side of some very bad people."

I breathed a bit easier. If Leo was warning me against a possible course of action, then perhaps I'd have a future outside this filthy room that reeked of stale smoke. I affected indifference. "If he's dead, so much the better. We think he may have killed our mother."

I felt the force of Susan's gasp. Leo let the gun drop a few inches, but I didn't attempt an escape. Aside from the deep respect I had for his resolve and his aim, neither Susan nor I had the skills to take down an armed man without getting ourselves shot.

"We all got along just fine without any family reunions." He drilled into me with the force of his stare. "I'm warning you, we ain't gonna start now. If you're lucky, I'll let you go back to your life."

I leaned forward. "You don't want us to talk to Ralphie. No problem there. And it's not like I want to keep talking to you. But what about Velma? I thought you were taking us to meet her."

Leo's smile was more chilling than the cruelest of sneers. "You lift one finger to talk to my mother, and I will blow your head off. What will your kids do without their mama?"

A shuddering weakness took possession of me. Over and over, I'd promised myself I would never do to my kids what my parents had done to me. The irony crushed me, and I was silent.

Susan pressed her elbows against the sides of her body. "We came here because we were curious about you, your mother, and our father. I think we've learned everything we need to know." Ignoring the gun pointed at her, she showed him the phone she'd palmed when she retrieved the matches. The screen read 911, and her finger hovered over the call button.

Leo laughed. "Go ahead. You'll get to meet my buddies at the precinct."

I rose to my feet on knees that threatened to buckle. "We're not one of your street dealers. Put the gun down, let us go, and that'll be the end of this."

His voice was indifferent. "I got a team of guys. They'll take you for a swim at Sheepshead Bay, and no one's the wiser."

Susan nearly dropped the phone. I grabbed it from her and said, "You think the disappearance of a New Jersey suburban mom and her sister won't make headlines? You think we came here and didn't tell anyone? We hired a dick to track you down, you moron. If we disappear, he's gonna be asking a whole lot of questions. You may own this crappy neighborhood, but cops from all over the tri-state area will be combing through The Club. Sooner or later, they'll find you."

Leo's eyes darted about the room as if these imaginary detectives had already descended upon him. "I was just kidding about takin' you out to the Bay. But I wasn't kidding about the rest." He pretended to think. "I'll tell you what. You two get the hell out of here, and we'll call it even. You don't bother me, and I won't bother you."

I stepped back toward the door. "Deal."

And with that, Susan and I left. When we reached the sidewalk, I looked up. Leo was standing by the window, watching us, as if to let us know we hadn't seen the last of him. He hadn't seen the last of me, either. I wanted Mom's lighter. It belonged to me, and someday I'd get it and him.

Susan and I sprinted past MarVel's Coffee Shoppe, but our progress came to a stumbling halt when we stepped off the curb and into a busy intersection. A police car, lights flashing and sirens screaming, ran through a red light. Sick with fear, I crumpled to the ground.

Susan helped me to my feet. "What's the matter with you?"

After a few weak steps, I was able to run again, and we resumed our race to safety. "I was afraid Leo sent some of his buddies to either arrest us or beat us up. Leo is dangerous, even without his gun."

We had one more hurdle to go. The gang of boys who'd menaced us earlier were back. Susan and I ducked behind the car, and both got in from the driver's side. We counted ourselves lucky to have escaped physically unscathed, other than my scraped knees. The car, however, was not as fortunate. The side doors were keyed with a half dozen scratches. It could have been worse. It could have been us.

* * *

On the drive back to New Jersey, Susan was fretful. "Other than meeting our psychopathic little brother, who turned out to be older than we are, what did we accomplish today, other than get held up at gunpoint? We never got to meet Velma. I wonder where she was. Assuming Leo didn't have her tied and gagged in a closet. Or chopped into pieces and in the freezer."

Distracted by two busses whose drivers were hell-bent upon squeezing us out of the middle lane of the access road to the Holland Tunnel, I had no choice but to let her continue to ramble.

She kicked off her shoes. "If I'd known in advance we'd have to run a marathon, I would have worn sneakers."

Outside the gym, my sister didn't wear sneakers. She also didn't know how to drive and was oblivious to the peril we faced as six lanes of traffic merged into a single open path that led to the tunnel. As I risked life and limb to cross in front of a fanatically aggressive driver, she continued the conversation without me.

"Mom didn't do drugs or abuse alcohol, although how she stayed married to Lousy without the help of psychotropic intervention is beyond me. It's reasonable for us to conclude someone drugged her before she got behind the wheel." Susan looked unseeingly out the window. "We also know that Velma and her kids were living in the same general area we did. The big takeaway from today's adventure is that Leo was old enough and mean enough to, er, you do know where I'm going with this, don't you?"

I felt my heart beat faster, but this time, the increased pressure was unrelated to city driving. "With Mom out of the way, Leo would gain a full-time father. The only problem with that theory is no one, not even someone who so closely takes after Lousy, could want to spend more time with him. In other words, my money's on Velma. She had the most to gain. Maybe Velma put Leo up to it."

Susan drummed her fingers on the dashboard. "I think it was Lousy. You thought the same thing, until today."

I had an uneasy feeling we were missing something. "Lousy didn't have to kill Mom or any of his women. He dumped them, ditched his kids, and moved on. Let's try a different scenario. Mom finds out about Velma. Being Mom, maybe she goes to see her. Velma gives her a Mickey Finn special and then sends her on her way."

"In that case, Velma killed Mom." Susan finished.

"That's a definite possibility. But this doesn't let Lousy off the hook. Or Leo. Maybe one of them planned it with Velma. Don't forget, our enterprising father coopted our Social Security checks after Mom died. So, he did benefit from her death. And Leo said something about money. I wish I'd thought to ask him about that."

Susan frowned. "What's the point? Maybe we cut our losses."

With uncharacteristic boldness, I swerved into an open space to the right. This maneuver got us into the tunnel. I waited for the drivers behind me to cease their furious honking before resuming my argument. "The only way we could nail the killer is if there was a witness."

Susan nervously twisted the rings on her fingers. "How could there have been a witness? Surely if someone had seen Velma poison, or at least doctor Mom's drink, that person would have come forward."

I gripped the steering wheel so tightly my fingers ached. "Not necessarily. Not if the guy who suspected Velma of murder was secretly in love with her. Or if it was someone who had a lot to lose if Mom found out he had criminal secrets of his own. We have no idea how much Mom knew about Lousy's business dealings."

We exited the tunnel. Staring at the panoramic cityscape across the water, Susan said, "Are you thinking of Ira Goldfarb? We looked up to him! He was the kind of father we wished we had."

When New York City's skyline receded from view, the scenery that lay ahead of us provided no balm to our raw nerves. Susan, who rarely paid attention to signs or exits, yelped as we passed two signs that indicated contradictory directions to Oak Ridge.

I reassured her that, geographically, we were going the right way. "The photos Arlene showed us were pristine, but the ones I swiped from Ira were worn, like he'd taken them out a bunch of times to look at them. They meant something to him. So now, we have to ask ourselves if Ira is hiding secrets more incriminating than a few pictures. We assumed he scrimped and saved to afford a house in the suburbs, but what if he got the money through less legal means? And Mom found out about it? He had a lot to lose. As for the peace-and-love- hippie life he's living now, I think he's in it for the weed, the magic mushrooms, and the yurts."

I didn't want to further stress out my sister, but I also didn't want to hide anything from her. "Ira is one possibility we can't ignore. But Leo and Ralphie, knowingly or not, may also be implicated. It's weird how they turned out. Leo's a cop, although a dirty one, and Ralphie's in prison. We should find out what he's in for."

Susan shuddered. "Even without a gun, Leo is scary. He looks so much like Lousy."

I moved my head from side to side, trying to release the tension in my neck and shoulders. "Yeah, I was creeped out by the resemblance as much as you were. But I was more creeped out by him. As scary as Lousy was, I don't remember him carrying quite that level of sadism. Leo seemed more malicious. More threatening."

"I wonder why he took us to his apartment. Was it just to torture us?" Susan leaned back and closed her eyes. I wished I could do the same.

Traffic slowed, which gave me time to think. "Leo wanted information from us as badly as we wanted it from him. He released us because we knew nothing that could either help or hurt him."

Susan opened one eye. "So, what have we learned? Are we any further along now than we were before we started?"

"Yes. We talked to a lot of people today. The one thing everyone agreed upon was that Lousy made off with their cash, which brings us full circle. Maybe Mom's death, like the ones at the country club, had nothing to do with jealousy or hurt feelings. Money might have been the motivation for both crimes." I felt as if every effort to release myself from my childhood demons ended up drawing me closer to them.

Susan brought me back to more immediate dangers. "You can't separate money from emotion. Don't discount Leo's threat to send us to the bottom of Sheepshead Bay."

"I won't."

My sister's breathing slowed, and she fell asleep. Alone with my thoughts, I came to a few conclusions. The first was that I might never be able to prove that my mother had been murdered. That failure didn't mean we'd wasted our time. I'd justified our investigation as something I owed to Susan, to my mother, and to my kids. But it was, in the end, something I owed to myself.

There was plenty I could do if I could summon enough courage to follow through.

Leo's teachers and classmates could tell me if he was as brutal a teenager as he was an adult.

The men at The Club might have information about Ira Goldfarb and his relationship with both Lousy and Velma.

Arlene Goldfarb, like her husband, might be hiding a few secrets of her own.

I decided against contacting the police officers who responded to my mother's accident. Leo's clout at his neighborhood precinct rendered that line of inquiry too risky. Like the power brokers on the board at the Meadowfields Country Club, the people in charge of safety posed the most danger.

Chapter Twenty-Seven

Purpose is but the slave to memory
—William Shakespeare / Hamlet

S usan woke as we turned onto the tree-lined street where I lived, so different from the bleak neighborhood where we'd spent the day. She rubbed her eyes and said, "If Mom left Lousy, she'd probably still be alive. She wouldn't even be that old. Look at the Goldfarbs. They've got ten years on her. And the Weinstocks are even older."

"Let's not think about what might have been." I raised the volume on the radio.

She turned it off. "You bottle things up. It's healthier to air them out. I hope you don't do this to your husband."

Stung, I said, "My marriage is not an issue that concerns you."

Susan had no business critiquing my relationship with George. She had three ex-husbands and a string of unsuitable boyfriends. Following her advice would be like hiring King Henry VIII as a relationship counselor.

She dropped the subject of my marriage and reverted to one that was of equal interest. "What's our next step? It will be a cold day in hell before I return to Mel Weinstock's club."

"The Club may look like paradise compared to our next outing." I steeled myself against her likely reaction.

Susan took out a cigarette but didn't light it, as I won't let her smoke in the car. "I'd rather meet in the bowels of the Cross Bronx Expressway than make a return visit to The Club, the Weinstock apartment, or Velma and

Leo."

I waited until we were in my kitchen before telling her what I planned. "We're going to Rikers Island to meet Ralphie."

"No! I'm putting my foot down. That is never going to happen!"

Two glasses of wine later, she agreed to visit the fearsome prison.

* * *

Although we didn't get back to Oak Ridge until past five o'clock, George hadn't returned from the country club. When I called, he said, "I'm still here," without any other greeting. Before I could respond, he added, "I'm not coming home. We're eating dinner at the club. Be here by seven thirty."

I didn't argue, although I had no appetite for George's friends or another elaborate meal. "Add one more to the reservation. Susan is coming." I disconnected without a goodbye since he'd greeted me without a hello. While Susan made herself beautiful, I graded essays to alleviate my guilt. I should have spent the weekend doing schoolwork; instead, I'd expended my time and energy on two impractical and dangerous quests.

When shysters and criminals tell you they're scared of someone, nervous people like Susan and me were unlikely to succeed. Or survive. Eliminating Leo and Velma from our investigation left Ralphie as our best source. Although Susan agreed to visit Rikers Island, I hadn't fully convinced myself it was the right move.

As for the country club murders, Miguel's refusal to answer my calls and texts demonstrated the utter futility of my attempt to help him. I could continue to question potential suspects, but maybe Ben was right. I would report to the detective information that came my way, but going after a killer was foolhardy. It was time to quit.

My decision to retreat from amateur sleuthing lasted until I read Jack Tumbleson's essay on *1984*. Over the years I've learned people can't write a grocery list, let alone an essay, without revealing their character. Jack's rambling summary of that brilliant book revealed two important points. One was that he'd imperfectly copied online sources. The other was that he would have been a worse torturer than the fictional character he'd attempted to analyze. When Ben Sorkin added Jack to the list of suspects in Elliot's murder, I didn't believe my student was capable of killing his father. After reading Jack's essay, I was less certain.

I told this to Susan, who was blow-drying her hair.

She hit the off button. "Essays and class discussions are no substitute for really knowing another human being. You said yourself he copied half of what he wrote, which means you can't judge Jack guilty based on his essay any more than you can decide Miguel is innocent based on his A+ grade."

The front door banged open, and Zach charged into the kitchen. I left Susan and greeted my son. "How was the Mets game?"

"We won. It was close, but a homerun in the ninth inning clinched it." He spread peanut butter on a slice of bread and, after demolishing it in three bites, said, "The game was awesome. It was a lot more fun to see it from box seats instead of the nosebleed section."

The Hopewell budget didn't run to expensive seats at sports events. When I was a kid, the only time I saw a live baseball game was when I was working a concession stand, but I didn't tell him that.

A few minutes later, Ellie pirouetted into the kitchen. I opened the refrigerator and offered the standard I'm-not-cooking-but-am-still-a-devoted-mom options of omelet, grilled cheese, and canned soup.

Zach made himself a second sandwich. "It's Saturday night, and we're in high school. We have plans."

Susan walked into the kitchen, looking as radiant and rested as if she'd spent the day at the spa instead of rooting in the garbage bin of our past lives. She hugged both kids and said, "Wish we could stay home with you guys. But it's Saturday night, and your mom and I have plans."

On a tide of laughter, the kids went their separate ways. Zach took a sleeve of cookies and left, saying only, "I'll be at a friend's house."

I followed him to the door. "Which friend's house? And what time will you be home?"

He lifted one shoulder. "I'll be at the Castleton's. They're ordering pizza. Home early. Maybe midnight."

Midnight didn't sound early to me, but I let it go. Ellie, who resembled Susan more than she did me, went upstairs to try on fifteen different outfits. She returned to the kitchen briefly, blew us a kiss, and announced, "Going to Sarah's house to meet up with the rest of the gang. We'll be binge-watching TV and pretending we don't care we weren't invited to the Castleton's party."

I stopped her. "What party? Zach said he was going over to eat pizza. He didn't say anything about a party."

Ellie updated me. "If enough people show up, it's a party."

"Why weren't you invited?" Susan was outraged on my daughter's behalf.

"It's mostly juniors and seniors who are going. I'm not popular enough. Only the really popular sophomore girls were invited."

My beautiful, smart, talented daughter was untroubled by her exclusion, but it bothered me. "I find it hard to believe that you aren't popular enough to score an invitation to anything happening at the Castleton house."

Ellie grinned. "Don't worry about it, Ma. And now, if you're done with the third degree?"

I let her go.

Susan removed a nail file from her bag and scraped at a minuscule imperfection. "What's on the agenda for tonight? Besides dinner, that is."

"Dinner is all we're going to get. I don't know what else we can do. Magda is out of the hospital but won't take my phone calls. I've yet to hear back from Miguel. Time to get back to our real lives."

I expected an argument, but Susan disappointed me. "I was thinking the same thing. Let's just enjoy ourselves. And by enjoy, I mean you need to introduce me to some eligible men. Preferably one that isn't a no-show because he's gotten himself murdered."

"Good plan. Especially since you haven't set the bar too high." I swiped a lipstick from her makeup bag and propped a mirror on the kitchen table.

She tallied her requirements. "I want someone good-looking, smart, and with a great sense of humor. Preferably, no kids, but I can deal with a dad who doesn't have full-time custody. And the kids have to be old enough not to be a nuisance."

Her comments reminded me of the conversation I'd overheard between Heather and Amanda, but they were much less offensive coming from my sister. "Haven't you forgotten something?"

"I hope you're not referring to my potential mate's finances. It goes without saying that he has to have money. Why else would I be looking for romance at the country club?"

I searched for my car keys, which persisted in not being where I left them. "You might want to do a credit check before committing yourself to a new man. We're not rich, and we're members. Of course, that's only because Cooper Aldridge got us a discounted rate. It didn't cost much more than a two-week summer rental in the Adirondacks."

Susan frowned. "Not possible. Membership fees at that club are way more than a rented shack by a lake."

I'd never questioned George too closely about how much it cost us to join Meadowfields Country Club. All I knew was that it was expensive enough to preclude our yearly vacation in the Adirondacks, which I considered a bonus. Instead of spending a mosquito and poison-ivy-infested summer by a frigid lake, I anticipated reading by a pristine pool. By July, George would surely have given up on getting me to play golf. Susan's comments about the membership fees, however, troubled me. I logged into our joint account and the kids' college funds but saw no unusual activity.

* * *

As I drove up the narrow circular driveway of the Meadowfields Country Club, a text message pinged my phone. Susan looked at the screen and reported, "Your husband is getting impatient."

My hands reflexively jerked in annoyance, and we swerved a few inches off the path. No humans were hurt, but a large stone urn surrendered to the impact. I exited to assess the damage. Aside from long scratches on the side of the car, which were a souvenir of our afternoon, there were no new dings or dents. With some effort, Susan and I returned the urn to an upright position. A slight crack in the base was hardly visible, although it did cause a bit of a wobble. The parking attendants helped us steady it. I detected an undertone of suppressed laughter, but they remained blandly courteous.

After relinquishing my key to the valet, Susan and I climbed the stairs toward the entrance. Distracted by the mishap with the urn, I tripped over a cast-iron, antique-looking shoe scraper that propped open one of the doors.

Bryony Aldridge was among the witnesses to my humiliation. She spoke with unconvincing concern. "Dear, dear. Are you okay? Do you need a drink, or have you started without us?"

Susan was fierce in my defense. "I'm sure the sight of you is enough to make anyone stumble. Or drink."

Bryony's Teflon poise remained intact. "Likewise, I'm sure." She coolly sized up Susan, who presented a more formidable opponent than most women. "I'm sorry, but I've forgotten your name. Even though I've seen so much of you lately. You seem to be here more often than people who are members and pay dues."

"And I'm afraid I've forgotten your name as well. Though I do remember how charming you were at our last meeting." My sister, in saccharine tones, added, "Yes! I have it now. You're the one who spilled wine all over her dress."

Bryony, now on the defensive, made a strangled effort to set the record straight, which was unnecessary since all of us remembered quite well that Melinda Tumbleson was the one who ruined Bryony's dress and handbag.

Susan cut her off and, with a dismissive flick of her fingers, said, "I'd love to keep chatting, but we have dinner reservations."

Bryony looked down her nose at us, an easy feat since my sister and I are both very short. "I know. Your reservations are with us."

Chapter Twenty-Eight

I would challenge you to a battle of wits, but I see you are unarmed.
—William Shakespeare / Much Ado About Nothing

I f George had told me we were having dinner with the Aldridges, I would have stayed home and ordered pizza. Susan grumbled a similar sentiment as we entered the dining room.

Bryony led us to a table set for eight, and I wondered, with grim resignation, who else was coming. If someone had offered me a choice between drinking schnapps at The Club with Mel Weinstock and Phil Fleishman, or eating dinner at Meadowfields with Bryony and Cooper Aldridge, I would have chosen the former. At least at The Club, forced courtesy wasn't on the menu.

George and Cooper rose from their seats as we approached. Bryony commanded them to separate as the rest of our dinner party arrived. The president of the country club, Mark Felician, reverently escorted Sonya Tumbleson to the table. He looked, in his middle-aged, red-cheeked, pleasantly plump aspect, like a Norman Rockwell kid who's gotten a two-wheeled bicycle for Christmas. Sonya looked fragile and very beautiful in a dark blue halter dress that bared her delicate neck and shoulders. They both looked a lot better than the last time I saw them, when he was consoling her after she found Ryan's dead body.

Bryony sat next to George and reserved the chair on her other side by placing her handbag on it. Ian distributed menus and recited the specials of the day. I itched to question him about matters more pressing than soup and swordfish but refrained until I could talk to him without other potentially guilty parties listening in. Although an hour earlier, I'd waffled on the advisability of continuing my investigation, the sight of him rekindled my resolve. He was my prime suspect.

Cooper clapped Ian on the back and said, "This guy used to be my caddy. He helped Bryony and me win last year's tournament."

Ian filled our water glasses. "Everyone says you're the favorites to win this year again."

Bryony ignored his compliment and gave her husband a bored smile. "It's not rocket science, darling. I'm sure there are plenty of caddies to take Ian's place."

An awkward silence followed her pronouncement. Sonya's presence prevented any conversation about the murders, and there was little else that united us.

Mark Felician, whose cordial manner and good nature got him elected president, appeared unaware of any tension. He pointed to the empty seat next to Bryony and asked, "Are we still waiting for someone? Because I don't know about the rest of you, but there's nothing like playing eighteen holes to work up an appetite!"

Cooper said, less agreeably, "Yes, darling, this is your party. Who is our mystery guest?"

We followed Bryony's gaze as a Nordic god entered the dining room. She waved to him, and he greeted her with enthusiastic kisses on both cheeks.

Bryony peeled herself out of his arms and said, "This is Evan Carlsson. He's new to town and needs some sponsors, so I thought I'd invite him to join us."

The men made appropriately welcoming noises. Susan, Sonya, and Bryony regarded the newcomer like a trio of kids eyeing the display at a candy store. I tried to remember where I'd heard his name.

He bypassed the others to greet me first, "Liz, I feel as if I already know you."

Since my social circle was abysmally narrow, I couldn't imagine how he knew of my existence.

Smiling widely, he explained, "We're going to be colleagues. I start at Valerian Hills High School tomorrow. I'm the new English teacher."

Susan glowed with enthusiasm. "How lovely! Liz, isn't that wonderful?"

I was less pleased than my sister. So this was the athletic phenom the principal described to me, the English teacher who broke football records in his position as a tight end. It was unfair of me to be prejudiced against him because Timmy liked him, but my hackles rose nonetheless.

I returned Evan's smile. "It's nice to meet you. I'm happy you were able to sub for Bill. Have you been teaching long?"

"Long enough to know better. I've been teaching for about five years." He winked at me as if we were in on a secret no one else knew.

My suspicions flared anew. No one leaves a tenured teaching position to take a job as a long-term substitute. Especially not at Valerian Hills, where we paid substitute teachers with the same munificence as most fast food empires. I wondered how he could afford to join the club.

Evan sensed my mistrust. "I hope I'm not telling tales out of school, but I feel pretty confident that I'll get a full-time gig at the high school very soon."

I toyed with my drink as I reviewed possible casualties in the English department. Maybe Bill wasn't coming back from his extended sick leave. Perhaps Caroline, the embittered head of our English department, decided to make good on her years-long threat to retire. I hoped Emily wasn't on the chopping block. Although she was tenured, she lived in fear of getting moved to the middle school. Thanks to Melinda Tumbleson, my position at the high school was no more secure than Emily's.

From across the table, George threw me a fierce look. I banished these unproductive thoughts and returned my attention to a conversation that had proceeded quite well without my input. Bryony told Evan, even more delightedly than Timmy told me, "The students are going to love you, I'm sure."

She pressed her arm against his. Given ten minutes alone with Evan, she probably would have ripped his clothes off with her teeth. I was embarrassed by her overt attention to him, but Cooper appeared unconcerned by his wife's behavior. It was George who watched them with tight lips and a creased forehead.

All of the women, except for me, deferred to Evan. Marital devotion had nothing to do with his inability to charm me. He simply wasn't my type. Show me a man who thinks doing the crossword puzzle and reading under a pile of blankets is a fine way to spend a Sunday morning, and I'm interested. But Evan's tanned, blue-eyed Scandinavian ruggedness left me cold. For a brief, unfaithful moment, I wondered how Ben Sorkin spent his weekend mornings.

Evan moved his chair closer to mine. "I'm counting on you to show me the ropes, Liz."

"Happy to help." I plucked a roll from the basket between us and asked, "So, how do you, uh, how do you know Timmy?"

I knew the answer, but I wanted to hear it from him.

"Timmy was my high school teacher and football coach. Over the years, we kept in touch, and when there was a potential opening at Valerian Hills, he called me."

I pushed the bread closer to him. "It's nice to have an in with the boss. But I'm surprised you'd leave a full-time gig for a substitute salary. Where have you been teaching?"

"I have no worries. And like I say, I look forward to teaching with you."

"I'm sure the students in your school will miss you." Unsure whether he'd not heard my question or chose not to answer it, I said, "Where did you say it was?"

Evan reached for the wine bottle and refilled my glass. He raised his in a toast and said cheerfully, "To new beginnings!"

We clinked glasses in that awkward way people do when there are too many participants and no way to avoid reaching across the table. As Bryony rather forcefully rammed her glass into mine I felt a slight vibration from my phone, which I'd placed in my lap. The text was from Miguel.

Susan, who was deep in conversation with Cooper Aldridge, at first didn't acknowledge the increasingly vehement way I jerked my head toward the exit. Annoyed, I rose and said I was going to the bathroom. Susan finally got the nonverbal part of my message and excused herself.

CHAPTER TWENTY-EIGHT

From behind us, Bryony called, "Hey, you two! Wait for me."

Under my breath, I muttered imprecations better suited to the dockyard than the country club. While Bryony admired her reflection in a three-way mirror, I entered a stall and sent a text to Miguel: **At the club-where are you?**

After a few seconds, he answered, **Parking lot.**

Although George would be furious if I ditched our dinner companions, I texted, **Be there in 10.**

I emerged from the stall, washed my hands with the care of a surgeon, and spent more time on my makeup and hair than I'd done since the day I got married. But there was no getting rid of Bryony. She chatted, made unnecessary adjustments to her immaculate makeup, and refused to leave without us.

We returned to the dining room. I couldn't remember eating much, but the dinner plates had been cleared, and everyone ordered coffee and after-dinner drinks. I rummaged in my purse and announced that I'd left a lipstick in the bathroom. Susan, heedless of censorious looks from our nonsmoking companions, said she needed a cigarette and wanted me to keep her company.

I showed her Miguel's message, and we retreated to the end of the parking lot to escape the camaraderie of the refugee smokers. Susan lit a cigarette and offered me one, but I refused.

"Suit yourself," she replied. "I'd rather have a cigarette than dessert."

Laughter floated across the grounds to where we stood. I stared at my cell phone, willing Miguel to text me again.

Susan blew a plume of smoke into the heavy night air. "It's getting cold. Let's go in."

I sent Miguel another text. **Where are you? I'm in parking lot near back exit.**

"Has it crossed your mind," she asked, "That Miguel might be here, watching us? And that he thought you'd be alone?"

I was exasperated. With myself. "I should have thought of that. He's probably waiting for you to leave. Go inside. I'll stay here and wait."

Susan ground the cigarette butt under her heel. 'For an English teacher and a would-be detective, you're not too good at deductions. Don't you see? Miguel is the killer. If you'd come out here by yourself, he would have gone after you."

Chapter Twenty-Nine

When we mean to build/We first survey the plot, then draw the model
—William Shakespeare / Henry IV Part 2

Susan and I had been absent from the dinner table for a discourteously long time, but no one appeared to either notice or care. The others were deep in a conversation about the club's upcoming golf tournament. The title of this much-anticipated event was the Spring Fling.

Bryony and Cooper modestly revealed they had won two of the last three competitions.

"Who knocked you out the year you lost?" I wanted to toast whoever had toppled them.

The Aldridges looked at me as if I'd committed a felony.

Mark Felician said softly, "Elliot and Sonya Tumbleson. It was Sonya who carried them. She has one of the best swings I've seen."

Bryony ignored Mark and informed me, in a faintly mocking tone, "I've heard that you and George may give us a run for our money this year."

I gagged on my coffee at the thought of competing in a golf tournament. If the event included a Jane Austen trivia contest, I would have been the first to sign up. But golf? I'd rather attend a four-hour meeting of the High School Prom Decorating Committee.

When I recovered the use of my voice, I said, "Thanks for the vote of confidence, but I've got a previous engagement. Maybe next year."

George's foot pressed mine. "Did I forget to tell you? I've signed us up. Should be a lot of fun."

I kicked him. "Yes, dear, I think you did forget to tell me."

In his defense, when George asked about the progress I was making, I may have slightly exaggerated my skill level. I suspected, however, that he anticipated my reluctance to compete and was hoping to secure a better partner without appearing to reject me.

Cooper said, "Liz, you don't know what you're missing. The Spring Fling is the highlight of the season. Bryony and I always have a great time. He looked brightly around the table. "There, now. It's all settled." He lifted his brandy snifter in tribute to Sonya. "And this brave lady will be playing with Mark."

Sonya bowed her head. "I didn't want to take part so soon after, well, you know." There was a sympathetic silence, and she continued, "But everyone's been so kind."

Mark patted her hand and said, "Best thing in the world for you. Nothing like golf to make you forget your troubles." Susan, who was sitting across from me, rolled her eyes.

"Sometimes you have to take care of you and not worry what other people think." Bryony emitted a longsuffering sigh as if her sacrifices were too numerous to mention.

Sonya fluttered her eyelashes. "Speaking of taking care of yourself, will you excuse me if I leave early? My little boy needs me." Mark jumped to his feet to take her home, but she insisted on taking a car service. He walked her to the main entrance to wait for her ride.

After the two lovebirds left, my sister said, "Someone should talk sense into that woman. She should stay away from the golf course."

Cooper looked puzzled. "Why on earth should she avoid the country club? Her friends are here." He slapped his hand on the table. "Sonya's an excellent golfer. It'll do her good. And Mark will take care of her. He was with her, you know, after she found Ryan. Terrible thing for Sonya to go through so soon after Elliot's, er, after Elliot's passing."

Bryony's voice had a malicious edge to it. "It is interesting, though, that Sonya's husband and lover were both murdered. Maybe someone's got it in for her."

I hadn't considered this possibility. "It's true that Sonya has many friends at the club. But Susan and Bryony are right. This might not be a safe place for her."

Cooper scratched his head. "There may be something in that." He added, with as much satisfaction as if he'd coined the phrase, "Hell hath no fury, and so on. Although a golf club isn't a woman's weapon. Don't they mostly go for poison?"

He'd misunderstood me. My goal was to protect Sonya from someone who could be masquerading as a friend, not to accuse her of murder. Mark Felician, who returned to the table in time to hear Cooper's comments, turned a shade pinker than his usual rosy hue. "You know I have a lot of respect for you, Cooper, but this is not acceptable. Sonya is a suffering widow, and I don't want to hear any nasty gossip about her. She's been an absolute angel."

Bryony put a sad expression on her face as if regretting the necessity of giving us information that was now common knowledge, "Elliot Tumbleson physically abused Sonya, and she was going to divorce him. So, I guess she sort of has a motive? Because instead of getting a divorce from a man in debt up to his ears, she'll scoop up a pile of life insurance money."

Mark's cheeks darkened from pink to purple. "None of that makes her guilty! The—she—the opposite. Sonya is the gentlest person I've ever met."

Cooper topped off Mark's wineglass. "You're right about Sonya. I don't know what some people are thinking of to make such wild and irresponsible accusations." He didn't acknowledge his and Bryony's attempt to do that very thing, not two minutes earlier.

Bryony was quick to follow her husband's lead. "It makes no sense to discuss Sonya when the prime suspect in the murder is that guy they fired from the club."

"His name is Miguel. And he's not guilty." I didn't trust myself to say more than that.

She winked at Evan. "Miguel was one of Liz's students from a million years ago. She thinks anyone who gets an A in English is, by definition, not guilty."

I had to unclench my jaw to answer. "What makes you so sure he did it? You admitted you know nothing about the waitstaff."

She took a deep breath and closed her eyes. When she opened them, she said, "Ryan told me he saw Miguel at the scene of the crime. And a ton of people suspected him of stealing from the club. What none of you seem to realize is that if Miguel is innocent, then Sonya also has a good motive. Spousal abuse is an excellent reason to want your husband dead. Facts are facts, Liz. You can't let romantic notions get in the way of the truth."

Evan consoled Mark, who was stricken over Bryony's casual reference to the violence Sonya suffered at Elliot's hands. "Hey, man. I'm sure it'll all work out for the best. Sonya doesn't seem like the type to murder anyone. Not that I have any experience with murderers, of course."

He laughed heartily at his joke, and Bryony laughed with him. I was more interested in Bryony's claim that Ryan was the one who'd seen Miguel at the scene of the crime since Ryan was dead.

Mark didn't crack a smile. "I saw Sonya right after she got the news that Elliot was murdered. She was devastated. And I was with her when she found Ryan with his head bashed in. All you have to do is look at her to know she's innocent."

The conversation died, as no one had an appetite to continue talking. People got busy checking their phones and fiddling with their spoons. A different waiter refilled our coffee cups, and as we passed cream and sugar, Cooper seemed to rethink his earlier dismissal of Sonya as a suspect. Or, perhaps, he was justifying his attempt to accuse her. "Forgive me, Mark, but unlike the rest of us at this table, Sonya doesn't have a cast-iron alibi. That might pose a problem for her."

I interceded, although my opinion did little to decrease the tension between Cooper and Mark. "If Sonya isn't the killer, and I don't think she is, then she could be the next victim."

Bryony covered her mouth in a yawn. "Let's hope the police put the finishing touches on their case before Liz's pet student strikes again."

I checked my phone for the dozenth time since returning from the parking lot. Nothing from Miguel. But something Bryony said earlier stood out from the drivel. What was it?

Chapter Thirty

Make not your thoughts your prisons
—William Shakespeare / Antony and Cleopatra

After the dinner party, all George wanted to talk about was how I'd embarrassed him in front of his friends. All I wanted to talk about was George signing me up for a golf tournament without my knowledge or consent. I also had a few choice words to share with him concerning his relationship with Heather and Amanda. And Bryony.

While we waited for the valets to bring our cars, I made my case for being the injured party. "If you heard some guy talking about having an affair with me, you'd be as angry as I was when I heard Heather and Amanda discuss you."

George gripped my arm so hard it hurt. "I don't pay attention to gossip. You eavesdropped on two very silly women. I can't help it if Heather and Amanda got the wrong idea about me."

By mutual consent, we took our argument behind one of the massive pillars that separated the foyer from the seating area in the lobby. Shielded from prying eyes, other than those belonging to the bored coat check attendant, I said, "What do you expect me to think? For the last year, you've been coming home late. You're more attentive to everyone else in your life than you are with me."

He admitted nothing. "Be reasonable! Of course, I'm nicer to them. I'm not married to them."

I wasn't sure if the sensitive guy I married was entombed deep within the clueless dolt in front of me, or if he existed only in my imagination. "When you're ready to treat me with as much respect as you treat women who aren't your wife, let me know."

I tried to twist away from him, but he held me fast. "Wait. I know what you're thinking."

"I don't believe you do. Because what I'm thinking is that if you had an affair with Heather or Amanda or, worst of all, Bryony, I could never forgive you." With a sharp jab, I succeeded in getting free of him. "Not because you were unfaithful, although that would hurt. No, I couldn't forgive you for choosing one of them over me. I'd lose all respect for you. If you're going to leave me for another woman, I would hope you'd pick someone smarter and nicer."

The remainder of my argument with George had to wait until we got home since we'd driven separately to the club. Susan, who'd given us a wide berth while we fought, joined me when my car arrived at the front entrance. She plopped herself into the passenger seat with a sigh of relief. I tossed my purse into the car but retrieved it when a glow alerted me to a new text message. I grabbed the phone, hoping it was from Miguel.

The message was from George: **Staying here for a short meeting. Don't wait up.**

I wondered if he was intentionally postponing the inevitable wrangle that faced him when he got home but said nothing about it to Susan. She yawned mightily on the drive home. "I feel as if ten years have passed since this morning. Did we really meet with Mr. and Mrs. Weinstock, the members of The Club, and Leo? The whole day feels like a dream that happened to someone else."

She rolled down the window and sighed. "Instead of that awful dinner, I wish we could have gone home, put our feet up, and drunk wine in our pajamas. Evan, your teacher friend, was a breath of fresh air, but the rest of them? Those are unpleasant people. Liz, I don't know how you stand it."

We stopped at a red light, which allowed me to take my eyes off the road. "Evan Carlsson isn't my friend. I never met him before tonight, and frankly, I'm not looking forward to working with him. When I asked about his previous district, he didn't answer me, which made me think he was hiding something."

Susan warmed to her subject. "Don't be so snippy and judgmental. I thought he was cute."

"I'm not being snippy. Unlike you and Bryony, I have to work with Evan, not fantasize about having sex with him." Cutting my sister off from further speculation about Valerian Hills' newest English teacher, I said, "Any one of today's events would have provided me with sufficient emotional trauma for an entire year. I, not to mention the car, have suffered enough to last quite some time."

I hoped our insurance would cover the cost of repairing the scratches on the side of the car. Or maybe, since we might revisit The Club, I should wait before having them fixed, in case a second assault on the paint occurred. It could have been a lot worse. I was happy the tires and both my knees remained in good working order.

Susan clasped her hands and then shook them out. "Liz, I want you to ignore any texts that Miguel sends you. Forward them to Tom Harriman or Ben Sorkin, and don't answer. I'm worried your former star student is knee-deep in this mess. His behavior is not that of an innocent man."

We rode the rest of the way in silence. I parked the car, and we entered the kitchen, blinking at the blaze of lights that greeted us. Tired as I was, I was too anxious to sleep. Plus, there was that unfinished argument with my husband, which would keep me awake no matter how long it took him to get home.

Since George wasn't around, I quarreled with Susan. "Despite Miguel's sketchy behavior in the aftermath of the murder, I can't believe he's guilty. He has no motive. And, as I've told you a million times, he doesn't fit the profile of a killer. He's a terrific kid with a close family, a lovely fiancée and a promising future. He's too smart to throw all that away."

Susan opened a bottle of red wine. We'd already had plenty to drink, but I didn't refuse her offer of another glass. After pouring the wine, we headed to the front porch so that she could smoke a cigarette.

The alcohol smoothed away some of the pressure that weighed upon me, but the relief vanished when Susan said, "Your entire line of reasoning is faulty. What if Elliot Tumbleson threatened the rosy future Miguel had planned for himself? That's a great motive for murder." She blew a few smoke rings into the air. "He could have a dozen other reasons you don't know about."

"That's pure conjecture. We have definite financial motives for Sonya and Melinda. Cooper is another strong candidate if he's the one who embezzled funds from the club treasury. A kid like Miguel doesn't figure into any of those scenarios, although I'm very suspicious of his cousin Ian. He's the one person who straddles both worlds. Ian told Miguel he didn't know Elliot Tumbleson, but Ian moonlights as a caddy. Maybe that's the connection between them."

Susan tapped her cigarette against an empty soda can, which she used as a makeshift ashtray. "Stop calling Miguel a kid. He's an adult. And you probably don't want to hear my advice, but I'm going to give it to you anyway." She took a deep breath and said, "I think your best bet is to put George on the case."

"You don't know George as well as you think you do. He would never involve himself in a murder investigation. Especially not one that involves his precious club members. Also, we're not partners in anything right now, least of all partners in crime."

The back door slammed. "There he is," said Susan. "Why don't you ask him?"

She took her glass into the guest bedroom, and I entered the kitchen. My husband looked cynically at the wine bottle and at me.

I ignored his look, poured him wine without asking if he wanted any, and got straight to the point. "George, I need your help. For the moment, I'm willing to temporarily put aside our discussion about the unworthy women you admire so much."

"In return for your kindness, I'm willing to temporarily put aside your unfair assumptions about those women." He looked to the ceiling as if expecting celestial help from our fake Tiffany light fixture. "What do you need help with? You're always so determined to do things on your own."

I ignored this patently false statement and said, "You've got access to the club finances and are now in the perfect position to investigate possible motives for Elliot's murder. There may be information about the missing money Cooper hasn't given you."

He switched his attention from the lamp to me but didn't answer. I said, trying to sound encouraging. "Despite all the talk at dinner tonight about Elliot's marriages, I doubt his personal relationships have anything to do with his murder."

George leaned his head to one side, "How did you arrive at this deduction?"

I spoke seriously and without anger, as the motive, if not the person, became clear to me. "Elliot was going to present his financial report to the executive board, but he was quite cagey about what he found. And yet he did tell several members, including you, that he'd uncovered some kind of scam."

George remained skeptical. "That's no help at all. Since he told a bunch of people, and those people probably told a bunch of others, it proves nothing."

"Don't you see? If nothing else, the timing of his murder provides our best clue. Elliot's miserable and abusive relationships with his wife and his ex-wife had been going on forever. But it wasn't until he threatened to reveal what he knew about the club finances that he was killed. You can do this, George! You can investigate the murder. You'll be the hero of the country club."

George pressed his lips into the narrow line of disapproval that was so infuriating to me. "That's your plan? You want me to investigate the very thing that inspired some homicidal maniac to bash Elliot with a golf club? Liz, this is very touching."

I hadn't thought about it in quite that way. Perhaps he had a point. But if he—if we—didn't act, then who would? "The detectives told me that a forensics accountant would review the books and the club's bank account. But how long will that investigation take? And how many more people are in danger? You've already got the same access the police do. And you've got something they don't, which is inside information about the people running the club."

"I suppose this brilliant plan was your sister's idea. Why can't you get her to put a lid on it? She was totally out of line tonight. These are our friends. I found her quite offensive. And I'm sure they did, too, even though everyone was too polite to say so. She can't get through dinner without leaving for a twenty-minute cigarette break." He got a mulish expression on his face as he delivered his ultimatum: "I don't want her at the club anymore."

This punishment didn't carry the same weight for me or Susan as it would have for him. "Put your mind at rest. I doubt she'd ever want to come back."

With unusual meanness, he retorted, "Good. Let's keep it that way."

Because I wanted George to investigate the club's finances, I didn't mention how petty his behavior was. Maybe Bryony, or Heather and Amanda, were having a worse influence on him than I thought.

"My sister did nothing offensive. If anything, she showed more consideration for Sonya than the rest of you. Your friends think that golf solves every problem. Susan was the only one smart enough to be concerned about her safety."

"Your sister has the brains of an amoeba. And you're equally dim for not seeing that."

"And you can't accept the fact that these people are not our friends. I don't understand why Cooper wanted us at his precious club. What's in it for him?"

His cheeks flushed with anger. "You don't value me. That doesn't mean other people don't."

I gave up on the unwinnable argument and addressed a less serious grievance. "I wish you'd asked me before signing us up for the golf tournament. There are plenty of things I do well and that we could enjoy together. Sign us up for a Scrabble tournament. Or a crossword puzzle competition. I'm no athlete, George, and I don't care if I ever get good at golf."

George looked as appalled as if I'd said I was joining a terrorist group, although something about his exaggerated reaction struck me as insincere. "Why don't you just say you don't want to share my life and my interests?"

My heart was beating so fast I could barely breathe. "I thought we already had a life together. Kids together. Are you telling me that to ensure the success of our marriage, we have to play golf together? I'm sorry, George, but that attitude is totally screwed up. I don't know where your values are. But maybe you should start thinking about what's important to you and why." I stalked out of the room and went to the den. I knew that women were supposed to exile their husbands to the den, but I liked the den. The last place I wanted to be was in our marriage bed.

Susan was sleeping in the guest room. I piled pillows and blankets on the sofa and turned the volume down while I watched a documentary on reptiles. Although I was afraid of snakes, I found the discussion of their food choices quite soothing. As the narrator expounded upon their various habitats, I started to relax and was nearly asleep when Miguel texted.

Ian hurt. In ER. Greenbrook Hosp.

Chapter Thirty-One

A fool thinks himself to be wise, but a wise man knows himself to be a fool
—William Shakespeare / As You Like It

M y first impulse, after learning Ian was in the hospital, was to eliminate him as a suspect. Upon reflection, however, I decided those suspicions remained viable. Miguel's cousin could have been an accomplice first and a victim second.

The news was too big to keep to myself. Susan was asleep, but George was awake. He was in bed, thumbing through a stack of papers. I showed him the text and said, "What should we do? Anyone could be next. And by anyone, I mean you or me."

"Don't jump to conclusions. For all you know, Ian could be having his appendix out." George yawned and went back to reading.

I texted Miguel, who answered, **Hit & run/ Ian in surgery.**

The information made no difference to George. He said, "That's a shame, but it's none of our business. Send a nice card and a gift basket."

His offhand comments pained me. "Elliot Tumbleson, the club treasurer, is dead. Ryan Walker, the golf pro, is dead. Magda and Ian, who both work at the club, were attacked. And you want me to sit back and do nothing?"

"The short answer to that question is yes. Magda was hit by a falling tree branch, and Ian got hit by a car. There's nothing to connect them with the person who killed Elliot and Ryan. Let the police handle the investigation. You'll only get in the way." He rubbed his nose and yawned again. "Keep your mouth shut, and don't do anything stupid."

189

"I'll do as you say under one condition. We quit the club and use the money to rent a damp cabin in the Adirondacks this summer." Too on edge to sit down, I paced the room, rearranging framed photos that didn't need to be moved.

George threw off the blankets. "Stop fidgeting! I don't know what's gotten into you lately, but you hate vacationing in the Adirondacks."

His sharp tone startled me, and I dropped a picture of us on our honeymoon. Careful not to cut myself, I swept the broken glass into the trash can. I was aware of the unintentional symbolism in the gesture but kept it to myself.

"George, please hear me out. I was wrong to complain about our summer vacations. There, at least, we had each other. I don't like the Meadowfields Country Club. Or golf. Or most of the people we've met." I didn't let myself cry. I didn't want to win because he felt sorry for me. I wanted him to understand and agree with me because he felt the same way.

"Let's not relitigate an issue that's been decided. The kids are going to love going to the pool this summer. And you'll make new friends. I've always wanted to join the club, and thanks to Cooper, who pulled all kinds of strings, I could." Behind his cajoling tone, I felt his anger. And his disappointment.

The solution to this problem, unlike all the others, was easy. "Fine. You go. Enjoy the country club all you want. But I quit."

"If that's what you want, I can't force you to do the one thing that would bring us together." His accusatory stare was as fierce as if I'd mortally wounded him. "But don't get involved with this murder investigation. Let Sorkin and Harriman do their job. No investigating. No interrogating. Send that gift basket to Ian and forget about it."

I didn't argue the point, because I had no intention of doing what he asked, and further discussion was unlikely to sway either of us. Instead, I looked over his shoulders at the reports he'd been studying. "Is Cooper involved with a new real estate deal?"

He bundled the papers into a folder. "These are some of the financial records from the club."

His hypocrisy floored me. "Have you been investigating without telling me?"

"Of course not. This has nothing to do with the murder. Our club is negotiating a merger with the one in Clairmont. I'm the new assistant treasurer, remember?"

I sat next to him. "How could I forget? So…what have you learned?"

George spoke without hesitation, almost as if he'd rehearsed the answer. "Thirty thousand dollars went missing, along with the last three months of any kind of paper trail. The online records appear to have been doctored. It has to get cleaned up before we can move forward with the merger."

This example of irony I didn't keep to myself. "How could you tell me not to get involved with the murder investigation when what you're doing is way more dangerous than anything I've planned? If you have the same information that Elliot did, who's to say you won't be the next victim?"

"What I'm doing isn't dangerous. I'm helping the club with their current financial reports, not with anything that happened previously."

I was loath to ask George the question uppermost in my mind, but, in the end, I was too worried about him to stop myself. "Did Cooper ask you to cover for him? Every time he snaps his fingers, you jump through hoops. It's demeaning. And now, it's dangerous. I'm scared that he's asked you to do something he doesn't want to. Is he trying to keep his hands clean by dirtying yours?"

George threw off the covers, and I followed him to the kitchen. He poured a large glass of water and gulped it down, along with two of my Excedrin. "You're dramatizing a very ordinary situation. The directors have decided to eat the loss and move on. It sounds like a lot of money to us, but it's not for them. That's what tonight's meeting was about."

He drummed his fingers on the counter and said, "Cooper now thinks Elliot took the money, cooked the books, and planned to pin the theft on someone else. That's the other reason the board wants to sweep this under the rug. Elliot was in a bigger financial hole than any of us knew, but no one wants to go after his estate to recoup the cash. Sonya has been through enough. If we delay the merger, that'll cost us more than thirty thousand dollars. It's not a decision they came to lightly, but it's the best way to deal with the mess."

This new evidence appeared to eliminate embezzlement as a motive for murder, but it all seemed a bit too convenient for Cooper to blame the victim for the crime. "Since Elliot can't defend himself, I'm going to reserve judgment. We don't know if he removed the files for safekeeping or if the killer did." I drank George's water, which annoyed him more than it should have since we were standing next to the faucet.

He massaged his temples. "My point is that what I'm doing is a routine part of my job and not as risky as you skulking around the club, looking for clues like an amateur Nancy Drew."

I corrected him, because literary references were important to me. "I'm not *like* an amateur Nancy Drew because Nancy Drew was an amateur. Like me. You, however, are underestimating the danger. Does anyone know you copied these records? You don't know what you're dealing with, and you don't have the kind of experience that would help you figure it out."

He rubbed his bloodshot eyes. "And you do?"

"Yes. My family lived from one scam to the next. Stolen goods, pirated cable connections, you name it, and they did it."

He patted my head. "You're out of your depth, Brooklyn girl. This is high finance. Not petty theft."

"The principle is the same, and so are the people." I told him about Uncle Milton, and how he torched his dry cleaning store to collect on the insurance, and how Aunt Rose skimmed money from the PTA. George didn't see the parallels that, to me, were obvious.

We returned to the bedroom. I grabbed his folder and removed several papers, which George tried to pry from my grasp. When he realized he would either have to relinquish his hold or allow me to tear them in half, he reluctantly let me have them.

Holding the papers behind my back, I said, "I'll make you a deal. I'll refrain from investigating the murder if you tell me everything you learn about the club finances."

He agreed, even though he didn't believe me. I handed the papers back, even though I didn't believe him.

After he fell asleep, I snapped a picture of each page. Then I tiptoed downstairs, too guilty about violating my promise to George to sleep. The motion-detector light on the back porch unexpectedly clicked on, bathing the rear of the house with bright white light. I assumed it was a raccoon and nearly fainted when a pale face loomed outside, a few inches away.

Miguel had finally shown up.

* * *

He refused to come inside. Anticipating a rebuke, he said, "I know what you're going to say. I should have been in touch with you. But Ian and Magda and the rest of my friends didn't want you involved."

I trembled, unnerved by his surprise visit. "Ian and Magda are in the hospital. Those plans didn't work out too well for them."

"You don't know the whole story of why we're so protective of each other. Three kitchen workers have undocumented family members. An investigation could put them in jeopardy." Miguel wiped his sweaty forehead with his sleeve. "I think I'm being watched."

"By whom? The police?"

The sound of the wind in the trees made him jump. "I don't know. Just like I don't know who reported me as being at the scene of the crime." He bounced on the balls of his feet like a runner ready to take off. "I have to get back to the hospital. Ian is in critical condition."

"Surely, you didn't come to my house in the middle of the night to say hello. Tell me why you're here."

"The police have called me in twice. They searched my house, but they didn't find anything, because there was nothing to find. They subpoenaed my bank records, and again, there's nothing to find, other than the fact that I'm in debt up to my ears with college loans. I want you to talk to the cops and find out who fingered me so I can talk to them."

Miguel's desire to confront Bryony was a literal dead end, as she had merely reported what Ryan told her. "If the police thought they had evidence from a credible eyewitness, you would have been charged. More important is the fact that someone stole thirty thousand dollars from the club. When the police find out who did it, they'll have the murderer. I sincerely hope your cousin makes a full and fast recovery, because I think Ian is the key to answering that question."

Miguel looked at the overhead light. "Is there any way to turn this thing off?"

I flipped the switches for the outside lights and dimmed the ones in the kitchen. Miguel retreated into the darkness of the back porch.

"Tell me," I implored him. "Let me help."

Miguel wiped his hands on his pants. "If I tell you, you have to swear not to tell anyone. Not the police, not anyone at the club. Swear to me."

I backed away from him. "If you tell me that someone else is in danger, I'll have to notify the police. You can understand that, right?"

"This doesn't involve hurting people. Physically hurting them, that is." He looked away from me. "But it is about money. That's not my secret to tell."

Initially, I'd suspected Ian of using Miguel as a fall guy. Another possibility, though, was that someone else was using Ian. Or paying him off.

I hesitated a moment too long. The kitchen light clicked back on, and Miguel fled.

Ellie screeched when I walked inside. "What were you doing on the back porch?" She had her hands behind her back.

"I needed some fresh air. What are you hiding?" Guilty Mother thoughts haunted me. Was my daughter drinking beer or guzzling whiskey in the middle of the night while her clueless parents snored?

She sighed and showed me the silver can. "I'm the one stealing your diet soda."

Chapter Thirty-Two

...every subject's soul is his own
—William Shakespeare / Henry V

I planned to see Ian early the following day, but visiting hours didn't begin until ten o'clock. The cocktails and wine I'd drunk at dinner left me with a cottonmouth, a dull headache, and a sluggish body. Because I'd spent the previous day in Brooklyn, instead of stocking up on groceries in Oak Ridge, the cupboard was without basic provisions. I went to the bagel store and purchased a feast.

Two cups of coffee and a bagel topped with lox worked magic on my mood and my hangover. Tossing aside the Sunday crossword puzzle, which was filled with clues less challenging than those surrounding Elliot's murder, I reread the notes I'd taken on each possible suspect.

Susan ambled into the kitchen and, after professing great anger that I'd bought such a fattening breakfast, helped herself to a bagel and butter. When I told her of Miguel's late-night visit, she was outraged.

"Why didn't you wake me?" She pushed her plate away with an impatient sweep of her arm. "He could have killed you!"

"Miguel is in a very fragile state. He would have run for the hills if he knew I'd dragged you into this mess." Thinking of his hasty retreat, I added, "He's scared, though not because he's guilty. He's trying to protect people who don't deserve his loyalty."

She sat back in her chair and crossed her arms. "You're as bad as he is. Miguel doesn't trust you because he knows how smart you are."

195

I told her about Ian's accident and showed her my notebook. If she could follow my reasoning, she would, hopefully, come to a similar conclusion.

I underlined the name that headed my list of suspects. "Elliot's death put Cooper conveniently in charge of the club finances. And now, there's a new wrinkle. Cooper is claiming Elliot stole the money and was going to accuse someone else of the theft to cover it up. That would also explain how and why the records were deleted."

Susan's reaction was the same as mine. "Cooper's theory very conveniently exonerates Cooper. I wonder if Bryony is the one who concocted that alibi, although I think she's more likely to turn on her husband than perjure herself to help him out."

I kept my promise to George and didn't show Susan the copies I'd made of the financial reports. As far as I could tell, they didn't reveal any irregularities, but my findings were far from conclusive. The mind-numbing columns of numbers and their explanatory notations needed an expert financial advisor, not an English teacher whose depth of accounting knowledge could be measured in microns.

I also couldn't discuss with Susan my fears about George's involvement. Did my husband know who embezzled the money? And if he did know, was he covering up Cooper's theft as payback for that country club membership we couldn't afford?

I banished these disloyal musings and said, "The simplest solutions are more likely to be correct, and when Bryony claimed she couldn't distinguish one waiter from another, she was probably telling the truth. This doesn't make her any nicer, but it does absolve her of deliberately plotting the conviction of an innocent man. Ben Sorkin and Tom Harriman are intelligent and experienced detectives. They probably already knew Bryony wasn't going to make an ideal eyewitness, especially since she claimed to have seen Miguel from a distance of nearly fifty yards."

Then I remembered what Bryony said at dinner, the niggling detail I'd missed. "She told the police she saw Miguel at the scene of the crime. Later, she claimed it was Cooper who saw him. But last night, she said it was Ryan who identified him, which she might have done to cover for her husband."

Susan's eyes widened in excitement. "We already know Cooper had the means and the motive. It looks now as if he also had the opportunity. Talk to George."

"Talk to George about what?" My husband's voice startled me. I wondered how long he'd been listening in.

I offered him a bagel. "Was Cooper with you all afternoon on the day Elliot was murdered?"

He hacked the bagel in half. "If you think I'm going to implicate my boss, who's shown us nothing but kindness, forget it."

Fear, combined with a too-large bite of bagel and cream cheese, stuck in my throat. "If your boss is a cold-blooded killer, then yes, I do think you need to implicate him."

"I don't know the precise time Elliot was killed." He jabbed his knife into the cream cheese and mumbled a few words about eating his breakfast in peace.

I gulped a mouthful of bitter coffee. "This isn't difficult. Did Cooper leave for any length of time?"

"He did. So did Amanda and Heather. So did I. Are you going to accuse me next? Maybe you want to talk to your boyfriends on the force, so they can haul me in for another of their little chats." His voice was soft. Perhaps it was Susan's presence in the room, or his fear that Zach or Ellie would overhear, that kept him from blowing up at me.

George hadn't told me the detectives did a follow-up interview with him. "This isn't an accusation. All I'm asking for is information you already have. You know the country club crowd better than I do. You've got access to the financial records. You were with Cooper at or about the time when the murder happened."

The next part of what I wanted to say was the hardest. I couldn't do it with my sister in the room. She understood what I needed without words and took her coffee and the newspaper to the guest bedroom.

When she was out of earshot, I said, "I don't want to destroy your job and friendships. I'm worried about you, because I think your boss may be guilty of theft or worse, and you're too close to him to see the danger. And I can help. I'm not like Bryony. I don't accuse innocent people."

When he spoke, it was as if each syllable had been dragged out of him. "I can't account for Cooper's whereabouts for the entire afternoon. Same for Amanda. That doesn't mean they killed Elliot. I don't know who embezzled the club funds, although Cooper's explanation is plausible. Are you happy now?"

His reluctant answer confirmed my growing suspicion about Cooper. George's boss had the opportunity, as well as the means and the motive, to kill Elliot. Cooper's uncharacteristically altruistic offer to employ Miguel at one of his buildings now looked less like a favor and more like a trap.

Susan descended the stairs with a heavy tread. She paused at the doorway. "Ellie and Zach are awake. I want to spend some alone time with them if that's okay with you. They're my favorite niece and nephew."

In an attempt to mask the thick haze of tension between us, George got busy reading the newspaper, and I stacked plates in the dishwasher. The bagels provided a further distraction for the kids. When Susan offered to take them shopping, Ellie was thrilled. My sister loved to shop and was a much better and more generous companion than I was. Zach was harder to persuade, but when Susan mentioned a sale on the pricey sneakers I'd never in a million years buy him, he was all in.

* * *

I didn't text Miguel before arriving at the hospital, but when I entered the crowded waiting room and took the chair next to him, he wasn't surprised to see me.

He sat, half facing me and half facing the wall behind him. "Thanks for coming, but only family members can visit Ian. I'll let him know you were here."

"I wanted to see you more than I wanted to see Ian. If you can't be honest with me now, after all that's happened, I won't bother you again. At this point, I care less about you and your cousin than I do about my family and my friends."

Although calling any of my suspects a friend was a stretch, I couldn't come up with a more precise description. How else could I term my relationships with the members of the Meadowfields Country Club? No single word sufficed.

He inched his chair closer to the wall. "I haven't lied to you."

"You lied by omission."

He worked his lower lip the same way he used to do when taking a test in English class. "Let's get out of here. I can't talk with all this noise."

I followed him into the elevator. We rode to the top floor and walked down a maze of hospital corridors that ended at an exit door that brought us to a deserted concrete seating area. A few scraggly trees in boxes provided a hint of green. He peered over the railing at the streetscape below. I stayed a few feet behind. I was afraid of heights and, for a brief moment, afraid of Miguel as well. The blank windows of the hospital complex were our only witnesses.

He turned and said, "Does anyone know you're here?"

"Yes. My sister knows." I held up my phone, because he was too far away to check if I was telling the truth. "She's downstairs, and at my signal, she'll send out an alert if she thinks I'm in danger."

His laughter had a hysterical edge to it. It didn't reassure me. But his words did. "You're in no danger from me, Ms. Hopewell. But if anyone finds out you've talked to me, you will be. No one close to me is safe. That's what Mr. Aldridge said, and he's right."

I sank onto the concrete bench. Although I'd suspected Cooper Aldridge was guilty, having Miguel confirm those suspicions took my breath away. "Tell me everything. Then we'll figure out what to do."

He gripped the railing with white-knuckled hands. "You can't do anything, and I'm too afraid of what might happen next."

"I swear, I won't do or say anything without your approval. If nothing else, telling another person what you're going through will help."

His words came in hesitant spurts. "Mr. Aldridge insists he saw me at the scene of the crime. But like I told you, I was late to work and didn't arrive until after the murder. Mr. Aldridge said he didn't want to get me in trouble and would tell the cops we were together at the snack bar in case anyone else saw me. I said okay, because I was worried he mistook me for Ian. Then someone, not Mr. Aldridge, did tell the cops. That's why I wanted you to tell me who blabbed. The only two people who knew the truth were both attacked."

"You're not thinking straight. Mr. Aldridge gave you an alibi you didn't need and made it look like he was doing you a favor. But the real reason he did that was so he could pressure you into covering up for him. Why didn't you come clean? You would have saved yourself a lot of trouble if you did." I pulled a few tissues from my bag and handed them to him.

He wiped his eyes. "The day after the murder, Ian said the club was going to let me go. He didn't know why. I was scared to tell the cops that I lied to them, but Mr. Aldridge said not to worry and that if I quit right away, he'd get me a better job."

It was a good thing Cooper wasn't with us on that roof. I would have been tempted to shove him off, not only for the murders but also for taking advantage of Miguel. "This seems like an impossible situation, but it isn't. I'll go with you to the police. Let them take it from here."

"No! It gets worse. On the day Mr. Walker died, Mr. Aldridge wanted Ian to caddy for him. There's a lot more money caddying for someone like Mr. Aldridge than there is at the snack bar, so Ian asked me to cover his shift." He shuddered. "It was like the same nightmare happening twice. I was on my break when I saw your sister fall onto the grass. I thought maybe she was sick. I ran to help. Do you have any idea how I felt when I found out there was another dead body? With me right there? It would have been my word against Mr. Aldridge's. I'd have to find someone who saw me sitting by myself behind the snack bar. Who do you think the cops are going to believe?"

Nothing in my experience equipped me for this situation, other than a lifelong addiction to books. If there was an answer to this conundrum, surely there was a writer much smarter than I was who could help us.

Only one that came to mind. "We need to beat the killer at his own game. *The play's the thing.*"

The iconic words didn't console or convince my former student. "Isn't that from *Hamlet?*"

"Yes. Well done, Miguel." I was pleased he'd remembered.

"Ms. Hopewell, didn't everyone die at the end?"

It was a legitimate argument. "There's a few left standing. And our plot doesn't have to follow the original that closely. If we set things up the right way, Cooper Aldridge will reveal himself as the killer."

Chapter Thirty-Three

That one may smile and smile and be a villain
—William Shakespeare / Hamlet

I believed Cooper Aldridge was guilty, but before moving forward, or talking to Ben, I wanted to get all the facts in order. In the messy tangle of interconnected relationships at the Meadowfields Country Club, the two murder victims played very different roles. Ryan Walker was a favorite among the women, including those who had limited their enjoyment of his company to the golf course. His amorous extracurricular activities also made him popular with the men, other than a few disgruntled husbands. Perhaps they admired his success. If the stories about him were true, he'd been a sexual superman.

Elliot Tumbleson, however, was widely disliked. His detractors included his ex-wife, the head groundskeeper, the caddies, the waitstaff, Bryony, and Cooper. His second wife gave a credible performance as a woman in mourning, but Sonya's actions told a different story. Days after her husband's death, she was back in the social swing of dinners, tennis matches, and golf tournaments. I didn't blame her. After suffering the torments of an abusive marriage, the woman was entitled to party.

Hardcore golfers like Mark Felician were more upset over the temporary closing of the course than they were about the murder, and they thought Elliot had shown extreme bad taste by getting himself killed on country club property. The consensus, according to the affable club president, was that a better-mannered man would have arranged to die on a publicly owned stretch of grass.

Although Elliot's familial relationships provided multiple motives for murder, the financial incentive remained the most credible. His ex-wife and current wife would collect on his life insurance, which would also benefit each woman's son. Melinda Tumbleson's angry words on the day Elliot died *I'll see you dead before I let you get away with this* may not have been an idle threat.

Cooper, however, had the strongest motive for murder. If he embezzled money from the club, and Elliot threatened to expose him, George's boss would stop at nothing to protect himself and his reputation. This theory presumed Cooper was a thief as well as a murderer, which required no great stretch of the imagination. It also explained his desire to have George, whose livelihood depended on him, join the club and be appointed assistant treasurer.

Although the motive for the first murder was an open question, the motive for the second was clear. Someone, probably Cooper, killed Ryan to keep him quiet. The golf pro had disappeared several times during my first lesson, ostensibly to replenish the supply of balls. Perhaps Ryan witnessed Elliot's murder. Or maybe he questioned Cooper after seeing him with Elliot. If that were the case, the only reasonable conclusion I could draw from Ryan's subsequent silence was that he'd attempted to blackmail the killer. This gave me an additional clue: if the person who killed Elliot Tumbleson did so in the heat of the moment, he or she quite coldly planned the second attack. That profile fit Cooper better than it did Melinda or Sonya.

Miguel was right to fear Cooper, and I understood better why my former student had avoided me. The two people he'd confided in had both been attacked. What I didn't yet know was the role Miguel's cousin played in Cooper's schemes. Ian was the wild card.

* * *

The house was empty when I returned from the hospital. I scrolled through my contacts and stopped at Ben Sorkin's name but didn't tap the number.

The information I wanted to share with him didn't rise to the level of an emergency that could justify interrupting a Sunday afternoon. I wondered if he was married or if he had kids. He didn't wear a wedding band but that was no guarantee he was single.

I took advantage of my solitude to plan a trap for Cooper, one that would lure him into confessing his guilt without using myself as bait. Despite my grand promise to Miguel, it didn't have to rise to the level of Shakespearean deception and tragedy to get the job done.

I was mulling over possible scenarios when Susan and the kids returned, bearing many packages. Ellie and Zach retreated to their bedrooms, and my sister lay on the sofa and fanned herself with a section of the newspaper. "They wore me out, and I'm too tired to take the train home. Is it okay if I extend my stay at Chez Hopewell?"

I took a pan of lasagna out of the freezer. "As long as you don't complain about the menu, you're welcome to stay as long as you like."

"What were you up to while we were gone? I hope it wasn't grading papers." She inspected my fingers and face. "I see it wasn't a manicure or facial."

My sister wasn't pleased to have been left out of the meeting with Miguel. "I'm thankful the police didn't have to clean your mangled remains off the sidewalk but angry that you were so reckless. What grand scheme have you hatched to nail Cooper?"

"It's a work in progress. I'm going to make up some excuse to meet with him. I haven't gotten much beyond that."

She closed her eyes and rubbed her forehead. I recognized the gesture as one I often used when I wanted to stimulate my brain cells. When hers became sufficiently engaged, she said, "Call Tom Harriman. Tell him everything and see what he says." She wagged a finger at me. "Is he still swooning over you and your literary references? You should leave him to me. Ben Sorkin sounds like he's more your type."

"You seem to have forgotten that I'm married." As if to emphasize my point, George pulled into the driveway.

Coolly, she said, "Yes. But you are *malheureux*." When I didn't respond, she translated, "But you are not happy."

I crumpled a piece of paper and threw it at her head. "You didn't have to translate for me. I got it the first time." My sister's habit of inserting French phrases was always mildly annoying, but when she went all Gallic on me during a serious conversation, it was infuriating.

She tossed the paper ball back to me. "I don't blame you for being aggravated. If I saw any of my husbands hanging out with those two good-time golfing girls, I'd ditch him. What were their names, again?"

Through stiff lips, I said, "Heather and Amanda."

George, as if to prove Susan's point about our marriage, walked in, grunted a greeting, and went upstairs.

I said, without my former confidence, "George would never cheat on me."

Susan made a shooing motion with her hand. "Of course, he would. I mean, it's possible he hasn't cheated on you. My purpose, however, in having this discussion is not to speculate about your husband's infidelities. I've always rather fancied your police detective. If you want him, then fine. But if you don't..."

Unwilling to address any of the issues that interested Susan, I left the living room and started cleaning the kitchen. She followed me, and although she didn't help, she did respect my desire to avoid discussions of infidelity.

I scrubbed the countertop and said, "I'm going to hold off contacting the detectives until tomorrow morning."

She blew a Bronx cheer through pursed lips. "Suit yourself. I'm out of here."

"That's easy for you to say. Right now, I'm worried more about George's safety than I am about his sex life." I threw the sponge into the sink, took out a broom and dustpan, and began sweeping the floor.

Susan assumed a penitent expression as she watched me clean. "Is George going to help investigate? He isn't a threat to anyone, so he should be fine."

"Thank you for your concern." George stood in the doorway. His hair stuck up in unattractive spikes, his eyes were red, and his skin had a greenish cast to it.

Susan smiled. "Don't take things so personally."

He poured a glass of water and sat at the table with one hand pressed against his abdomen.

"Stomachache?" asked Susan.

He nodded. "Stomachache and headache."

My sister inspected him. "Maybe you're feeling the effects of last night's alcohol. I have an excellent recipe for hangovers. You take two raw eggs, mix them with ketchup and Worcestershire sauce—"

"Stop!" George whispered in a hoarse voice. "One more word of that recipe, and I will vomit all over this table."

I moved a bowl of fruit to the other side of the kitchen and away from possible stomach flu germs. "George, I'm sorry you're not feeling well, but we have to talk." I blinked at Susan, who took the hint and retreated to the guest bedroom. "However good or bad our marriage is right now, it doesn't mean I want you dead."

His eyes watered. "While I appreciate the fact that you don't want me dead, I don't see how butting into a murder investigation is going to keep me safe. Probably the opposite."

I handed him a bottle of Tylenol. "You're too close to all the suspects. The only way to protect yourself, and any future victims, is to find evidence against the killer."

George swallowed the pills. "Once again, you're jumping to conclusions. It may be hard for you to fathom, but not everyone is as obsessed as you are. I tried talking to Cooper about untangling the club's financial records, but he wasn't interested. He even told me to forget about trying to balance the books. Said he'd hand it over to his personal accountant."

I gripped George's cold, damp hand. He pulled it away, complaining, "You trying to kill me? What's the problem now?"

I squelched the sarcastic response that rose to my mind and filed it away for a future argument. George's situation—our situation—was too dire for me to joke.

"Don't you see? Cooper must be the killer! He was the assistant treasurer when Elliot was treasurer. He had the best opportunity, after Elliot, to screw with the books. That's why he wants you to drop it. He's afraid of what you'll find."

He shaded his eyes from the bright sunshine that cut across the kitchen table. "You get an A for creativity. But an F for factual evidence. Cooper was with me and two of our clients for the entire afternoon."

"That's not what you told me before. You said he and Amanda went off together. Maybe they're both guilty."

"He, er, he did leave with Amanda, but not to commit murder." George drained his glass. "What are you thinking? That Cooper—and this is my boss we're talking about—that Cooper conked Elliot with your golf club in a brutal act of violence? Sorry, Liz. You're going to have to do better than that."

"It wouldn't have taken long for him to kill Elliot and return to the course. What are we talking about? Ten minutes? I saw him shortly before my clubs disappeared, which means he had the opportunity to grab one of them and hide it."

"If you're going to make unfounded accusations, pick someone who isn't paying my salary." He saw my face and added, in a more conciliatory tone, "What I mean is, you should focus on someone who is a better suspect."

George's words made me more suspicious of Cooper, not less. My husband had been in the company of two beautiful women. Cooper could have been gone for two days without George realizing how much time had passed.

I tried to keep the bitterness from my voice. "What about the two, uh, clients you played golf with? Can you vouch for them?"

"I know your opinion of Heather and Amanda. But I can't imagine either of them committing a violent crime."

I resisted the urge to beat him over the head with the broom. "The fact that you can't imagine something doesn't mean it's not possible. I repeat the question: Did either one of the two ladies and I use the term loosely, leave the golf course? And if so, for how long?"

George squinted as if trying to see the scene. "They did. But not singly. They left together and returned together. So unless you think they hatched a plot to kill a man neither had ever met, I think your suspicions about them are as off base as those about Cooper."

Susan wandered back into the kitchen in time to hear George's last words, although I suspected she'd listened to the whole conversation. She said, "What if the murderer's motivation isn't financial? Maybe money had nothing to do with it, and it was a crime of the heart."

I considered again this possible motive. "We shouldn't eliminate alternate explanations, but I keep coming back to the timing of the attack. Elliot was killed a few hours before he was due to present his report to the members of the board. To me, that's a powerful argument for a financial motive." Before Susan or George could poke holes in my theory, I did so myself. "But it's not conclusive. The timing could be coincidental. Or someone could have framed Cooper, knowing that his involvement with the club finances would cast suspicion on him."

Susan was impatient. "All we do is talk. What do we do? We need a plan. A way to test our theories."

George put his head in his hands. I handed him an ice pack wrapped in a dish towel. As a detective, I might lack skills, but there wasn't much I didn't know about treating a headache.

I picked at a leftover bagel. "Susan is right. We have to think of some way for the killer to implicate himself."

My sister grabbed my shoulders in an excess of excitement. "What if we send an anonymous note to each of the suspects? We say something like, I know what happened to Elliot. And…and then set up a meeting."

She steamrolled past our reasoned objections. "I'll wear a wire! And then we can catch the murderer on tape, and I'll be a hero. I can see myself now, on a late-night news show, talking about my upcoming true crime book." Susan went into the bathroom to reapply her lipstick, as if this imaginary television show appearance was scheduled to begin. When she returned, she said, "I know a lot of people in publishing. We'll make a killing. No pun intended, of course."

George slammed the ice pack on the table. "This is not a game. It's also not one of your online dating hookups. If the murderer shows up, he'll attack first and ask questions later. Do you want your head bashed in and your brains spilled over the pavement like the other victims?"

"Don't be so graphic. You know I hate blood, cruelty, and all violence."

"Given your sensitive and delicate nature, perhaps you're not the best pick as an investigator." He went back to propping up his head with his hands. "If anyone does take part in this insane plot, it should be me. The two of you don't stand a chance."

I felt insulted. "You're one of the worst liars I've ever met. I'm a much better liar."

In a tone that allowed no argument, Susan said, "I lie better than both of you combined. You said it yourself, George: I do a lot of online dating. No one's better at lying, or spotting a liar, than someone who's got six different profiles on six different sites."

My sister's claim of superiority had merit, and George ceded the field. "I'm going to take this horrible headache back to bed. Don't plot anything without me. And don't do anything without me. You'll get yourselves killed, and then I'll have to deal with a ton of paperwork."

I wasn't amused by his weak attempt at a joke. Nor was I consoled by his promise to help unmask the killer. His words reminded me of *Hamlet*. Like the tortured prince's mother, the guy protested too much.

Chapter Thirty-Four

Though I am not naturally honest, I am so sometimes by chance.
—William Shakespeare / A Winter's Tale

The following morning, Susan boarded an early train back to the city, and the kids left for school in a wordless, teenage stupor. George didn't get out of bed. He claimed he was sick and running a fever, but he looked fine to me.

Under his watchful gaze, I dressed in a new pair of black pants and a fitted shirt with a deep V-neck that wasn't in my usual workday rotation. A gold brooch kept the blouse closed at a level high enough to make it school-appropriate. I styled my hair with a blow dryer and a quart of expensive lotion, applied two coats of mascara, and swiped my mouth with Barcelona Red lipstick.

These grooming rituals annoyed George. "What's taking so long? You're going to be late."

"I've got my disciplinary hearing today, and I want to look nice for the perp walk." His impatience made me suspicious. "Are you trying to get rid of me?"

He retrieved his phone from the night table and sent a long text before answering. "Yes. I can't get back to sleep while you're futzing about."

"Then I'll go." I packed graded essays into my schoolbag and left, but not without wondering what George was plotting. As Susan noted the previous evening, he wasn't a good liar.

A full day of classes, a three-hour rehearsal of the school play, and a disciplinary hearing with the principal deterred me from following George's lead and calling in sick. Without those burdens, I would have spent the day staking out my house and husband. It's one thing to lie to your boss about why you're not showing up for work. It's quite another to lie to your wife. Did he think I'd out him to Cooper? Or was the subterfuge meant for me?

Teaching, rehearsing, and defending myself against Melinda Tumbleson's accusations of incompetence weren't the only reasons why I didn't take a sick day. It was the promise of a different sort of appointment that propelled me out of the house.

I took a deep breath, called Ben Sorkin, and asked if he and Tom could meet me at the end of the day.

Ben answered after the first ring. "Tom can't make it, but I'll be there. Three o'clock, okay?"

"I've got play rehearsals until six. Is that too late?" The nervous flutter that strained my vocal cords had nothing to do with the murder investigation.

"Even better. See you then."

I had many reasons for wanting to see Ben, other than the one that prompted the extra makeup and new clothes. With no assurance from Miguel as to when, or if, he'd tell the detectives about covering up for Cooper and Ian, it was up to me to do so. Miguel might view this act as a betrayal of trust, but he faced greater peril from the man who'd killed two people than he did from the police.

Although unsure about the method by which I would get evidence of Cooper's guilt, I was certain of where and when it would happen. There was no more appropriate venue for the killer's downfall than the scene of the crime, where every player in this tragedy would be present. I texted George to tell him I'd changed my mind about joining him, Bryony, and Cooper at the Meadowfields Country Club Spring Fling Golf Tournament.

* * *

My students were in a Monday morning fog of resentful exhaustion, which lifted when they learned I wasn't going to spend an hour talking at them.

Instead, I put them in groups to rehearse sections of *Hamlet*. Their interest level rose considerably when I handed out plastic crowns and cardboard swords. While they enacted fight scenes, I contemplated my looming disciplinary hearing.

Mrs. Sugarman's accusation of unprofessional conduct wouldn't have gotten as far as it did without Melinda's interference, but the timing, for me, was fortuitous. If the situation had arisen in September, Timmy would surely have decided in favor of the board president, her friend, and their two sons, who were stars of the football team. But with Jack and Kevin set to graduate in a scant two months, I was less certain Timmy would cave. He didn't care about the success of the school play, where Jack played a different sort of leading role.

The subject of these unsettling calculations abandoned his group and slammed his *1984* essay on my desk. "What's this supposed to mean?" Jack stabbed his middle finger on the notes I'd appended to the last page of his work.

"I'm offering you a second chance to submit your essay. If you don't want to rewrite it, I'll grade it as is."

Jack's homelife, not his writing, had made any fair assessment of his work impossible. Although he'd written the essay, or, to be precise, copied and pasted it, before his father was murdered, I couldn't bring myself to add to his troubles by charging him with plagiarism and giving him a zero.

He put his hands on my desk and leaned over me. "Why would I want to rewrite it?"

The online tool I used to check for plagiarized text lit up like Times Square when I uploaded Jack's essay, but I didn't want to embarrass him in front of his classmates. "Let's talk about it after school."

Jack sneered at me with the self-assurance of a conventionally good-looking boy who'd been told his whole life how wonderful he was. But he also was a kid whose murdered father had rejected him. I spoke softly. "If you don't want to talk to me, we can discuss this with the principal and your guidance counselor."

He rolled the essay into a thin tube and beat it against his palm. "Thanks anyway, Ms. Hopewell, but you're the one going to the principal's office."

He crumpled the paper and tossed it in the wastebasket. All but one of my well-behaved students gasped. Kevin was the holdout. He clapped his hands in a slow, amused rhythm.

The shrill clang of a fire alarm claimed our attention. Failure to obey the rules for a fire drill was one of the few infractions that earned swift and dire disciplinary consequences. Jack and Kevin, along with the rest of the students, trooped out of the classroom, leaving their backpacks but taking their phones. Their prompt departure was also fueled by the promise of a walk outdoors with their friends. Exits from the building invariably took less time than reentries.

I grabbed Emily, who was on hall duty and thus didn't have to escort an assigned group of students. "Can you do me a favor? Take over for me. My class lines up in the parking lot. The kids know where to go."

Emily knew I wouldn't have asked her to take my place if it wasn't important. The penalties for teacher noncompliance at fire drills were worse than for students. She prompted Jack and Kevin to catch up with the rest of the class and led them toward the closest exit. When the coast was clear, I locked the door, closed the shades, and opened Jack's backpack. I figured any dirt I could get on him would help me fight the trumped-up charges he and his mother were planning to perpetrate upon me.

I unearthed a half-finished math worksheet and a chemistry test that had a large red F written across the top of the page. Thanks to our online grading system, I already knew the extent of Jack's academic problems. I kept digging. A candy bar, a pack of rolling papers, and a box of condoms were in the front pocket. I hoped the last item was for show and not for use. The world wasn't ready for a new generation of Tumblesons.

I removed a large notebook and a smelly lunch bag to get at the zippered pocket inside, where I found a Christmas card from his father. On the front was a picture of Elliot, his second wife, Sonya, and Jack's adorable half-brother. Their bright smiles mirrored the sparkling winter wonderland backdrop. Underneath the photo was the caption *Seasons Greetings from the Tumbleson Family.*

The sentiment that inspired Jack to keep the card was explicit and ugly. Each face had a thick black X across it. The bodies of his father, stepmother, and half-brother were pockmarked with ragged holes. He must have used a pen, or something sharper, to stab the thick paper.

Jack had stored the card in his backpack since December. Four months had elapsed since he received it. Some of the holes in the card were frayed, but others had clean edges, which suggested his rage hadn't abated.

The drumbeat of footsteps accompanied by peals of raucous laughter jolted me out of my trance. I replaced the card, the lunch bag, and the books in Jack's backpack and unlocked the door. When the kids returned, I told them since the class was due to end in five minutes, they could enjoy some free time.

Jack waved at me as if flagging a taxi. "Hey, Ms. Hopewell, how come you didn't go on the fire drill? Isn't that against the rules?"

"The only rule that should concern you is the one that requires a passing grade in all your classes to participate in the school play. I'll let you know later today if you're eligible."

His face lost its arrogant complacency. "You can't do that! My mother won't let you! She'll get you fired."

I leaned toward him and spoke in a stage whisper that could have been heard in the neighboring county. "I hate to think what your friends would say if they knew you were the reason the show got canceled."

He opened and closed his sulky mouth, like a fish that can't believe it got hooked. "But I'm the star."

I corrected him. "You were the star."

* * *

The exchange with Jack wore me out, and I needed all the strength I could muster to teach the next two classes. When the bell rang for lunch, I walked to the main office feeling as if I'd aged fifty years. I took two sharpened pencils and a folder of Jack's work as a first line of defense against Melinda.

I pinned my hopes on Caroline, the English department chair, to provide more potent protection than pencils and paper. She was the vice president of our union and had been assigned to represent me. I disliked Caroline's bossy manner, but there was no teacher better suited to do battle with Melinda Tumbleson than my supercilious colleague.

Timmy and Melinda stopped talking when I entered the office. Caroline hadn't yet arrived, but Emily, whom I wasn't expecting to see, was there. I wondered why my friend hadn't told me she was coming. Emily looked miserable, but misery was her set point, in the same way that malice was Melinda's.

It wasn't an easy room to read. Emily picked at her fingernails and refused to meet my eye. Timmy stared past me at a poster from his college football days, as if communing with that two-dimensional representation of his younger self. Melinda wore what could only be described as a Resting Twitch Face. The cords in her neck tensed in an uneven rhythm that pulled at her mouth and stretched the unnaturally tight skin over her jawline.

Timmy tore himself away from the poster and rubbed at a grease spot on his tie, which, in addition to the food stains, was spattered with tiny baseballs and mitts. "Welcome, Liz! Glad to see you. Let's get started."

His jovial manner wasn't a good sign. I remained standing and said, "I refuse to begin without my union rep. If Caroline can't make it, we'll have to reschedule."

Melinda stopped twitching and smiled. Like Timmy's cheerful greeting, it didn't bode well for me. "Caroline has been unavoidably detained, and Emily is taking her place. It doesn't much matter who's here, because the resolution of this issue is simple. You will give Jack a B in English for the year, and you will apologize for your sarcastic remarks, which caused him extreme emotional suffering when he's already so fragile. In return, I will allow all other disciplinary measures, including those involving Kevin Sugarman, to be placed on hold pending further investigation."

Caroline was a pit bull and would have sunk her teeth deep into Melinda's flesh after shoving the board president's words down her throat. Emily was a quivering spoonful of marshmallow fluff. The only concession my friend left out of her counteroffer was the sacrifice of my firstborn child.

My feet hurt, my stomach was buzzing with too much coffee, and an epic headache occupied most of the prime real estate inside my skull. All of that discomfort made me reckless. How else to explain what happened next?

"I quit."

Chapter Thirty-Five

I am gone forever. [Exit, pursued by a bear.]
—William Shakespeare / The Winter's Tale

When I told Timmy and Melinda I wanted to resign, my surprise was greater than theirs. The words came out of me without the benefit of prior thought, but I didn't take them back.

The principal recovered first. "You can't quit. There's less than two months left before the kids take the AP exam." The gaze from his watery blue eyes, too shallow to support a minnow, sharpened. "You have to give us sixty days' notice."

My mouth, not done with burying my career, answered, "Sue me."

The cords in Melinda's neck stuck out so far they resembled a relief map of the Andes. "Well done, Ms. Hopewell. Might I remind you, however, that you're in an office and not onstage? If you're finished with this melodramatic scene, let's get down to business."

She was the president of the Valerian Hills Board of Education, the ex-wife of a murdered man, and, as she noted in the signature of her poisonous emails, Jack's Mom. In none of those roles had she ever uttered a single statement that didn't fill me with loathing, but I was impressed with her coolness.

I matched her frigid tone. "I refuse to comply with your requests. I will, however, remain in my position under the following conditions: Neither of you will interfere with how I conduct my class or my rehearsals. Jack will treat the staff and students with conspicuous courtesy, and any failure to do so will be just cause for me to remove him from the cast of *Grease*."

Melinda gnashed her teeth but surrendered without suing for better terms. So few people challenged her, she was probably out of practice. Timmy wasn't as quick to agree. I wondered if he was calculating the odds of getting a replacement AP English teacher at a lower salary who also could coach lacrosse. Perhaps he already had someone in mind, but after an extended consultation with his baseball-patterned tie, he sighed and assented.

Giddy with success, I pressed forward. "Timmy, you will give three detention periods to Jack, where he will rewrite his *1984* essay without the aid of electronic devices. If he doesn't complete the assignment, he will fail English for the year and will have to attend summer school to graduate."

Melinda fussed over the horror of her son spending three consecutive days in detention, doing the work he should have finished during class and at home. She said she was speechless, but her voluble retort didn't support her claim.

To my surprise, Timmy didn't quibble. "That seems reasonable, Ms. Hopewell." He laced his fingers and leaned back in his chair. "I think we're done."

I almost tripped over Emily. She'd made herself so small I forgot she was there. Shocking all of us, she brandished a notebook. "I wrote down everything you said, so there's no going back on what you promised Liz. I'm writing up a full report for the board and the union."

We walked out together, and I linked my arm with hers. "I am so proud of you! And so grateful. What's next? After that performance, I won't be surprised if the dinosaurs make a comeback."

She managed a brave smile. "We've got seven minutes left to eat lunch. My place or yours?"

When we arrived at my classroom I dropped the shades on the door window, but this precaution didn't deter Caroline from barging in on us. She offered no apology for abandoning me in my hour of need. My colleague spoke with a bored, upper-class British accent that was an accurate reflection of her world-weariness. "How did it go with Timmy the Terrible and Melinda the Meanie?"

Her indifference exasperated me more than her failure to show up at the meeting. "If you're that interested, you should have been there."

"Sorry, darling. Timmy needed me to take charge of the Jock Table at lunch. He didn't trust anyone else to keep them in line. Unlike the rest of you, I enjoy the challenge of putting those miscreants in their place." Caroline clicked her teeth together as if she were about to bite into a misbehaving student. "Compared to Jack, Kevin, and their gang of future felons, Timmy and Melinda are pushovers, even for weaklings like you and Emily."

I'd counted on Caroline's ruthless competence to help me during the disciplinary hearing and suspected Timmy had engineered an excuse to prevent her from being there. After the fact, however, I didn't regret her absence.

It was a day of surprises. Before I could frame an answer, Emily piped up, "Liz did great. She didn't need you."

"Delighted to hear it." Caroline's narrow eyes and pinched nostrils contradicted the cheery answer. She couldn't hide her disappointment that without her expert piloting, I hadn't gone down in flames. With a brisk wave, she said, "Tata, darlings," and left.

Emily wolfed down her sandwich. Between bites, she said, "I can't believe you told Timmy and Melinda you'd quit. I'd never have the guts to do that. My husband would kill me if I gave up the pension."

My stomach was knotted too tightly to accept food. "George would do the same. I'm happy they didn't call my bluff."

She pushed my lunch bag closer to me, urging me to eat. "You should be proud of yourself. You made them do the right thing. For once."

I couldn't delude myself that anything substantive would change. "You were no slouch, yourself, but our meeting today won't change much. If I gave Jack a failing grade, Timmy would change it. That's what happened to Bill during the last marking period. I wouldn't be surprised if his heart condition was directly related to that little episode of administrative power."

"Were you serious when you said you would quit? I don't know what I'd do if I wasn't teaching. I love my job." With less sentiment and more pragmatism, she added, "I have five years to retirement. I'll probably stick around a few years after that, until after my daughter graduates college. Hopefully, I'll be able to leave before I get as jaded as Caroline or Bill."

I tossed my lunch in the garbage. "It isn't teaching I want to quit. It's everything else."

* * *

I wished I could cancel rehearsals for *Grease,* but opening night was two weeks away. As with every high school production at that point in the process, the play was a mess. Many kids hadn't memorized their lines. Entrances and exits were ragged, and the dance sequences resembled *Night of the Living Dead* more than they did a happy sock hop.

Jack wasn't a skilled actor, singer, or dancer, but his natural swagger made him a credible lead. Melinda and Timmy must have scared him straight, because he was polite and subdued. He accepted my notes on his performance without mugging or mocking.

In anticipation of Ben Sorkin's arrival, I dismissed the kids ten minutes early, but Jack lingered after the rest of the cast left. I was uneasy at being alone with him in the auditorium and stationed myself at the door.

His face, which had a puckered, babyish scowl on it, sat atop a man-sized body, and he towered over me. Jack blocked the exit and said, "I bet you didn't know I was acting, even when I wasn't onstage. You can't change me, Ms. Hopewell."

I reached around him and opened the door. "I don't care how you feel or what you think. But maybe, if you pretend to be a kind person, you'll get used to it, and it'll stop being an act."

He smirked. "You don't care that I'm lying?"

"Of course not. Your actions are what's important. Rehearsals went much better today, thanks to your improved attitude. Keep it up."

He followed me into the hallway and said, "I'll walk you to your car. Wouldn't want anything to happen to you."

Jack was as skilled as any playground bully I'd ever seen. He was limited, however, by an imagination that wasn't expansive enough to project an outcome that didn't favor him. Unlike my fellow English teachers, I could knee him in the groin and stab him in the face with a pen in less time than it took Hamlet to wield his bare bodkin.

Ben Sorkin entered the building in time to avert any intensification of hostility. "I'll see Ms. Hopewell to her car, Jack. You go home. And stay out of trouble."

Jack started at the sound of Ben's voice. "Okay, yeah, sure." The boy's attempt at nonchalance was undercut by a flush that stained his neck and ears red.

When the door snapped shut behind him, I took a deep breath, held it for a few seconds, and then exhaled. I was afraid of Jack, tired from a day filled with tension and conflict, and self-conscious about the damage that those stresses had on my appearance. I ran my hands through my hair to confirm that the long, shining mane I'd possessed at seven a.m. would now do Medusa proud. Jack had cost me the time I needed to repair my makeup, and I didn't need a mirror to know the mascara and lipstick were history.

If Ben was put off by my disheveled appearance, he hid it well. Through the glass exit door, he watched Jack climb into his car and roar off at double the speed limit. The detective turned back to me and cocked his head as if weighing the impact his next words would have. "I don't like him. I suppose that's not the kind of thing teachers can say. You're in a more optimistic line of work than I am."

Ben's mild teasing distracted me from worrying about how I looked. "Publicly, teachers err on the side of sympathy, but you should hear us in the break room. Not only do we trash the kids we don't like, we keep tabs on their parents, so none of us is caught unprepared when someone like Melinda Tumbleson is on the horizon. The entire staff is going to heave a huge sigh of relief when Jack graduates."

His eyes, always so serious, crinkled in amusement. "That's good to know. I imagine your break room, and mine aren't so different after all."

I paused as the elevator pinged, and the nighttime custodian emerged, pushing an industrial-sized vacuum in front of him. I greeted him and suggested to Ben that we continue our conversation in my classroom.

He leaned closer as a roar from the vacuum echoed down the empty hallway. "Are you hungry? I'll buy you dinner."

My poker face deserted me, and I looked at my feet so he couldn't see how pleased I was. "Sure. But let's not eat in a Valerian Hills restaurant. I don't want any of my students or their parents to see us."

He agreed and texted me the directions to a diner equidistant between Valerian Hills and Oak Ridge.

* * *

The waitress at the Delish Diner greeted Ben by name, escorted us to a corner booth, and handed us a twenty-page, spiral-bound, plastic-coated menu, which offered a dizzying array of food, from blueberry blintzes to spinach pie.

Ben didn't bother with the menu. "The sandwiches and breakfast dishes are great, but if I were you, I'd give the beef bourguignon a hard pass."

The waitress plopped a metal coffee pot in the center of the table and brought two cups and saucers. He ordered a stack of pancakes, scrambled eggs, and hash brown potatoes. I settled on an English muffin.

When Ben asked why I wanted to meet with him, I opened the photos on my phone and showed him the mangled Christmas card Jack kept in his backpack. The detective gave a low whistle and said, "Where did you find this?"

"In his backpack. Jack doesn't know I saw it."

I wished I could read what lay behind his inscrutable expression. Unlike George, Ben would have made an excellent poker player. The detective said, with no perceptible emotion, "Jack has enough rage in him to kill, but he didn't murder his father. He's guilty of lying to his mother and the police, but she's claiming we pressured him into making a false statement, and we're not going to pursue it further. He said he was getting tutored in English at the time of the murder, but he was with one of his buddies. Kevin's parents vouched for both of them."

I drank some of the Delish Diner's excellent coffee. "I'm glad Jack isn't guilty, but only because I've got a much better suspect in mind."

Ben's fork stopped midway between the plate and his mouth. "I'm happy to consider all of your theories, especially the ones that come from books. At the same time, let's keep those ideas in the theoretical realm. Leave the investigation to me."

I told him of my encounters with Magda and Miguel and why I believed Cooper was the killer. "He had the same opportunity as all the other suspects and a much better motive. I think he embezzled money from the club, and when Elliot discovered what happened, Cooper killed him. Cooper is a proud man, and the loss of status, not to mention the threat of legal action, pushed him over the edge."

A flicker of what looked like amusement illuminated Ben's face. "Surely you also have some literary analysis to prove his guilt."

"Of course! I have two. One is from *Frankenstein*, and the theme is doubles. The other one, which I like better, is connected to *Hamlet*. This murder looked like a crime of passion, but it was as carefully planned as Claudius's poisoning of Hamlet's father. It's all about revenge and ambition."

"Ms. Hopewell. *Liz.* As long as your pursuit stays inside the covers of a book, I'm willing to listen. But you can't act on those theories. That's my job. I can't reveal our leads or the details of our investigation, but rest assured, Cooper remains a person of interest."

"Under other circumstances, I would agree to step aside. But I can go places you can't, and people like Miguel will tell me things they wouldn't tell you. The Meadowfields Spring Fling Golf Tournament is happening this Saturday. I'm supposed to be in a foursome with Bryony and Cooper. It's the perfect time to confront him." I didn't mention George would be part of the group. My husband was unlikely to be of much help, and if he knew what I was planning, would try to stop me.

Ben's voice rose above its customary low pitch. "That's out of the question. If you're right about Cooper, that's the wrong place to challenge him. The killer murdered two people and seriously injured two others at the club. There were no witnesses to any of the attacks. Tell your foursome you have other plans."

"Do you have a better idea?"

My phone lit up with a text, and as I reached across the table, our hands touched. A sharp sting of static shocked us both. As my AP students would say, it was, like, a symbol.

Chapter Thirty-Six

There is something at work in my soul, which I do not understand.
—Mary Shelley / Frankenstein

The English muffin I ordered at the Delish Diner turned to ashes in my mouth when I saw George's angry text. Ben paused, his fork halfway between the plate and his mouth. "Is everything okay?"

My first impulse was to leave, to rush out of the restaurant, and to appease my husband. Instead, I texted George the same message he sent to me each time he arrived home hours later than he'd promised. **Don't wait up.**

I turned my phone face down. "Of course not. How can anything be okay when we've got a killer to catch?"

The faint lines that surrounded his eyes and mouth deepened. "Wrong pronoun. You have to lay low and trust me to do my job."

"Tell me one thing, and I promise not to press you for more information. The killer used my golf club to kill Elliot. Did you find the weapon that killed Ryan?"

"Is this a test?"

"Yes. I have to know if you also trust me."

He lifted his cup with a steady hand. "The club that killed Ryan Walker was part of a loaner set in the caddy shack. It should have been covered in fingerprints, but it had been wiped clean. The killer left behind nylon fibers consistent with certain types of golf gloves, which eliminates no one. They came from a popular brand that's sold in every major sporting goods store. Everyone at the club presumably owns a pair of golf gloves."

My hands were nowhere near as steady as his. "That might not tell us who killed Ryan, but it surely eliminates Miguel."

Ben hesitated before answering. "It doesn't completely rule him out. Miguel could have gotten his hands on a pair of gloves, but it's a moot point because he's no longer a suspect. We haven't officially cleared him, because we don't want the killer to know how close we are."

I wished I could tell Miguel what Ben told me. "Are you going to arrest Cooper?"

His voice was tight, his face grim. "All I can say is that you should keep your distance from him and the club."

"I promise not to say anything to Cooper, or make any move to ensnare him, but I have to attend the golf tournament. I don't know any other way of protecting my husband. He's determined to go, and I doubt I can persuade him otherwise. I'm afraid Cooper will see George as a threat and go after him next." Talking about George to Ben was painful, but there was no way to avoid it.

He loosened his tie. "You said you trusted me."

If only it were that simple. "I do. Unfortunately, George doesn't trust me, which is my fault, not his. I've asked him to believe things I can't prove and to act in ways he sees as contrary to our best interests. Cooper is his boss and has been really good to him. George can't see past that, and it's made him vulnerable."

I couldn't admit my guiltiest secret, which was that I feared George was complicit in covering up the embezzlement at the club. If I admitted these doubts, that might be the last straw for him. And our marriage. For sure, I couldn't tell a cop about it.

With a quick goodbye, I left the food, the coffee, and Ben, and drove home. For many months, I'd told myself that my marriage was solid and that time would mend the seemingly impassable rift between us, but I was no longer certain we'd work things out together. Maybe we'd have to work them out separately.

George was sitting at the kitchen table when I arrived. "Where were you? I expected you home over an hour ago."

The lie came as easily to me as if it were the truth. "Rehearsals ran late." I cut off further complaints by reminding him I'd changed my mind about participating in the Spring Fling Golf Tournament.

As I suspected might happen, he wasn't pleased to have won his point. "Are you sure you want to go? I don't want you to bail at the last minute when it's too late for me to get another partner."

"Stop lying, George. You're no good at it. Did you already ask Amanda to partner with you? And was that before or after I turned you down?"

Thwarted in his attempt to ditch me, he slammed his fist against the table. "I've been sick all day. I don't want to hear any more stupid accusations."

I put my arms around him. "Why don't we both skip it? Let's go into the city instead. We can see a movie and eat out and forget about this, um, this other stuff."

He disentangled himself and said, "How would you like it if I asked you to skip your students' performance? Or one of the kids' events? This is important to me, Liz." He passed a shaky hand across his eyes, which made me unutterably sad and sorry for him.

I wasn't surprised he turned me down, but I wished he'd at least been tempted.

* * *

The rest of the work week passed in a tacit, uneasy, marital truce. George and I didn't fight, but we didn't talk things through, either. He had a fake recovery from his fake illness and made up for his single day of truancy by staying at the office, or some other location, until long after the kids and I ate dinner. I cooked his favorite meals and left tiny portions of leftovers on the countertop so he could see what he missed.

Daily rehearsals for *Grease* kept me at school until past six o'clock. I missed Zach's baseball game and accumulated significant carpool debts to the parents of Ellie's ballet buddies. George appeared unaware of the effect his absence had on our kids. Zach was resentful, and Ellie tearful. Like their father, they didn't want to talk about how they felt. They were, after all, teenagers. Emotional drama was a given and, perhaps, was a consequence of hormones and not their parents' problems.

* * *

The gloomy skies that greeted me on Saturday morning matched my dark mood. I half-hoped the threat of rain would postpone the Spring Fling Golf Tournament, but George assured me the competition would proceed as planned, as the approaching thunderstorms wouldn't arrive until evening.

Ben called while the kids were still asleep and George was in the shower, but I took the phone outside anyway.

He spoke with quiet urgency. "The more I think about you going to this golf tournament, the less I like it. Miguel is no longer a suspect, and even if he were, finding the killer isn't your responsibility. Why are you going? And don't tell me it's to protect your husband. We can do that better than you."

I sat on the back porch as the wind whipped through the trees. "I was the first person on the scene for Elliot's murder and a short distance away from Ryan when he was killed. What if my presence wasn't a matter of chance? What if the killer targeted me, as well as the more obvious victims?" This thought hadn't occurred to me before, but it seemed as good a reason as any to attend the golf tournament.

After a pause that stretched so long I thought the call dropped, he said, "That's not it. What's driving you to put yourself in danger? Most people would run screaming in the opposite direction."

"I can't tell you. Not yet." I liked Ben, but it was too soon to share with him all the ways I was trying to make up for my cowardly failure to protect my mother and sister. I wanted him to know about my good qualities first.

His response was resigned but not angry. "Tom Harriman, a few plain clothes, and a half dozen uniforms will be at the club. You won't see me, but I'll be watching you."

A call from Bryony pinged through. I told Ben I'd get back to him and answered Bryony before the voicemail cut her off.

The woman who could have won first place in a competition for Miss

Cool, Collected, and Contemptuous sounded as if she were crying. "Liz, I'm in trouble, and I didn't know who else to call. It's Cooper. He's totally out of control. I'm scared to death of him."

Of all the unspeakable things I suspected Cooper of doing, I never imagined him capable of hurting his wife. I was terrified for her. "Call the police. Or, even better, go to the police station. I'm on my way. I'll meet you there."

"No! I can't do that. It's—it's too big a step. I'm not ready to blow up my life. Where will I go? What will I do?" Her voice cracked, and her sobs grew louder.

My heart ached for her. "Where is Cooper? Is he home?"

"No. He left the house in a rage. Liz, if I don't show up at the club, on time and looking perfect, he'll kill me. I'm afraid to go and afraid not to go. Will you meet me there? I'll wait for you in the parking lot. I don't want to walk in by myself. He won't touch me if other people are around."

I checked the time. George also would kill me if I reneged at this late date, although, in my husband's case, the threat wasn't literal. "Yes. I'll meet you." Ben's promise of protection made me brave. "Other than the police station, the club might be the safest place for you until we can sort this out. Pack a bag before you go. You're welcome to stay here."

Sounding more like the confident woman I knew, she said, "You're a good friend, Liz. I won't forget this."

I ran back into the house and entered the steamy bathroom. I pulled back the shower curtain and said, "Phone the club and tell them we're not coming to the tournament. If you must, tell them you have a family emergency. I'll explain later. Stay home and wait for me. Don't accept any calls or texts from Cooper." I didn't want George alone with his boss.

I checked the guest bedroom, which was passably neat. I grabbed some clean sheets and towels, dropped them on the bed, and got dressed.

Dripping wet, George exited the bathroom and watched my hasty toilette. "What are you talking about? If we miss our tee time, we'll have to forfeit."

"Our tee time is no longer relevant unless you want to end up Cooper's next victim. I'm going to the club to pick up Bryony. Please, George, trust me to do the right thing. The golf tournament isn't as important as your safety." I grabbed my purse and left.

By the time George wrapped himself in a bathrobe and laced up his sneakers, I was already in the car. He tapped on the window. "You're delusional. Cooper is not a killer. Get in the house, change out of those ridiculous clothes, and stop this nonsense."

George's critique of my clothing, which consisted of a perfectly respectable pair of black cotton drawstring pants and a gray t-shirt, wasn't as upsetting as his refusal to credit my accusations against Cooper, but it bothered me that this was the focus of his complaint.

"Do you trust your boss more than me? Bryony called a few minutes ago. I don't have the whole story yet, but I think Cooper has been terrorizing her in the same way Elliot did to his wives. Don't you see? That's why Sonya confided in her. She knew Bryony would understand what she was going through."

I started the engine, but George didn't budge. "If anyone is doing the terrorizing in that marriage, it's Bryony and not Cooper." He spoke with quiet calm, perhaps sensing that any increase of emotion would send me roaring off. "Since when are you and Bryony best friends? You told me you didn't trust her. And now you're rushing off to rescue her? Liz, slow down and think this through."

"I don't have time to think. I have to act."

Chapter Thirty-Seven

The facts, if not true, were well invented; the arguments, if not logical, were
seductive.
—Anthony Trollope / The Way We Live Now

When I arrived at the Meadowfields Country Club, I pulled into a spot near the snack bar and did a quick reconnaissance. The tournament hadn't yet started, but several golfers were on the driving range, unfazed by the dark clouds and damp air. Cooper stood on the perimeter of the putting green with Sonya Tumbleson.

Although Sonya had professed reluctance to attend the tournament, her smile was bright. She was gaily dressed in a white collared shirt and red skirt. A red scarf bound her yellow curls in a long ponytail. Cooper was facing away from me. A remark from Sonya caught his attention, and he picked up a club and swung lightly at a ball. His answer, which was inaudible to me, made her laugh. Cooper's callous indifference to his wife sickened but didn't surprise me.

Relieved to see Bryony's cheating, murderous husband caught in Sonya's charming web, I drove to the farthest lot, the one I'd used on the day Elliot was killed. Bryony's low-slung car was behind a weeping willow, near a half-closed gate that gave out onto a narrow dirt road. It was too early for anyone to have to use this deserted area to park, and the curve in the road rendered me invisible to the golfers who'd arrived before I did. I peered through the window of Bryony's car, thinking perhaps she was hiding inside, but it was empty.

The silence scared me. I texted her, but she didn't answer. My heart beat faster, and I feared I was too late. Cooper could have killed her, left her body in the woods, and been back on the putting green in minutes, with Sonya there to provide an alibi. I cursed myself for wasting precious time in stocking the guest room with clean sheets and towels. I should have left the house immediately.

The logical place to look for Bryony was in the grove of trees that bordered the dirt path, but I was too afraid to search for her there. If Cooper had a murderous accomplice, which I'd long suspected, I'd be dead before I found her.

I screwed up my courage and called her name, hating the tremble in my voice and the fear in my heart. Truly, I was no hero. If I were brave, there were so many things in my life I would have done differently, but this was neither the time nor the place for useless regrets. I couldn't change the past, but there was plenty I could do going forward after I rescued Bryony. A good first step would be finding and confronting the Lousy Bastard. Everyone claimed he was dead, but I felt in my bones that he was alive. I couldn't see him, but he was out there somewhere. Just as Bryony was.

With renewed strength, I yelled, "Bryony? Where are you?"

She stepped out from behind a tree. In a high, tight voice, she said, "Stop shouting. I had to make sure you were alone and that no one followed you."

Was it instinct, or some atavistic sixth sense that made me draw back? Perhaps my upbringing was the reason for my caution. Spend enough time with criminals, and you learn pretty quickly that suspicion keeps you safe and trust will kill you. That held true even—especially—when criminals wear fancy clothes and drive expensive cars, because they're the ones who are most successful at scamming others.

The explanation for my wariness might have been much simpler. Bryony sounded the way a scared woman would, but behind the soft words, I heard the unmistakable thump of danger. What if she wasn't alone?

I tensed and took a step back. A jumble of thoughts and fears fogged my thinking. Unable to decide on a course of action, I turned to the writer who had all the answers to real-life problems. Shakespeare understood indecision. He wrote a whole play about it.

How much time passed while I, like Hamlet, wavered? Probably not more than a few seconds, but those seconds cost me. I didn't want to be like Act II Hamlet, who acts too quickly and ends up killing the wrong guy. But I also didn't want to be like Act V Hamlet, who fails to see the danger in a friendly sword competition and ends up dead.

Bryony didn't wait for me to finish my unspoken version of the Danish prince's *to-be-or-not-to-be* soliloquy. She stepped out of the bushes and checked the surrounding area. Her eyes swam with tears. She brushed her hair to one side and showed me her neck, which had a line of purple bruises around it. With a sob, she said, "Look. Look what he did to me."

I hadn't taken more than one cautious step toward her before she grabbed a club hidden in the brush and aimed for my head. My hand-eye coordination was poor, but my instincts were good. The blow missed my face but cracked against my uneased arm. The pain brought me to my knees.

The Lousy Bastard's voice, which I'd tried my entire adult life to silence, roared in my ears. I followed his directions and tackled her ankles, using my uninjured shoulder to topple her.

Caught off guard, Bryony dropped the club and made a typical rich girl mistake by grabbing a handful of my hair. No kid from the projects would do that unless the intent was to bully and not to kill. I jabbed my finger in her eye and punched her upturned nose.

She scrambled away and tried to grab the golf club. I stuck out my foot and tripped her. She fell on her face, which looked pretty bad already.

I picked up the club. Without rancor, I said, "You should have gone for my dominant side. I'm right-handed."

She cursed with indelicate thoroughness, which wasn't against club rules but was not encouraged. When she was finished maligning me, my husband, and our children, she changed tactics. Blinking furiously with the eye that wasn't swollen shut, she said, "Don't be too hasty, Liz. This doesn't look good for you. I'll claim you attacked me first, and you won't be able to prove otherwise. I'm sure we can come to some agreement."

I hesitated, not because I was tempted by Bryony's offer, but because I was weaker than she realized. I couldn't call nine-one-one with the arm she'd smashed, and my uninjured arm was holding a golf club. My best chance of survival was to keep her talking long enough for the parking lot to fill up with people attending the tournament. It was a popular event.

The skies opened, and a torrent of rain drenched my hopes of a speedy rescue. Anyone foolish enough to show up would surely head for the clubhouse.

Bryony sensed my vulnerability and edged closer. "We have more in common than you know. We both married men who are beneath us. I can help you fix your problem if you help me fix mine."

My head was spinning. "What does that have to do with Elliot? Or Ryan? You killed two men. Why? What did they do to deserve that?"

"You disappoint me, Liz. I thought you were supposed to be so smart. But when you hear me out, you'll understand why Elliot Tumbleson deserved to die." She smiled and nodded as if we were co-conspirators and not deadly opponents. "As you might have guessed, Cooper borrowed money from the club treasury. I want to be perfectly clear about this: He didn't steal it. He was going to give it back, but Elliot wouldn't listen to reason and threatened to expose him."

Tears of rage poured from her swollen eyes. "That filthy worm laughed at me. Said he was going to press charges. He gave me no choice. I made the necessary arrangements to get rid of him, but my pathetic husband didn't have the guts to follow through. In the end, as always, Cooper left it to me to do the dirty work."

Bryony made her cold-blooded murder sound like the act of a wife whose lazy husband refused to take out the garbage. She wagged her finger at me. "Whatever you do, spare me any moralizing. Who's going to miss Elliot? The wife he beat black and blue? The kids he ignored?"

I didn't let her see my horror and spoke with the same conversational tone she used with me. "What about Ryan? Did he also deserve to die?"

She smiled approvingly. "Absolutely. He saw me take your golf club and threatened to tell the police unless I paid him off. Trust me, Liz, a blackmailer doesn't deserve to live." She wiped a trickle of blood from under her nose.

"Think it over. If we work together, we can pin the murders on Cooper and George. And then we'll both be free."

I clutched the golf club with wet, freezing fingers. "If you hate Cooper so much, why didn't you let him take the rap for the theft? Why commit murder to save a husband you loathe?"

Her blue eyes were flinty with rage. "If Coop got caught stealing, as most certainly would have happened, people would suspect I put him up to it. They know he's too dumb to do it on his own. We'd both be disgraced, kicked out, a laughingstock. I could never show my face at the club again."

My arm threw out knife-sharp lashings of pain that were difficult to mask. "Before I agree to anything, explain why you tried to kill me."

She blinked as if surprised by the question. "You were getting too close for comfort. Every person I tried to blame, you tried to exonerate. It was incredibly annoying, and I was getting worried you'd put it all together." With a regretful sigh, she added, "I don't like you."

Like a gambler with two crappy cards in the hole and everything to lose, I bluffed for all I was worth. "I don't like you either, but I accept your offer. We'll figure it out together."

"Put down the club." Her ice-chip eyes narrowed as I bent my knees to lay it on the ground.

I knew what was coming and was ready. The second she sprang, I used a stabbing motion to plunge the end of the club into her stomach. It knocked the breath out of her but didn't kill her. Just to be on the safe side, I whacked her kneecap. It wasn't the most sporting move, but I didn't want her following me, and shattering her joint was preferable to cracking open her head. Bryony howled in pain and threatened to kill me. But that wasn't exactly breaking news.

I wished I had a clever Shakespearean quotation to offer her, but it was The Lousy Bastard's mocking boast that came to mind. *Don't kid a kidder.*

Chapter Thirty-Eight

Poetry makes nothing happen.
—W.H. Auden

Ben Sorkin, followed by Tom Harriman, Cooper Aldridge, George, and a half dozen cops swarmed across the parking lot. Bryony couldn't get to her feet, but she held her arms out to George. "Thank God you're here! She tried to kill me."

Ben cuffed her. She screamed as he recited her rights. "You've got the wrong person! Her husband stole money from the club, and she killed Elliot to cover it up!"

Two medics lifted her onto a stretcher. She twisted her head and said to the detective, "I want my lawyer. I'm suing you, the department, and everyone else who's taken part in framing me." When the EMT tried to examine her, she bit him.

George didn't notice my broken arm. He hugged me, which sent thunderbolts of pain through my body. I passed out. When I regained consciousness, I had an ugly bruise on the side of my head from where I hit the ground. It wasn't George's fault. I slipped out of his embrace before he could catch me.

I opened my eyes to find myself inside an ambulance with Ben on one side of the stretcher and a medic on the other. The medic shined a light in my eyes. She spoke slowly and asked easy questions. Who I was. Where I was. I was pleased to be able to provide her with answers, although my voice took a long time to travel from inside my head to my mouth.

Ben's question was harder. He gazed at me and said, "Can you tell us what just happened?"

My throat was dry, and my voice hoarse. "She had her other face. Don't you see? It was always about doubles."

The medic exchanged a look with Ben. "That's fine, Ms. Hopewell. We're going to take you to the hospital now, where you can rest and recover."

George clambered into the narrow space. "I'm going with her." He grabbed the hand that was attached to my broken arm, and I passed out again.

* * *

Other than George and the detectives, I wasn't allowed visitors until the following day. Susan was the first to arrive. She brought a change of clothes, makeup, a hairbrush, and three bunches of daffodils, my favorite flower. George bought me a dozen roses, my colleagues at Valerian Hills High School sent a splashy spray of lilies, and the waitstaff at the country club sent daisies. I hoped the bouquets would last long enough for me to repurpose them for the opening of *Grease*.

My sister alternated between fulsome praise for my bravery and sharp criticism for facing off against a killer without her. "You should have waited for me. I could have helped you."

I was woozy from the pain meds, the broken arm, and a slight concussion. "To my everlasting shame, I didn't think Bryony was the killer. When she called to tell me Cooper threatened her, I figured I could enlist her to get evidence against him. Not my proudest moment, I can assure you."

She sat back and said, "Well, I'm here now. I want every detail, from start to finish."

A tap on the door interrupted my recitation. Ben and Tom entered, followed by a scowling nurse, who shooed them out of the room while she took my blood pressure and checked other signs of life. Susan helped me into a pair of black yoga pants and a stretchy tank top. With the air of a conjurer, she pulled a shawl in rose-colored cashmere out of her bag and draped it over my shoulders.

My sister asked the nurse not to allow the detectives into the room until my face met with her approval. Susan did her best to mask my chalky skin and pale lips, but there was only so much she could do with the material at hand.

When she opened the door, I was surprised to see George walk in with Ben and Tom. I didn't expect him to arrive until the afternoon. My husband kissed my cheek and took possession of the sole chair in the room. Tom greeted me warmly.

Ben's eyes had dark shadows under them. "We need a preliminary statement, Ms. Hopewell. Let's start with the phone call from Ms. Aldridge."

I drew the shawl closer around my shoulders. "Bryony said she was afraid Cooper was going to kill her. She was crying and said she didn't know what to do."

Not a muscle on Ben's face moved. "Why didn't you tell her to go to the police?"

The implicit criticism smarted. "I did! She said she was scared and wasn't ready to blow up her life, but I thought I could convince her to leave him. I should have realized she was setting me up."

George hitched his chair closer to my hospital bed. "Too bad you didn't think that through before you left. It might have tipped you off that the whole thing was a trap and not a very good one. If you'd listened to me, none of this—"

In an even tone, Ben said, "I'll get to you shortly, Mr. Hopewell. Please let your wife finish." Turning to me, he said, "When you were in the ambulance, you said something about doubles. Were you loopy from pain and shock? Or did you have something else in mind?"

"That was Hamlet talking. Hamlet and Frankenstein. Bryony showed us her painted face, but it wasn't real. And the stuff about doubles? Like Frankenstein and his Creation, she and Cooper were both monsters. One of them was a killer. The other stayed silent, covered it up, and let innocent people die."

My sister blinked at me. "Assume it's been a while since we read those books and tell us what you mean in English. Not English literature."

238

Although there was much I didn't know, I figured the detectives could fill in the blanks. "I was certain Cooper stole money from the club and killed Elliot to prevent him from reporting it. And I thought Bryony helped cover up the theft, not because she thought he was guilty, but because she believed he was innocent and didn't want him to be a suspect in a murder case. The only way to get her to admit this was to gain her confidence, which wouldn't have happened if I refused to help her in what I thought was her hour of need."

I paused to organize the rest of what I thought I knew. "Cooper pressured Miguel to leave his position at the club and seemed to be conspiring with Ian to pin the murder on him. The evidence appeared to point in only one direction. It was stupid of me not to realize the roles could have been reversed, and it was Cooper shielding Bryony and not the other way around."

Tom looked up from his notebook. "Don't beat up on yourself. We were thinking the same thing. But the earring your sister found near the scene of Ryan Walker's murder had a partial print that matched Bryony's, and when we rechecked her alibi, it didn't hold up. Without you, though, we would have had a hard time convicting her. There just wasn't enough evidence."

George looked as sick as I felt. I hoped it wasn't because he was in love with Bryony. He got up from his chair and positioned himself between me and Ben. "You guys also found a nametag at the scene of Ryan's murder. Were Bryony's fingerprints on that as well?"

Ben's mouth barely moved as he answered George's question. "No. It had been wiped clean. So no matter what, we knew Miguel hadn't accidentally left it, because then his prints would have been on it. And he wouldn't have planted a clue that could be traced only to him or his cousin. Don't know if we can prove one of the Aldridges swiped the nametag, but if we can, it'll help."

Susan took George's place. "Liz already told me that Ryan tried to blackmail Bryony after he saw her take Liz's golf club. But why did she attack Magda and Ian?"

An uncomfortable silence ensued. Since no one else wanted to assign blame to the person who deserved it, I did. "Miguel thought anyone who was close to him was in danger. But it was anyone close to me that got attacked. Bryony was on the patio overlooking the course when I met Magda. She saw me enter the kitchen and talk to Ian afterward. Bryony thought that Ian and Magda would tell me stuff they wouldn't tell the police, and she was constantly needling me about being friends with the help. She didn't kill Miguel because she wanted to frame him for the murder."

Ben turned to George. "Were you aware that Cooper stole money from the club?"

"Was I aware of it?" George turned his head and pulled at his ear. "I, er, no, I had no idea. Cooper asked me to look after the finances of the club, so why would I think he was guilty?"

Ben put down his notebook. "There's more than one way to interpret a request like that."

George kept his head down and directed his answer to the daffodils next to my bed. "The money that was missing has been found. It was an accounting error. The board of directors has closed the case."

I was shocked. "You know that's not what happened. How can you be silent about this?"

When George didn't speak, Tom answered for him. "Cooper admitted to taking the money. Said he it was a loan that he planned to pay back with interest and that Elliot approved it. There's no way to prove otherwise, but like it or not, the club won't be able to cover it up. It's with the DA now."

My head ached with the effort of processing this new load of information. "In other words, Cooper is still trying to cover for Bryony. If no one challenges him, it will look as if Bryony had no motive to kill Elliot. Will it work?"

"No." Ben's wooden exterior didn't crack. "It won't work. We would have had a harder time proving it if you hadn't put yourself in harm's way, but we would have gotten there eventually. We will, however, need a more complete statement from your husband." He stared at George, who couldn't quite meet the detective's eye.

A crowd of tears blurred my vision. "George, why didn't you tell me? I wanted to protect you."

He put his hand to his head and shaded his eyes. "I tried to stop you. As usual, you refused to listen to reason. That's on you. But thanks to me, you didn't end up the third murder victim. When I got to the club and couldn't find you, I called the cops."

And then, the man I married got up and left the room.

Chapter Thirty-Nine

If we do meet again, why, we shall smile.
—William Shakespeare / Julius Caesar

L ife didn't return to normal after I left the hospital. My concussion made it impossible to resume rehearsals for *Grease*, and Caroline had to take over. I'd often thought our department chair missed her calling as a dictator of a repressive regime, but I was wrong. Caroline belonged in the theater. She was a born director, and the play was a huge success.

There was plenty of other unfinished business in my life. The biggest change occurred when George and I agreed to a trial separation. I wanted to wait until the kids left for college, but he refused. For once, he was right. I'd been so consumed with my dissatisfaction and unhappiness I'd failed to see his.

George broke the news after we had the best and most honest talk in years. With equal parts regret and resolve, he said, "We're not the same people we were when we met. It's time to move on."

What he said wasn't what I wanted to hear, but I couldn't deny the truth of it. And although I didn't think I still loved him, some part of my battered heart disagreed. "Do you want a divorce?"

"Not sure yet. Do you?"

Although I'd fantasized about a life free of him when that option seemed distant, I wasn't ready to make the final cut. "Not now. Not yet. We lived together for years before getting married. Maybe we can live apart without getting divorced until we know for sure that it's the right move." A thought struck me. "Unless there's someone else? If that's the case, I agree we should make it official."

His oblique answer told me what he didn't want to openly admit. "Let's take it one step at a time."

I dreaded telling the kids. For days, we debated the best way to break it to them. When we finally sat them down and told them George would be moving to a nearby apartment, I braced myself for tears and anger. Instead, they seemed relieved.

Zach said, "What took so long?" He raised one eyebrow. "This might be a good time to get me a car so I can help out."

Ellie was more thoughtful. "Does this mean we'll have to spend alternating weeks with the two of you? I'm auditioning for the summer program at the ballet school, and I want to board with the rest of the girls."

I assured both kids our separation wouldn't interfere with their social lives, and they went off to do their homework and share the news on social media.

Was that the end of it? No. Life is never that simple. I consoled myself, in moments of crushing guilt, that whatever else we'd failed at, George and I hadn't lied to our kids, hadn't pretended things were great when they were terrible, hadn't shut them out of important decisions. I wondered how much better my life would have been if my parents had done the same.

* * *

Several difficult tasks remained, and after putting them off as long as I could, I got started. On the first day of summer vacation, I waited until George picked up the kids for the weekend and then called Rikers Island. When I asked to speak to my half-brother Ralphie, the operator told me he'd been released and was residing in Vallen Kill Falls, in upstate New York.

Susan shuddered, although the afternoon was balmy and the sun bright. "That's the town where Lousy died. Is supposed to have died." She squared her shoulders. "I guess it's time for another road trip."

I put two coffee cups on a tray, and we moved to the front porch. "I have a better idea. Let's make them come to us." I was sick of chasing shadows. "If there's one positive thing that came out of the last few weeks, it's that I learned a lot more from Lousy than I realized. He was a con man, and if he's alive, the only way to smoke him out is to beat him at his own game. I propose we send a letter to Velma that says Lousy inherited money from a long-lost relative. If that doesn't get one or both of them to come forward, nothing will." I wasn't sanguine about our chances of learning who was responsible for our mother's death, but I wouldn't rest until we'd exhausted every possible path to the truth. And maybe not even then.

Susan gazed over the railing at the bushes below, as if fearful our closest relatives were lurking in the azaleas. "We don't know Velma's last name or where she lives."

After missing all the clues that pointed to Bryony, I was proud of coming up with a lead in the case that meant so much to us. "I tracked down the original owners of MarVel's Coffee Shoppe. The 'Vel' in MarVel was Velma. I knew I'd seen her before. She used to work behind the counter, which was how Lousy, Ira, and the rest of The Club got to know her so well. And, you'll be happy to know, only one Velma lives in Vallen Kill Falls."

Ben pulled up in front of the house. I was a long way away from introducing him to the kids, but figured it was time for him and Susan to get to know each other better.

The arrival of a homicide detective, even one bearing a box from the bakery, wasn't enough to calm my sister's nervous response. "These people are dangerous. Aren't you afraid?"

"Not anymore."

Acknowledgements

This work of fiction was inspired by my high school English teacher, Linda Arkin, whose devotion to all things academic didn't preclude her from encouraging me to leave school and pursue a career as a dancer. Her voice was the one that spoke to me then and still does. Professor Nancy Dean of Hunter College (1930-2017) also has my heartfelt admiration and thanks. I began my post-secondary education years after my peers graduated, and when we met I was thoroughly disenchanted with life in English 101. She handed me an exemption for every class that had the word "Survey" in the title and mentored my independent study of British Literature. I did, of course, take her storied classes on Chaucer. Nancy, I owe you. I'm also grateful to the City University of New York, which continues to provide opportunities to non-traditional students like me.

Most of all, I thank my family. Their patience, humor, and love of intrigue and wordplay make everything I write better. Although they're devoted to drama they can spend endless hours together without generating any, and food fights are limited to opinions on pie crust. (My recipe wins.) In my mind, Becky, Jesse, Gregory, Geoffrey, Jacob, and Luke are still kids. Which may come as a surprise to their lovely partners Emily, Natalia, and Kris. As for the newest generation: Skylar, Viola, Ava, Alice, Ella, and Henry love a good story (and pie) as much as I do.

For creative inspiration and unstinting support (in addition to oceans of coffee, and gallons of wine) I'm indebted to my fellow writers and the organization that unites us, Sisters in Crime. At the top of that long list are Mariah Fredericks, Beth Mannion, Cathi Stoler, and Alison von Rosenvinge. And then there are my Level Best "Besties" Mally Becker and Lori Duffy Foster.

On the topic of sisters: If I had my choice of siblings, I couldn't do better than the ones I grew up with and those I got through marriage: Richard Smith, Karyn Boyar, and Barbara, Lisa, Jane, Gail, and Lolly Robbins.

Much gratitude is due to the many people who provided their expert advice. Chief among these is my editor, Shawn Reilly Simmons. Many thanks are also due to my longtime critique partner, Corey LaBranche. Thank you, from the bottom of my heart.

This book is dedicated to Glenn, who still thinks—after all these years—that he's the one who got lucky.

About the Author

Lori Robbins is the author of the On Pointe and Master Class mystery series. She won the Indie Award for Best Mystery, two Silver Falchions, and is a finalist for the Daphne du Maurier Award for Excellence in Mystery and Suspense. Short stories include "Leading Ladies" in *Justice for All,* which received an Honorable Mention in the 2022 Best American Mystery and Suspense anthology. She also is a contributor to *The Secret Ingredient: A Mystery Writers Cookbook.*

A former dancer, Lori performed with a number of modern dance and classical ballet companies, including Ballet Hispanico and the St. Louis Ballet. Her commercial work, in featured spots for Pavlova Perfume and Macy's, paid the bills. After ten very lean years onstage she became an English teacher and now writes full-time.

Lori is a co-president of the New York/ Tristate Sisters in Crime and an active member of Mystery Writers of America. You can find her at lorirobbins.com and sign up for her newsletter at The Great Books Guide.

AUTHOR WEBSITE:
lorirobbins.com

SOCIAL MEDIA HANDLES:
https://www.instagram.com/lorirobbinsmysteries/
https://www.facebook.com/lorirobbinsauthor/
https://twitter.com/lorirobbins99
https://www.bookbub.com/profile/lori-robbins
https://www.goodreads.com/author/show/16007362.Lori_Robbins

Also by Lori Robbins

Lesson Plan for Murder

Murder in First Position

Murder in Second Position

Murder in Third Position

Murder in Fourth Position

www.ingramcontent.com/pod-product-compliance
Lightning Source LLC
Chambersburg PA
CBHW020616110726
47899CB00002B/527